CW00854880

DEAD AND GONE TO BELL

A Samantha Bell Mystery Thriller

JEREMY WALDRON

All rights reserved.

Copyright © 2019 Jeremy Waldron

No part of this book may be reproduced or transmitted in any form or by any means, electronic or mechanical, including photocopying, recording, or by any information storage and retrieval system, without permission in writing from the author and/or publisher. No part of this publication may be sold or hired, without written permission from the author.

This is a work of fiction. Names, characters, places and incidents are a product of the writer's imagination and/or have been used fictitiously in such a fashion it is not meant to serve the reader as actual fact and should not be considered as actual fact. Any resemblance to actual events, or persons, living or dead, locales or organizations is entirely coincidental.

The author acknowledges the trademarked status and trademark owners of various products referenced in this work of fiction, which have been used without permission. The publication / use of these trademarks is not authorized, associated with, or sponsored by the trademark owners.

jeremy@jeremywaldron.com

CHAPTER ONE

HE SAT IN THE CORNER CHAIR NEXT TO THE DIM LIGHT. IT was all he needed. Just enough to keep the darkness from spooking his imagination.

The room was silent except for the sound of his faint breath.

Covering his mouth, he yawned then turned to look out the large window to his left.

The city lights twinkled against a black backdrop. Sounds of sirens and the weekend parties echoed off the tall buildings, reminding him that there was a life outside of this small single-queen motel room. A life waiting for him to return to.

His fingers drummed on his swinging knee. He was excited to get on with his night, disappear back into society and act like nothing had happened.

He checked the time on his digital wristwatch. Rolling his neck, his bones popped before he extended his arm and took his glass between his fingers. Sipping his Tom Collins, the lemon juice puckered his lips and the carbonation caused him to hiccup. It was the night cap that would close out his day. The last call before the real work began.

A smirk pulled his lips up.

The alcohol made his head spin. Adrenaline had his heart pounding.

Closing his eyes, he slumped further into the chair, threading his fingers together over his stomach. Inside his mind, he could see the beautiful woman he'd picked up earlier dancing and twirling around him. He could feel her pulse tick against his fingers as he held her close. He could still see the look in her eye after their first kiss. The scent of her perfume clinging to his clothes.

He reached to his crotch, adjusting his manhood as it grew hard.

Just thinking about her curvy figure was enough to destroy a man. A vixen—his trophy—the woman whose luck ran out.

He inhaled a deep breath, filling his lungs with pride.

Picking up women wasn't always this easy for him. Once, not long ago, he was the awkward gangly teenager who blushed every time a beautiful woman looked his way. Now, their cheeks bloomed a rosy red when he stared at them.

The bed sheets rustled. He casually opened his eyes, rolling his gaze to the motel bed. The woman dug her face deeper into the pillow and mewed a sexy sound. He watched her struggle to open her eyes, her lids heavy from the sedative he'd slipped into her drink.

He spread his knees further apart, the blood pumping hard and fast in his groin. Tipping his body forward, he rested his sharp elbows on his knees and stared for a moment before unclasping his cufflinks and setting them on the end table next to his chair.

The woman whimpered, sending his heart into a flutter.

Rubbing his moistened palms together, his gaze traveled over her smooth legs, across her tight bare stomach before stopping on her firm, perky breasts. His lips parted as he licked them. She was gorgeous. Young and beautiful. Glancing to her face, he found himself staring into her almond round eyes. They glistened with fear and he swore he heard the moment she stopped breathing.

He took one step closer—his confidence increasing by the second.

Her head turned as she jerked her arms against the binds. The restraints tightened around her wrists as her body flapped like a fish out of water. She glanced to her feet, her ankles bound in the same fashion as her arms. The whites of her eyes grew into large discs as panic set in. "What did you do to me?"

His heartrate ticked up a notch as excitement flushed through his body. He continued inching his way closer to the bed, rolling up his sleeves along the way. Tilting his head to the side, he soaked in her innocence in one deep inhale.

She was incredibly attractive. A shame she was so naïve to trust him, he had thought. She never saw it coming. Just another night out. Another fast hookup with a complete stranger. Little did she know that a monster lay hidden beneath the charming good looks she lusted after. She should have known better.

"Nothing yet," he said with a grin.

The woman held his glare. Terror flashed across her eyes, tightening her face into something ugly and unattractive. "Who are you?" Her voice cracked.

He chuckled and moved closer. His knees touched the side of the bed and he extended his fingers straight so he could rake them up her legs. Her stomach quivered as she breathed harder. Then he touched her mound and she screamed.

He lunged forward and covered her mouth with his hand. Bucking her hips, she thrashed against the bed. The binds only tightened around her limbs and his erection grew harder.

Reaching behind him, he grabbed the silicone ball gag and worked it into her mouth before clasping the strap around her head. She fought, nipping at his hand with her teeth. He was too strong; there was nothing she could do to stop him.

He leaned close to her face. "I told you," his hot, alcohol-filled breath swirled into her ear, "they call me The Lady Killer."

CHAPTER TWO

A CHILL WORKED ITS WAY UP MY COLLAR AND SENT A shiver down my spine.

Outside, a cold autumn wind blew. The leaves that had already fallen gathered against the curb and swirled in puddles left over from last night's rain. The black pavement glistened from the street lights when I glanced to the dashboard clock—6:53AM.

I turned my head and flicked my gaze out my window.

Nothing about today felt right. The sun should have lifted over the eastern horizon by now. And it would have on most days. But today wasn't beginning like most days. Not only did the weather make me feel off, I was still without a story. No copy to hand in to my editor. Nothing to show for my efforts except this cheap coffee and tired eyes.

I zipped up my jacket tighter. It was an unusually gray for Denver, and the low hanging clouds threatened to spit out more rain before the storm broke. We needed the rain, especially after the scorching summer that had left the state in a drought, but I wished it would have come another night, a night I was tucked peacefully inside my bed, sleeping.

Curling my lips over the rim of my gas station to-go coffee, I was already missing the sunshine. I welcomed both the warmth and the caffeine the dark roast offered as I took a moment to appreciate the change of seasons—a brief reprieve from the darker reality I was both hoping to discover, yet praying to keep astray.

Turning my head back to the motel entrance, I knew this was where my next story would begin. I'd caught word of it unfolding on my police scanner just as I was tucking myself into bed for the night, and though I hadn't wanted to leave my son home alone—again—I knew I didn't have much choice.

My gaze darted to my mirrors between glancing toward the clock. Twisting my silver rings over my knuckles, I kept expecting other members of the media to arrive any minute. I flipped between websites on my phone. One was my personal blog, the other *The Colorado Times*—my current employer. A constant anxiety kept me on edge as I wondered which one would be my future with the paper's survival looking bleak.

I caught movement out of the corner of my eye and I lifted my gaze over the dash.

The chaos from a few hours ago was too big to pass up. Police cruisers filled the parking lot and I watched as the medical examiner came and went, wheeling out a body on a gurney.

I drummed my feet on the car floor unable to control my excitement. I knew it was a strange response to death—maybe even murder—but without it, I would be planning my own funeral for the death of my career.

Someone had died—perhaps was even killed—and I wanted to be the first to break the story.

I inhaled a deep breath of air and blew out a heavy sigh of anxiety.

There were still a few uniformed officers hanging on, and

a couple detectives lingering beside them. I watched, deciding who to take my chances with first—the cops or the motel staff? The crime scene investigators were still inside and, from my experience, I suspected they would be finished soon. A single body had rolled out; how bad could it be?

Adrenaline rushed through me and I could feel the coffee beginning to perk me up.

When my feet stopped tapping, I drummed the wheel, keeping an eye open for other reporters. I couldn't believe I was still alone. Maybe it was the weather, or perhaps I was just that lucky.

I finished my coffee just as the detectives got in their vehicle and finally left the scene. It was almost time. I pulled myself up in my seat, keeping a close eye on the motel entrance. The last members of the CSI team followed shortly after and I gathered my hair in my hands, tying it off in a ponytail before leaving my car and braving the chill.

Scampering into the motel front lobby, I pulled my hands out of my jacket pockets and greeted the young manager working the desk. "One night of rain and I'm already over it."

He gave me a knowing look. His eyes were still bugged and rattled by whatever happened here last night. The young man was looking through me as he stared. I was thankful for it. It made my job easier as I befriended those I needed to give me the story I wanted.

"I'd like to check out a room," I said.

He blinked and he was suddenly somewhere else. Recognition flashed over his pupils and I held my breath, hoping he didn't recognize me from my crime and court column. I glanced to his desk and saw his cellphone. I doubted he read newspapers. He seemed more like a social media addict than a print kind of guy. But who really read newspapers anymore, anyway?

"A room?" He blinked.

I nodded.

"For the night?" he asked as he brought his fingers to the computer keyboard.

"I'd like to check out a particular room." His eyes lifted and he cocked his head to the side. I paused and stared for a moment before saying, "The room the police were just inside of."

His left hand started to fidget when he frowned. "I... uh..." he stuttered.

Reaching to my back pocket, I pulled out my media badge and told him I was with *The Colorado Times*. "Just a quick look around. That's all."

He barely glanced at my credentials. "I'm sorry. That room is unavailable." His young age was really beginning to show.

I brought my hands to the counter and leaned against it. "Then maybe you can tell me what happened here last night?" I smiled.

The young man glanced to the front double doors as if longing for the police to come back and save him from me. He wasn't going to get off that easy—especially since I had chosen him to speak with first. It was always a gamble, but the cops were generally assholes in the beginning stages of their investigations. They never told me anything. At least not when it mattered.

"I can't afford bad press," the young man stammered.

His answer surprised me and I had to give him a little bit of credit for connecting the dots.

"I understand." My voice was sincere. "It's bad for business."

His innocent eyes stared as he nodded in agreement.

I dropped my gaze to his nametag. "Brian, let me tell you what's really bad for business." He swallowed hard. "Hiding the fact that a murder took place on your watch." Calling the death a murder was another gamble but, in doing so, I hoped he would confirm it for me.

His face paled. "I wasn't working. My shift didn't start until five."

I rubbed at an eyebrow.

"I swear."

Then I turned to face the opposite wall and said, "I could always write about how this motel in particular is a favorite spot for sex workers to take clients." Swiveling my head back around to face Brian, I continued, "And, of course, I would have to mention your name since you were the manager I spoke with."

"Fine. I'll let you inside the room." He reached beneath his desk and came up with a room key. "But you can't mention to anyone that I gave you this. The cops told me I couldn't say anything to anybody."

"You can trust me." I smiled and took the key into my hand. My brows pinched. "Does this place have surveillance cameras?"

"The cops already took it."

"What else did they take?"

His shoulders rounded. "The guest register and a list of potential witnesses. That's all I know. Like I said, I wasn't here when the murder happened."

A knowing smirk pulled at my lips. *Bingo*. That was all I needed to hear. Someone was murdered. Just as I suspected. An all too familiar numbness wrapped around my heart like a cocoon. "Do you know the deceased's name?"

He drew back, making himself appear smaller. Then he nodded his head once. "Mallory Madison."

"Thank you, Brian. I'll return the key when I'm finished."

CHAPTER THREE

EVERY GREAT STORY HAD A STRANGE BEGINNING AND A tragic end.

I told those stories. Better than anybody. It was how I'd made a name for myself and the reason I was first on scene today. My instinct brought me here, and this was what I loved most about my job. The chance to play detective. Uncover that story hidden in the rubble. Brush it off, give it life, and provide enough detail and narration to get people invested in knowing more.

A tingle rolled down my arm. My heart beat faster and every sense in my body was now on high alert. Feeling my eyes narrow and my lips curve upward, I lowered my chin and marched toward the stairs with a lengthening stride.

There was something about walking in the footsteps of evil that made you feel alive. It was like stepping into a haunted house on Halloween, your nerves jumping and anticipating when a monster or ghost would reach out and scare you. It could happen around the next bend, or never happen at all. You never knew and always had to be ready.

When I reached the staircase, I began climbing to the

top, moving closer to my next story. I listened to my heels
click-clack up the two flights before landing on the carpeted
second floor hall.

I stopped and stared.

The florescent light lit up my path and I could still smell
the swarms of police and lab units that had roamed this hall
before me. It was a strange, yet familiar, mix of cologne,
energy drink, and chemicals.

I wiped my clammy palms on my thighs, lifted my foot,
and began moving.

My vision narrowed and the hallway walls closed in
around me as I prepared myself for getting in and out as
quick as possible. Brian made a mistake in granting me
access. I shouldn't be here. I knew I wasn't allowed. But it
was important to see the scene of the crime to understand
the atrocity that had been committed. Besides, I needed to
work with the facts the police were given—including the list
of potential witnesses, the guest register, and a list of the
evidence found. I could ask the police myself but I knew I
would be denied this early in the investigation. Going
through Brian was a risk I was willing to take if it meant
uncovering the truth.

I stopped at the door for room 2C and glanced to the
key firmly grasped in my hand. The leather keychain
matched the door number. I rolled my neck from side to
side, glancing up and down the hallway, listening for
activity.

There was nothing. Only silence. I grinned.

*How many of these rooms were full at the time the murder took
place?* I slid the room key into the lock, my head full of questions. That was information Brian would give me before
I left.

Pushing the door open, it swung on its hinges as I ducked
my way through the yellow police tape. Immediately, I was hit

with the intense smell of the sickly-sweet decomposition of death.

I took shallow breaths through my mouth as I flicked on the overhead light and latched the door closed behind me. Pulling latex gloves out from my jacket pocket, I pulled them over my fingers as I scanned the room.

My heart thrashed in my ears.

Heat bloomed across the backs of my shoulders.

The hairs on the back of my neck stood on end.

I turned to the wall, glancing to the thermostat. It had been turned way down and I doubted it was done by the police. Reaching to my back pocket, I pulled out my cell-phone and readied it for pictures.

I dictated along the way, noting how the bed sheets were tossed and there were no signs of blood or bodily fluids. Flipping the pillows, they were clean. Nothing stood out. Not even a stain. Everything else, swept clean by CSI. I both admired the lab and was frustrated at the same time for their thorough work.

I edged around the bed and noticed the phone line was pulled from the wall jack. I took a photo and moved on to the digital clock persistently blinking 12:01. I took a photo of that, too, before stepping into the bathroom.

The sink and shower gave the appearance that they hadn't been used. I opened the sink drain and dug out some hair. I did the same with the shower. Both were dry as a bone, confirming that they hadn't been used in quite some time. Turning on a heel, I found the towels still hanging perfectly folded on their rack. Convinced the murder took place on the bed, I moved back to the bedroom and flicked on the television with the remote. A national news channel came on, its talking head spitting out fiery political hysteria. I quickly turned it off and took a closer look at the bed.

Running the tip of my finger around the edge, I stopped

at the first solid groove. Dropping to my knees, I took a closer look. It was unmistakable what I was seeing—feeling. The wood stain had been rubbed completely off and a fresh hole had been drilled on all four of the corners.

My stomach churned.

With a pinched expression, I pulled back and turned my head around to stare at the empty armchair sitting in the corner of the room, trying to make sense of it all. *Another sex crime gone bad? Or was this the work of something else? Who was this person who had died and who did they come here with?* I had nothing but the name Mallory Madison. Everything seemed fresh but, strangely, the air was absent of the dank smell of sex.

A cool breeze swept in under the door.

Shadows followed.

I held my breath, feeling my eyes widen as I stared, hoping my presence remained unknown. Suddenly, I doubted my being here was a good idea. I could feel the clock ticking, my time about to expire. Pressing my lips together, I waited to move until the sounds were gone.

It was now 8AM and I could hear the pellets of rain hitting the window.

Standing, I pulled back the thick drapes. I had the strange feeling of being watched. The parking lot seemed to be no different from the way I had left it. No cops. No news vans.

Outside, the mood was still damp, a perfect metaphor for the day. This neighborhood seemed to attract the worst and, though I had covered many stories in the area, I had never felt as anxious as I did now.

A shadowy figure appeared from behind a nearby tree.

I swallowed and felt my throat close.

The rain came down harder and made it impossible to make out a face. But I knew that I was being watched. It was no coincidence that this person—whoever they were—was staring up at this particular room like they knew what had happened.

Was it the killer? A witness I could tap for information?

I released the drapes with a surge of adrenaline opening up my veins. I rushed out of the room and ran down the stairs as fast as I could. Tossing my key to Brian along the way, I slammed my way through the glass doors and sprinted around the building, hoping to catch the person before it was too late. But, by the time I arrived, there wasn't anybody around. The person had vanished.

CHAPTER FOUR

I WAS STILL WORKING TO CATCH MY BREATH WHEN I received a call from my son's high school principal. "Mr. Craig, is everything all right?"

"Ms. Bell," his deep voice was grim, "you know I wouldn't be calling you if it wasn't important."

My eyes darted over cars, behind trees, and to the corners of nearby buildings still looking for that mystery person. "No, of course not." My eyebrows drew together. "Is this about Mason?"

There was a pause followed by a sound of what I imagined to be Mr. Craig rubbing a hand over his face. "It is."

"Is everything all right?" I asked again as I wiped my forehead with the back of my hand.

"Ms. Bell, I was hoping I could speak with you in person."

I wet my lips. The rain had finally let up as I glanced to my watch. I should have been home when Mason left for school. Instead, I was sitting here by myself chasing my next story. A pain in the back of my throat formed when I said, "I can be there in twenty minutes. Is Mason there?"

"Mason is in my office. I'll see you soon, Ms. Bell."

I pulled my cellphone away from my ear and muttered a curse. Retreating into my nearly twenty-year-old Subaru Outback, I glanced into the mirror, thinking I looked as awful as I felt. My hair was damp from the rain, my eyes swollen from the lack of sleep.

The engine cranked over on the second try. Every misfire was one day closer to the end of my vehicle's life. I could feel the car on its last legs, sputters, hisses, and whines coming from underneath. It had over 200K miles on it and, though I knew I could benefit from an upgrade, I didn't have the money for something new. At least, not on my current salary.

Making my way to the highway, I didn't like the suspense Mr. Craig had left me with. I knew that Mason was safe, but something had happened. I was walking in blind, and that kept me on edge. *What did he do? Why could it not be solved over the phone?*

Rush hour was stop and go out of Aurora. I didn't have far to go but it took much longer than I'd anticipated. By the time I arrived at North High School, I was already 10 minutes behind schedule. There was nothing I could do about my appearance and wet hair so I rushed inside and checked in at the office, anxious to know what kind of trouble Mason was in.

"I'm here to see my son, Mason Bell," I said as I filled out the visitor form. "I was called by Mr. Craig."

The secretary turned her head toward the principal's office. Mr. Craig caught my gaze through the glass and waved for me to come inside.

"Appears he's ready for you." The secretary smiled.

Mason was sitting with his back to me when I entered the office. My son barely looked at me. Mr. Craig stood from behind his desk and greeted me. We shook hands and I apologized for running late.

"Please. Have a seat." Mr. Craig motioned to the empty seat next to Mason.

I leaned over and kissed Mason on the forehead before sitting. His spine was curled in the chair and he had an angry teenage look on his face. "What couldn't you say over the phone?" I asked.

Mr. Craig threaded his fingers together on his desk as he rolled his eyes to Mason. "Would you like to tell your mom, or should I?"

Mason was quiet. I darted my gaze between them. "Somebody please, speak."

"There was a fight between periods." Mr. Craig's eyebrows raised with concern. "Ms. Bell, your son punched another student."

Mason jumped forward in his chair. "Mom, this guy deserved it."

I held up my hand and felt my muscles quiver with sudden anger. I turned to Mr. Craig and asked calmly, "Is the other boy all right?"

"He got knocked in the face pretty good." He tipped his chin back. "There was a lot of blood but I think he'll be okay."

My jaw clenched as I stared at my son, wondering what happened to the well-behaved boy I'd raised.

"Unfortunately, it didn't end there for Mason."

My brows shot up as I gently turned my head back to Mr. Craig.

"Mason then left school grounds, ditched half of second period, and came back trying to fool us into thinking he never left."

I inhaled a deep breath through my nose. "I'll handle this, Mr. Craig."

"Ms. Bell, we have a zero-tolerance policy when it comes to school violence."

"I'm aware."

"I spoke with Mason before you arrived and we came to an agreement." Mr. Craig's eyes landed on my boy. "Haven't we, son?"

Mason glared at the school principal from under his brow before nodding.

Mr. Craig rolled his eyes back to me. "His classroom assignments for today have already been provided by his teachers."

"Excuse me?" My head angled to the side. "Are you saying—"

Mr. Craig nodded. "I'd like Mason to take today to cool off. He's welcome to come back tomorrow as long as he comes in peace. But, if this happens again, I can assure you that his suspension will be much longer."

I balled one hand into a tight fist. "I'm truly sorry," I said as the bell for the end of second period rang.

Mr. Craig stood. "Live and learn, isn't that right, Mason?"

Mason nodded, stood, and slung his heavy backpack over his shoulder. I shook Mr. Craig's hand and thanked him for calling me. He apologized for interrupting my work and I did my best to not seem annoyed.

I headed to the car, wondering what I was going to do with Mason. He was quiet. I was going to be pulling teeth to get him to talk. Falling behind the steering wheel, I stared at Mason as he gazed toward the school.

"How are you feeling?" I asked as soon as I started to drive.

"How do you think I'm feeling?" he barked.

"I don't know what has gotten into you, but your bad attitude has got to change."

Mason looked ahead. "He deserved it, Mom. You should have heard what he said."

I shifted gears and changed lanes. "I would like to see you

get involved in some kind of activity. I think it would be good for you."

"I'm not cut out for varsity sports."

"It doesn't have to be sports. It could be a club of some sort. Or individual sports like skateboarding."

Mason turned his head to me with an annoyed look filling his face. "That involves a skateboard, which I don't have."

I pulled into the grocery store parking lot and stopped the car. "I don't know what to tell you, Mason. I'm doing the best I can for you—for both of us. But you can't just go around punching kids in the face because you don't like something they said."

Mason opened his door and stepped out. I met him on the other side of the car and together we entered the supermarket and headed to the frozen food aisle.

I picked up a handful of frozen meals when I heard Mason grumble, "Can't we eat something fresh for once?"

"I just picked up a case this morning."

"Is that why you weren't home?"

"Yeah," I said, unable to hide the shame I was feeling.

We made our way to check out and stood behind a man handing the cashier a fist full of coupons. I watched the cashier tally up his final bill and the man counted his cash. "It appears I'm short," I heard him say, embarrassment coming through on his cheeks and in his voice. "Can we take these off?" He reached for a bundle of bananas and a carton of milk.

"Don't worry about it, I'll pay for that," I said, stepping forward. The man smiled and said he couldn't let me do that. I insisted and told him to pay it forward sometime when he could.

After paying for our own groceries, Mason asked, "Why did you pay for that man's food?"

"Because it's the right thing to do."

"But you can't even afford the things I ask for."

I stopped at the car and locked my gaze on Mason. "You get your act together and you might start getting some of the things you ask for."

He rolled his eyes and shook his head just as my cellphone rang.

"Sam," Detective Alex King said as soon as I answered, "I don't know if you've heard, but there's been a murder and it has your name all over it."

CHAPTER FIVE

I WAS CAUGHT BETWEEN WORLDS—EITHER DECISION I MADE would come back to bite me. I could stay home with Mason and be a present mother. Or I could chase down this story and know that I would have a job next week.

"Don't forget to feed Cooper," I yelled through the open car window as Mason scampered up to our small single-story house on the north side of the city in the Highlands.

Mason held up his hand without bothering to turn and look.

Cooper, our yellow Labrador retriever, needed a walk, too, but I wasn't going to push my luck. I didn't want to do it, but I had no other choice but to leave Mason at home, alone, and head back out to meet up with Detective King.

I couldn't stop moving. I needed this story. Needed it for my career, but also to take my mind off of Mason.

Having two murders occur on the same night wasn't that unusual for the size of our city. But Detective King's urgency was. I couldn't wait to see what he had. It had to be something big—unusual.

This time my GPS took me south of downtown. It didn't take me long to arrive in the ritzy part of Cherry Creek where life seemed to be perpetually better than everywhere else, no matter the current state of our economy. The only difference today, due to the gloomy weather, was that the otherwise bustling sidewalks were void of pedestrian traffic.

I hadn't realized it until I arrived, but as soon as I pulled into the hotel parking lot, I knew this couldn't be coincidence. I guess my mind was preoccupied with what I was going to do with Mason to get him back on the straight and narrow before I could focus on thinking about another murder.

Reaching across the seat, I gathered my cellphone and voice recorder before stepping out of my car. With each hour that passed—and still without a solid story—I expected to be getting a call from Dawson, my editor, wondering if I still wanted to keep my column.

I weaved my way through the parked cars and edged around the area the police had sectioned off. Scanning the crowd for King, he was nowhere to be found. The CSI mobile lab had their vehicle parked next to the ME's van and I waited for the right moment before ducking the tape and hurrying inside.

I kept my head down and my eyes peeled for leads as I pushed my way through the front lobby.

The place was buzzing with activity. Murmurs from the crowd filled the room with muffled white-noise, making it difficult to hear. Uniformed officers circled around the hotel guests that had huddled in small circles to the side. It didn't take me long to find my opportunity. But I had to act fast because, this time, I knew that other members of the media were soon to follow.

Stepping past the potted plants, I found myself eyeing a young female staff member who'd just finished speaking with a detective. Looking around, I made my move. She had shoulder length hair and was nervously biting her nails. "Hi. I'm Samantha Bell with *The Colorado Times*. Do you work here?"

Her eyes glanced at my media badge. Then she nodded.

"Can you tell me what happened?"

Her gaze rolled over to the far reaches of the room. "I'm not sure I should be talking to you."

"It's okay," I said in my friendliest voice. "I was invited here by Detective King."

She bit her lip, paused, and then agreed to speak. "It's awful. A woman was murdered."

"Did you see it?"

She shook her head.

"Approximately what time did this occur?" I asked, thinking of the motel murder early this morning.

"I don't know." Her shoulders shrugged. "Early in the morning, I guess."

"Were you the one who called it in?"

She shook her head again.

"Can you tell me what floor and what room it happened in?"

She gave me a questioning look. "I thought you said you were invited by a detective?"

"You're right," I said, catching a buzzed-headed detective glaring at me from across the room. "Thank you for your time." I turned and left, confident I could figure it out myself before I was asked to leave.

Edging the back wall, I hid behind the crowds, overhearing the hotel guests talking.

"How could this have happened?" one guest asked.

"We were in the same building and the killer is still somewhere out there," another guest said.

They were afraid, and had every right to be. Two women

were dead and, without having any facts to prove otherwise, it could have been any one of us.

I walked past the elevators and began climbing the stairs. I stopped on each floor, peeking my head down the hall until I found what I was looking for on the fourth stop. I pushed my way through and the heavy door shut behind me. I was immediately met with resistance. A female cop hurried toward me with small beady eyes. "You're not allowed here."

"Relax." I showed the female officer my palms. "I'll stay out of your way."

"Like hell you will." She put her hands on me and said, "I know who you are."

"You read my column?" I said, feeling amused.

"Not anymore." She shoved me closer to the door when I heard a familiar voice call out.

"Hey. She's with me."

The female officer took her hands off me and we both turned to find Detective Alex King staring straight into my eyes. The female officer rolled her eyes and said, "I should have known."

"I'll escort her out of the building," King said.

My mouth pinched as King reached around me and pushed the staircase door open. What was he up to? Why had he bothered calling me here in the first place if he wasn't going to let me in?

King turned his head and raised his brows when I didn't move. I sighed and reluctantly stepped off the floor I'd come to investigate.

"What is going on?" I asked.

"Just what I told you." His hand was still on the door.

"Then why call me here if I'm not allowed to see it for myself?"

He rooted both of his hands into his hips. "You were at the motel this morning, weren't you?"

I put on my poker face but he knew me well enough to know I was there. He didn't have to ask. "Is this related?"

He scrubbed a hand over his face. "Christ, Samantha."

"How many suspects are you looking at?"

He gave me a look like he didn't know what to do with me. "This conversation is over."

"But you must have evidence to make you believe the two murders are related?"

"I never said that. You did." King held my stare. "We're still waiting to receive word back from the ME about estimated times of death." Suddenly, voices echoed up the staircase chamber. King stepped forward and peeked over the side. "C'mon. It's best we talk somewhere more private."

I pointed at him with my index finger and reluctantly followed him back to the lobby. He led me outside, past the crowds and news vans where we couldn't be heard. Then he stopped on the grass and said, "It's always the worst when we have weather like this."

"I need something, Alex," I said, needing to cut through the twine. "You can't just call me down here and expect me to leave without getting a story I can work with."

He kept his head down and his eyes up as he scanned to see who might be listening. "I'm sorry. I can't. You should have got here sooner."

I clenched my jaw and wanted to hit him. "Did you call me down here because you had something for me? Or did you just want to see me?"

He inched closer and lowered his voice. Suddenly, I was completely aware of his presence and I crumbled inside. "Her name is Veronica Mills. She discovered the body."

My brows shot up. "Is she still here?"

"Over my left shoulder." He wagged his head toward the lobby windows. "Red hair. Pony tail. Wearing the hotel uniform. Talk with her and you'll have your story."

I pivoted around him and hurried back inside before I lost sight of Veronica.

"Sam," King called. I stopped at the door and turned to look at him. "If anyone asks, you didn't get it from me."

CHAPTER SIX

VERONICA MILLS WAS TUCKED INTO A CORNER AND surrounded by cops.

I slithered between the people like a snake, going undetected across the floor. I couldn't take my eyes off of her. I wanted to know what she knew—what she'd seen and if it would provide me with any clues to confirm that we'd had a double homicide committed by the same perpetrator.

The murmur of voices dimmed the closer I got to Veronica.

My vision tunneled and, with each step closer to my star witness, the easier it was to see her vulnerability. I circled like a shark, waiting for the perfect moment to strike. She was young and bright-eyed. A frail little woman with porcelain skin. Her hands trembled and, when our eyes met, I made my move.

I walked over to her quickly, knowing my time was limited. It was important I built her confidence back up before the trauma wiped her memory clean.

"Hi Veronica, my name is Samantha Bell and I'm with *The Colorado Times*."

Her head floated toward the ceiling as she stared at me.

"I understand you were the one to find the body?"

She did a quick once-over. I was casually dressed, my hooded sweatshirt still damp. "I did," her meek voice squeaked.

"Can you tell me what time that was?"

"A little after six." She swallowed. "I received a call at the front desk saying there had been an accident and the guest was in need of new sheets."

"Do you know who made that call?"

"I assumed it was from the guest."

"Male or female?"

"Honestly," her eyes glistened, "I don't know."

"That's enough," a man barked behind me before I could get a name.

Veronica ran a jerky hand through her flaming red hair as I flipped my head around and found the buzzed-headed detective from earlier staring me down. He hovered over me with the pompous authority most men in this room shared when it came to dealing with reporters. Maybe it was just women they despised. Or, perhaps, just me.

"Detective John Alvarez," I said cheerily. "How great it is to see you."

His brow wrinkled as he chuckled, acting semi-impressed that I knew him by name. "What do you think you're doing, Bell?"

"Nothing important." I figured I might as well say what he wanted to hear, not wanting to waste valuable breaths.

Detective Alvarez rolled his eyes to Mills. "You know she's a reporter, right?"

Mills's hands fidgeted around her waist as she nodded. "She told me."

"Come on, Bell. You'll have your chance to ask the department questions, but I can't have you speaking with witnesses."

"It's just girl talk."

"Then this girl talk has to wait." Alvarez lifted his arm and corralled me toward the herd.

I turned to Veronica. "Don't let these men push you around. If you want to continue our conversation, I'll be right over there," I said, pointing to the coffee machine.

Veronica nodded, folding her arms tightly over her belly before lowering herself back into the chair I'd originally found her sitting in.

"You're lucky I don't kick you out completely," Alvarez said from behind as he followed me across the room.

"You have a strange way of flirting," I told him.

"Who told you about what happened here, anyway?" He looked around as if just now noticing no other members of the media were on the scene.

"It's just my natural brilliance." I raised one brow and grinned.

Alvarez gave a hard smile and turned his head. But, before he left, he said, "If I find you inserting yourself into the investigation again, I really will kick you out."

"Understood, Detective." As soon as he turned his back, I rolled my eyes and snatched a coffee cup off the table. A quick brew and a minute later, I had my lips curling over the rim.

I'd had Veronica just about to open up and I liked that she was willing to talk. I needed to finish my interview but there was no way I was going to get back to her any time soon. Especially with Alvarez breathing down my neck.

An hour of pacing the room passed and still no one was making any fast moves. I wondered what they had found in the room and why I hadn't seen King. This crime must have been more gruesome than the last because one thing

Veronica said stuck with me. The guest called down requesting new sheets.

Veronica stood and my heart began to race.

I watched as she whispered something into the ears of the two uniformed officers tasked with keeping an eye on her. Alex was right, this was my story. It had my name all over it. I couldn't miss my opportunity.

Keeping my head down, I watched Veronica from afar. And, when I realized she was heading to the women's room, I double-checked Alvarez's position before tossing my coffee in the trash and making a run for it. I wasn't going to let this story slip through my fingers.

I moved swiftly and with purpose. Pushing through the restroom door, I surprised Veronica. "Are we alone?"

Her eyes flitted across the white walls. Nodding, she said, "I think so."

"Look, we don't have much time." Without taking my eyes off of Veronica, I reached behind my back and locked the door. "You have to tell me what you saw."

Her nostrils flared as she gasped for breath. Her eyes watered as she muttered, "I can't believe it happened here."

I stepped forward and took her trembling hand inside of mine. "What did you see?"

"A woman. She was... uh... tied up and naked."

"Dead?" Veronica nodded as a whimper passed over her dry lips. She covered her mouth with her free hand and I squeezed her shoulder. "It's all right. What else?"

"There was a ball or something stuck in her mouth."

"A gag?"

She nodded as her brow furrowed. "And she was bound by restraints attached to hooks that had been drilled into the corners of the bedframe."

A knock on the door sent my pulse racing.

"How was she killed?"

"I don't know."

"Was there blood?"

She shook her head. "I don't think so."

Another hard knock on the door.

"Here's my card," I said, pushing my contact information into her hand. "Is it all right if I contact you again?"

Her eyes bounced with mine. "I'm scared."

"I know, sweetie. You didn't do anything wrong." Veronica nodded. "I have to go, but please call me if you remember anything else about what you saw or who might have committed the murder."

"Shit." She tipped her head back and shoved a hand through her thick locks. "Okay."

Releasing her hand, I turned to the door.

"Are you going to publish what I told you?"

I stared into her brown eyes, not knowing how to answer. "Take care of yourself, Veronica." Then I stepped out and headed toward the exit.

My mind was reeling with what Veronica had seen. King had led me to believe these two murders were connected and now I was certain of it. I didn't know how these women were killed or why but, clearly, somebody's kink had gone terribly wrong.

"You're not leaving me, are you?" Alvarez called after me.

"Sorry, but I have to run."

"Put in a good word for me, will you?"

I waved and smiled. "Kiss my ass," I said beneath my breath.

Suddenly, I froze like a deer in headlights when I caught sight of the same mystery figure from the motel. *Was this the killer?* Again, it was impossible to determine a gender with how they wore their hood over their head and how they hid their eyes with mirrored sport sunglasses—unnecessary on this rainy ray. They were average height, average build. We stared for a moment as if deciding what to do next. Without warning, the person turned on a heel and split.

My eyes popped. I couldn't believe what I was seeing. I dug my toes into the pavement and began chasing after them. Only the guilty ran. And, as my lungs burned to catch up, I questioned what I would do if I did catch whoever this was. I had no way to protect myself. Before I could change my mind, they jumped on a city bus and disappeared.

CHAPTER SEVEN

I STAYED UP LATE TRANSCRIBING MY NOTES FROM THE LAST 24 hours. When I was finished, I lay awake staring at the moonlit ceiling, questioning if I had the angle of my story correct.

Minutes turned to hours.

I tossed and turned.

My mind was unable to rest.

I thought about what I had seen in the motel room and what Veronica had found in the hotel. King knew more than what he was saying and, though I knew answers would soon come to me, I was stuck on the mystery figure that kept showing up.

Who was this person and what did they want? Were they following me or the police?

Though I had only seen them twice, both times they left my stomach churning. Something about them was off. The fact they kept running away from me left me feeling exposed.

When my alarm finally went off, I slung my arm across the empty bed and slapped the buttons blindly until the noise went away. Silence filled the room but my head still rattled.

I covered my face with a pillow and groaned. Then, without realizing what I had done, I found myself lying flat on my back with my arms and legs extending to the corners of the bed—exactly how Veronica said the second victim had been found.

When I blinked, I felt my toes curl.

Sex crimes always left me with a sour taste in my mouth. The victims, nearly always female. The perps, nearly always men. But before I jumped to any conclusions, I needed to know more about who these women were and why they had been targeted.

On my way to the kitchen, I knocked on Mason's door. "You awake? Don't forget, you have school today." I waited for an answer as Cooper moseyed on up to me. Nothing came from behind the door. "Your ride is leaving in thirty minutes."

Again, there was no response but when I heard his covers hit the floor, it was enough for me to get Cooper fed and quickly plow through a bowl of cereal. By the time I finished eating, Mason stepped into the kitchen and tossed his school bag to the floor. He opened the fridge and quickly shut it.

"You're not going to eat?" I asked.

He fell heavily onto the wooden bench at the table. "Can I have some money?"

"Did you complete yesterday's assignments?"

"Mom, c'mon. I'm not an idiot."

"No one said you were." I sighed. "What do you need money for?"

"I'll get something to eat at school."

He held my gaze and I hoped he was being sincere. Standing, I moved to the counter, dug in my purse, and pulled out a twenty. Handing it to Mason, I said, "I need you to have a better day today."

"I will, Mom," he said, stuffing the crumpled bill into his front pocket.

"C'mon," I smiled, "we're going to be late."

Mason was quiet for the short drive to school. I encouraged him to keep his focus on himself, to remain positive and not let what others said get to him. I wasn't sure he was listening but at least I felt better, knowing I'd tried.

As soon as I pulled to the curb out front, Mason hopped out barely saying goodbye. I let it go as I watched him catch up with a friend. He glanced over his shoulder one last time, getting me to smile. Parents around me said their goodbyes and, when I caught a father fist bumping his son, my heart broke.

Dropping my face into my hand, I felt like I was losing control of my son. I didn't know what to do to make him feel happy—to get him to stop blaming himself for being raised by a single mother. Mason needed more than what I could offer, and I hoped that I could help him find whatever it was he was looking for.

Reaching for my cellphone, I typed up a quick text message.

Can you meet me today? I would really like to speak with you. I'm available when you are. Call me.

The car behind me honked and I knew it was my time to leave.

CHAPTER EIGHT

I WAS STILL WAITING FOR A CALL BACK WHEN I WALKED into the newsroom.

The chaotic chatter stopped me in my tracks. Phones were ringing like crazy and every person seemed to be tugging their hair or pacing in circles like a chicken whose head had been cut off.

A part of me hoped it had something to do with these murders, but I knew better. The police were tightlipped with their investigations and hadn't given anything away. No one was going after a story they didn't know much about. And, as far as I was concerned, I still knew the most outside of the department.

One step forward and I nearly collided with my colleague, Trisha Christopher. "Sam, you're the only calm face in this room."

I didn't react. "Is there a reason for me to be acting crazy?"

Trisha barked out a laugh. "You haven't heard, have you?"

"I guess not," I said, casting gaze to my palm, checking my phone for messages.

Trisha's head swiveled around on her shoulders. "We're all going to be out of a job soon if this buyout goes through."

My gaze swept up to hers. "It's really happening, then?"

"The rumors were true, girl." Her head bobbed like a buoy in the ocean. "*The Colorado Times* has now become *The Desperate Times*." Trisha hurried away, clinging to her manila folders as if someone was out to take them away.

I wasn't at all surprised by the news. There had been talk for several months now and, with the way our audience had drifted away from print and onto free digital content, frankly, I was surprised we had lasted this long.

Heading to my desk, I ignored the collective feeling of fear spreading from the potential mass layoff. We were all overworked, the paper was understaffed, the employees underpaid. And though I couldn't afford to lose my job, it wasn't my decision to make.

I sat behind my desk and got to work.

The first victim's name popped into my head and I quickly plugged Mallory Madison into the search engine. The pages populated but I soon realized that working with only a name wasn't going to be enough. I turned to Facebook. Several minutes of searching later and I had a hit. I was certain I had found her, and completely lucky that her profile hadn't been made private. Scrolling through her photos, she seemed like a decent young professional. Wasn't a huge party goer but appeared to enjoy a fancy drink from time to time. Men were common in her life and I couldn't place her profession. But, what I did notice, was a close friend, Abby Wales. She was everywhere. Tagged. Commenting. You name it. She was all over it. Several more minutes of research and I had Abby's home phone number and was giving her a call.

The line rang until clicking over to voicemail. Frustrated with having to leave a message, I introduced myself and told her I was calling to ask her a couple questions about her friend, Mallory Madison. When I hung up, I made a quick note to myself to follow up if I didn't hear back from her soon.

"Sam," I turned to find Dawson standing over me with a grim look on his face. "Can I speak with you in my office?"

I openly stared, worried my time here might be about to expire. The lines on Dawson's face deepened and my stomach sank. Whatever this was about, I knew it couldn't be good.

CHAPTER NINE

I DISCREETLY CHECKED MY PHONE FOR MESSAGES ONE LAST time before stepping into Ryan Dawson's office. There was still nothing from King and the longer he ignored my text, the more frustrated I became.

Dawson shut the door, closing off the perpetual sounds of keyboards clicking and printers whirring. "Sam, please, have a seat."

I dragged my feet over the floor and did as he said. I didn't like how Dawson kept referring to me by name. Perhaps I was overthinking this request of his to meet privately. But there was too much on the line. Not to mention the added stress of my challenges at home. The last thing I needed was to be let go from a job I loved.

Dawson leaned his tailbone against the edge of his desk, folded his arms over his chest, and lowered his head. "I assume you've heard the paper is changing ownership."

I felt my throat close up when I nodded.

"We've been bought out by a group of New York hedge funders." He inhaled a sharp breath of air. "I'm afraid our future around here doesn't look promising." He paused and stared which made me hold my breath for what was coming next. "I'm afraid our best days are probably behind us."

"Why did you call me in here, Dawson?" I tried not to sound defensive but my tone came out much harsher than I intended.

He lifted his chin and laughed lightly.

My brows knitted as my core temperature spiked.

Staring over the newsroom, Dawson had a longing gaze as he said, "I don't know how this industry found itself facing extinction. But that's where we're headed." He flicked his gaze back to me. "In its last days."

Realizing Dawson didn't call me in here to fire me, I felt a renewed sense of courage bubble up inside. "That may be, but I'm not going to let it stop me from doing my job. And neither should you."

He gave me a knowing look. "You have something for me?"

I opened the folder clenched between my fingers and handed him the copy I'd written up last night.

"What's this?" His eyes quickly read the first paragraph.

"Tomorrow's headline." I cocked an eyebrow and told him how I believed the two murders were connected. He had listened to the police scanners but he also knew that the police had yet to make an official statement in either case. "You have to trust me on this," I said.

"I can't take any risks." Dawson rounded his desk and set my story in front of him.

"We'll break the story first."

He leaned forward, perching his weight on his splayed fingertips. "You're speculating, Sam."

"I have a credible source and I was there. Inside the motel room. I saw it all, Ryan."

"Christ, Bell." He shook his head.

I turned to look at the muted television screens Dawson

had flickering on the wall. They were stuck on local and national politics. As annoying as it was, it was also encouraging to see as I wanted to be the first reporter credited for linking the two murders to the same killer.

"I can't."

"What? What do you mean? You know my word is good."

"It's not that."

"Then what is it?"

Dawson blew out a heavy breath. "I'm reassigning you."

"You're *what*?" My neck craned. "You've got to be kidding me."

He raised his brows and opened his eyes wider. "Aren't you the least bit curious to what job I'm tasking you with?"

"Not really."

"Charles is working a tight deadline." His shoulders rounded. "I need you to fill in for him."

My entire body tensed. "I work the crime and court desks. Not politics."

"Not if you want to keep your job, you don't."

I hadn't realized how tightly I was squeezing my phone until it vibrated with a text inside my hand. Casting my gaze to the screen, I saw it was King.

You have 20 minutes to get to me or I split.

I read the address and knew the spot.

"Here are the details." Dawson handed me the assignment. I reluctantly took it. "And, Sam, keep your head down. I need you to do your job and walk a tight line."

"Understood."

A serious expression crossed his face. "None of us are safe. We could all lose our jobs tomorrow."

CHAPTER TEN

I RUSHED TO THE MICROBREWERY NORTHWEST OF THE CITY with no time to spare.

Something told me that King would actually leave if I was one minute late. He didn't even know why I had asked to meet with him but he wasn't a fool, either. I needed to know more about what happened at the hotel. The news crews had dipped their toes into the story but the juicy details were yet to be told. I wanted to be the one to break the story open and King could be the one to make that happen.

Gathering my purse and phone, I left my car and scampered to the front entrance, pulling my sunglasses off my eyes. Yesterday's storm had lifted and it was back to feeling like an Indian Summer. Clear blue skies and comfortable temperatures. Just the way I liked it.

I took a moment to let my eyes adjust to the dim lighting inside. Sounds of laughter billowed from somewhere in the back and, as my vision cleared, the salty citrus smells of fresh beer whetted my palate.

"Sam." King lifted his hand and waved.

He was putting me on the clock when I'd been the one

who messaged. I hated when he knew I needed him more than he needed me. And that was exactly what was happening here today, whether he recognized it or not.

King held my gaze, watched me approach and take a seat opposite him at the table. There was a playful glimmer in his eye that had me feeling breathless. He pulled up his sleeve and checked his watch without comment.

I clasped my hands on the table, twisting my wedding band around my finger, saying, "Sixth Ave was slow moving, and let's not even talk about Wadsworth."

One corner of King's mouth lifted, deepening his dimpled cheeks. Chuckling, he lifted his full glass and took a sip from his beer.

"Breakfast?" I teased.

"Of champions." He winked.

It wasn't more than ten past ten and he was already drinking. I wanted to roll my eyes at the ridiculousness of it but I knew King was a responsible man by nature. Besides, I liked this playful side of him that I rarely got to see. He wore it well—if not too well.

"You weren't going to leave if I was late, were you?"

He wagged his dark brows and licked the froth off his top lip. "If I didn't threaten it, you'd make me wait."

I glanced up at him from beneath my lashes. "I don't like to procrastinate."

He cocked his head to the side.

"Okay, maybe a little." I bit my lip. "But always with good reason."

When King set his glass down and leaned back, I reached my arm across the table and stole it for myself. He watched me drink his beer like it was my own, swallowing down two tasty gulps before saying, "This place makes an amazing stout."

"What's amazing is watching you enjoy a dark stout." He grinned.

"The best." I pushed his glass back to him thinking how King knew me better than most. It was what I loved and hated about him. I couldn't keep anything a secret. We may have begun our friendship outside of work, but it had quickly turned—and continued to be—professional. His look this morning made me think there might be something else he was considering.

"So, what did you want to talk to me about?" He rested his arm on the back of the chair next to him, calmly leaning back as if settling in for a casual conversation.

I cast my gaze down and leaned forward. My knee bounced under the table as I murmured, "Mallory Madison."

The air between us paused. King looked away and scrubbed a hand over his face. After a minute of complete silence, he flicked his gaze back to me. The playful glimmer was gone, replaced with dark beady pupils that instantly put out the fire burning inside of me.

"What about her?" he asked.

"Veronica Mills told me what she saw inside that room." I could feel his muscles tensing beneath his collared button-up shirt. "I saw the holes drilled into the bedframe at the motel and, if what Veronica told me is true, I know that the two murders are related."

"Damn you, Bell." King dropped his elbows to the table and tipped his body forward. "That room was sealed off."

"Who is killing these women?"

King held my gaze before rolling his eyes to his beer. He didn't make a move. His nostrils flared. "You can't keep doing what you're doing. This is still an active investigation."

"I know that." My voice was calm, my tone soft.

"Do you?" His tone, on the other hand, was harsh but not

condescending. "Because if you tampered with an active crime scene, the repercussions could be severe."

I knew all that and had gone in anyway. I was desperate. "Why is it that the department seems to want to keep these murders quiet?"

"I should have left," King said, turning his head away.

My brows slanted as I stared.

King glanced to my cellphone. "Is that thing recording?"

"It's off," I assured him.

"Everything we discuss is off record." He locked eyes with me. "Got it?"

"Roger that." I turned my phone off for added measure. King trusted me, and I him, but there was a reason no one wanted to say anything about these murders and I needed to know why that was.

King filled his lungs before whispering, "You're right about the murders having similarities."

"Any leads?"

"There's enough evidence to get us started."

It was a weak response so I squeezed him for more information. "Suspects?"

"I believe we're looking for a male with dominance issues." King was an excellent profiler so, as I listened, I began taking notes inside my head to reference back to later. "Both victims were lured in—probably trusted the person who took them to the hotels. There weren't signs of struggle and I'm still waiting to receive the toxicology report."

"What about the security tapes?"

"We're studying the surveillance videos of both scenes but, honestly, we don't have a clear image."

"How many suspects are you looking at?"

"At least one. Could be more."

"How were they murdered?"

King's eyes drooped. "Strangulation."

Instinctively, I reached for my neck and touched my jugular. I could feel my blood pumping hard and fast as it entered my brain. "Did it happen during sexual intercourse?"

"That's what would naturally make sense, however, the ME assured us that there weren't any signs of any kind of intercourse on either of the victims."

My mind raced around the track with a slew of thoughts brewing. "I did a little research on Mallory Madison." King's head floated up. "She didn't strike me as a sex worker. What about the second victim?"

"Her name was Darcy Jean. To my knowledge, she wasn't in the skin trade either."

"But there's a chance?"

King shook his head. "I'd be surprised."

"Why is that?"

"Because she was a canvasser working for gubernatorial candidate, Philip Price."

My heart stopped. Price was the man Dawson had assigned me to interview. Did Dawson know about the connection and that was the reason he sent me instead of Charles? Or was the entire city being purposely left in the dark because of who might be involved?

"Sam, what is it?" King gently touched my elbow with the tips of his fingers.

I blinked and met his gaze. "I'll be interviewing Price this afternoon."

King gave me a knowing look as he leaned back. "If we can't get a wrap on this soon, Lieutenant will have no choice but to call in the FBI."

I reached for my phone, suddenly itching to get to my interview with Philip Price.

King intently stared. "Then neither of us will have anything, and we'll both be out of work."

CHAPTER ELEVEN

KING DIDN'T HAVE TO SPELL IT OUT FOR ME. I KNEW WHAT he was asking me to do. I had access to sources he didn't and could approach people who might be close to the murders in a less threatening manner.

Disguised as a reporter, I left King alone to finish his beer, promising to report back to him if I managed to uncover something of interest. He promised me the same.

I didn't mind doing him a favor, especially considering he'd given me more of a reason to meet with Price than I had before our quick meeting.

My Subaru sputtered and slowed considerably the moment I passed the town of Golden and started heading up the hill on I-70. Not thinking much of it, I turned my thoughts to how great a team King and I made.

He'd been good to me throughout my career and we had developed a tight bond over the years, but his request today was different. And it wasn't just the glowing look he was giving me, either. The wrinkles around his eyes were deeper, the bags heavier, and I knew these two murders were weighing heavily on him. He would never admit it—putting justice above his own health—but he'd seen the women and how they had died. I hadn't.

That was a luxury I wasn't about to take for granted.

A chill shot down my spine.

I wished King had photos of Darcy Jean. If only to put a face to her name. I liked seeing who I was fighting for. Though I had Mallory's image ingrained in my head, having Darcy's would only amplify my desire to find the person who'd done this.

Feeling my bones ache, I put on my blinker, switched to the middle lane, and passed a semi crawling its way to the top of the mountain. My tires rolled steadily as I gained altitude with each mile my car climbed. Not long after, I exited the highway and meandered my way across the hillside to Philip Price's gated driveway and requested entrance. "Samantha Bell, with *The Colorado Times*, here to see Mr. Philip Price."

The gate attendant checked his security log. Glancing at the clock on the wall he said, "You're early."

"Guess my clock is running fast."

The dark-complexioned man smirked. "Just head around the bend and you'll be able to park in the front."

I thanked the man, rolled up my window, and found myself sweeping my gaze across the front of the sprawling five-thousand square foot, three-level mansion as my tires crawled around the bend. I had heard about Price's wealth from his many car dealerships, but hearing it and seeing it were two different things. This place was incredible.

I parked off to the side, next to a stallion-black Escalade with tinted windows. The view was impressive from this vantage point. The city of Denver sat squarely in the middle of the canvas and it wasn't hard to imagine the thousands of twinkling lights at night.

Unbuckling my seatbelt, I reached across the console and

pulled my assignment sheet out from my handbag. Going over Dawson's notes, I took a minute to collect my thoughts.

Though I was here to ask him about his policies and what he was going to do for the state of Colorado, I couldn't stop thinking about Darcy Jean and my discussion with King.

I lifted my head and stared at the ponderosa pines for a brief moment before finding the courage to step out and face the man who might know something about his staff member's murder.

The front door opened unsolicited and I was met by candidate Price's campaign manager, Christy Jones. "Samantha Bell." She shook my hand. "I've heard so many great things about you. Your editor called me earlier and said you would be filling in for Charlie. It's so great to finally meet you in person."

I thanked her and extended my own pleasantries before following her inside the house. It was hard not to be impressed. The foyer was as large as my own house and the cathedral ceilings it opened up to were bright and welcoming as we passed a well-stocked library.

"I hope you don't mind," Christy said as we walked, "but I made a check-list of points Mr. Price would like to discuss."

As soon as she handed me the printed paper, I put my nose down and read through the bullet points. Christy suddenly stopped, turned, and faced me. I nearly walked right into her. Tucking my chin into my chest, I gave her a funny look.

"And there are also some subjects that are off limits," she whispered, pointing to the box at the bottom of the page.

I quickly scanned the text. "I can't discuss his wife's death?"

Her brows raised as she shook her head.

"But that's the juicy stuff," I said, dropping my head back

to the page. "With the right angle, it could show how Price was drawn to a higher cause in her honor."

"I like how you think." Christy smiled. "But no." She began walking again. "It's a sensitive subject. I do hope that you can respect that."

This was the very reason I didn't want to cover politics. There were always unwritten rules about what was and wasn't allowed. His wife's sudden death was over five years ago, and not being able to ask him about her didn't jive with me. I liked going against the grain. But I let it go because what I really wanted from Price was to know if there was an apparent connection to Darcy's murder and his campaign. Of course, I couldn't tell Christy that.

"Price is here to debate the issues the Colorado people want addressed. His personal life has been covered enough already. It's time we get him looking—and speaking—like the next governor of Colorado."

"Fair enough," I said as the hall opened up into a gigantic chef's kitchen with granite countertops, recessed lighting, and a crystal chandelier hanging impressively over the dining room table.

"Mr. Price," Christy announced cheerily, "the reporter from *The Colorado Times* is here."

Price had a small team surrounding him when he held up his finger and turned around. His lips pursed, if only for a second. I almost missed it. He was dressed in a perfectly pressed three-piece suit. His salt and pepper hair barely moved as he glided over to me with a cocked head. There was a certain arrogance radiating off of him and it was clear that he was accustomed to commanding whatever room he was in.

"You're a woman," he said.

I flicked my gaze to Christy. "That's not a problem, is it?"

"No. No. Of course not." He laughed, reaching for my hand. "It's just, when I heard the name Sam, I assumed—"

"Samantha," I said, pulling my hand away.

He paused and leaned in. "Beautiful name."

"Where would you like to sit for the interview," I looked around the room, only Christy paying any attention to what Price was doing, "or do you prefer to stand?" I landed my gaze on his. "Either way works for me."

A deep chuckle rumbled past his lips. "No B.S. I like it."

"We have drinks and snacks waiting in the living room," Christy said. "Why don't we all head in there?"

"Very good." Price smiled, still staring at me as he raised his eyebrows.

I didn't like the idea of walking in front of Price. I didn't trust his gaze to stay where it should be. He was a man of privilege and, because of his bachelorhood, I had the suspicion he believed his advances weren't anything but innocent.

Once in the living room, Christy stepped to the side. I took the leather sofa chair opposite the coffee table, knowing my decision left Price with having to take a seat on the couch—far enough to be out of reach. I geared up for my interview, arranging the recorder close to Price, and put pen to pad.

"I understand you would like to make today's interview about the issues our state is facing. Is that correct?" I began my interview.

Price leaned forward and covered the microphone piece on my recorder with his hand. In a hushed tone he said, "What I would like to see is that you get today's interview on tomorrow's front page." His smile hit his eyes.

I rubbed my brow as if warding off the impending headache I was sure to have once this interview was completed. "That's not my decision to make."

Price reeled his hand back in and leaned back. "I disagree."

My brows pinched. "I'm sorry?"

"If you tell a good story, the people in charge will have no choice but to put it out front." He grinned.

I blew out a heavy sigh and glanced to my empty notepad, already thinking of my exit strategy. "So, where would you like to begin?"

"Let's begin with the economy," he said, ironing his hands over his thighs.

Over the next half-hour, I painfully went through the call and response that came naturally with interviews. We discussed a wide range of issues, rounding the bases of state economics, his stance on natural resource management, the opioid crisis, and his plan to combat them all before I had grown bored.

Crossing my legs, I bit the end of my pen cap, staring at Price. "You know what I find strange?"

"What's that, sweetheart?"

Inside, I cringed. "Not once today has anyone mentioned anything about Darcy Jean." My eyes narrowed as I stared. "Why is that?"

"Let's keep the interview on point, shall we?" Christy intervened.

I glanced to Christy but I couldn't stop myself. "Mr. Price, when was the last time you saw Darcy?"

"That's enough." Christy lunged forward and hit pause on my recorder.

Price stared unwaveringly as his face paled.

I knew I had hit a nerve. Something about this guy had my alarm bells ringing. "A woman on your campaign is dead and you have nothing to say?"

"I think it's time for you to leave." Price's voice suddenly went soft.

"I'll show you to the door." Christy stood, glaring.

"Don't bother." I collected my things and stood. "I can find the exit myself."

CHAPTER TWELVE

MY HEART KNOCKED AND MY INSIDES FLOPPED AS I REFUSED to look over my shoulder one last time to see the blank expression filling Price's face.

Price hadn't moved since I asked about Darcy Jean. Frozen stiff with dull eyes staring out, he had the look of a guilty man experiencing sudden remorse.

As I exited the room and headed toward the front door, I knew I was onto something good.

Feeling slighted by my sudden departure, I heard Christy's heels clacking behind, hurrying to catch up with me. I didn't bother to turn around. Instead, I kept marching toward the front of the house, reliving the way Mr. Price greeted me when I'd arrived. If he treated all women like the way he treated me, I didn't doubt that maybe he had made an advance on Darcy. And, if he had, how did she react?

Two men in suits saw me coming and stepped to the side. A third asked if I was leaving and, when I said yes, he reached for the door and kindly opened it for me. Hurrying down the front steps, I felt my hair bounce off my shoulders as I picked up the pace and made a beeline for my parked car.

"Samantha, please, wait," Christy called after me.

I felt my lungs expand and my cheeks flush as I wanted to turn around and give her a piece of my mind. But with Dawson and my career's future to think of, I tightened the lid, sealing my anger inside.

Swinging my driver side door open, I tossed my purse into the passenger seat and dropped my bottom behind the steering wheel.

Christy grabbed my door before I could close it. "I'm sorry for what happened back there," she breathed heavily.

"Are you?" My head snapped in her direction. "Because it seems like this campaign is more concerned about hitting news cycles than they are about Darcy's death."

"You must understand." Her gaze danced with mine and I couldn't decide if it was desperation I saw or just plain panic. "Darcy's death was a surprise to us all."

"Then why did Price not want to discuss it?" I felt my knuckles go white as my grip tightened on the steering wheel. "He could have at least said his condolences. Instead, he said nothing."

Christy held my stare, a knowing look in her eye. It was just the two of us, alone, left with our scrambling thoughts and the magnificent view in the backdrop. Then she glanced over her shoulder and stared back at the house for a moment before saying, "Because he didn't know."

My mouth fell open. "What?"

Christy sighed. "The police notified me after they contacted Darcy's family but Price hadn't heard the news."

My brows slanted. "You kept it from him?"

Her head bobbed slowly. "His schedule is incredibly busy and I didn't want to distract him from the upcoming debate —or this interview—and cloud his mind with guilt, knowing one of our own had been murdered."

I flicked my gaze forward, shook my head, and felt my

stomach clench with disbelief. In Christy's attempt to protect her candidate, she was doing more harm than good. It didn't make sense and I knew for certain she wasn't as stupid as she was making herself out to be. What was really going on here?

"You think the other side doesn't know?" I turned back to face Christy. "They'll use it against him in the debate. Price will be made to look like a fool."

Christy backed away from the door, tucking her upper lip in while she did.

"Christy, what are you not telling me?" I locked eyes with her, refused to let go until she gave me a story I could actually believe.

Her eyes watered as her mouth twitched in an attempt to smile. "Darcy was a talented, brilliant young woman." She wet her lips with a quick swipe of the tongue. "Attractive, too."

"Did she have a known boyfriend?"

Christy looked to the house again. "From what I heard, she had many men in her life."

"What was her relationship with Price like?" She glanced to her feet. I could almost hear what she wasn't saying. "Were they together?"

Christy stared as I watched her mouth tremble. Her lips parted just as the front door to the house opened. Price stepped outside and quickly found us. "Christy," he called. "Come back in the house. We're done speaking with Ms. Bell."

"I have to go," she said.

"Christy, was Price having an affair with Darcy?" I said just loud enough for Christy to hear.

She slowly backed away from my car, her eyes glistening in the light. I held my breath, waiting for a nod that only I could see, but nothing came. Her face was frozen with an undefinable expression I couldn't place. Was it fear of Price? Or her own guilt of knowing what happened to Darcy and not being able to say? I didn't know.

"I'd like to have an advanced read of the column you write up from today's interview." Her professional voice was back, strong and on point.

Staring at her, I said, "Yeah. Okay." Then on my next breath, I went for it. "But if Price had something to do with Darcy's death, I can't stop the media firestorm that would surely follow."

We both glanced at Price. He stood with a twisted brow, staring, but I was sure he was too far to have heard our conversation. Taking one step forward, Christy shut my door and, with it, my chance to know what she was hiding.

I left the Price property with my mind reeling. I was swimming in theories about the men in Darcy's life and why it seemed Price was being protected by those who surrounded him.

Reaching for my cellphone, I called King. The line rang but he didn't answer. "Alex, it's Sam. I just met with Price. I think you'll want to hear about my interview. Did Price have a connection to Mallory Madison, too? Call me back."

My cell chirped with a message as I stopped at an intersection. *Where are you? Still coming?*

I held my foot on the brake and ran my hand over my head, having completely forgotten my promised date with the girls. I messaged back. *I'm on my way.*

CHAPTER THIRTEEN

HEADING BACK DOWN THE HILL, MY CELL STARTED RINGING as soon as I parked at the Mexican restaurant on the west side of town.

"Is this Samantha Bell?" the female voice asked when I answered.

"Yes. Who am I speaking with?" I glanced around the parking lot, looking for my friends' vehicles. I spotted Susan's first, then Allison's—a slight regret twisted my gut that I was running late.

"My name is Abby Wales." Her voice quaked with uncertainty. "You called me earlier about Mallory Madison."

Recognition flashed across my mind as I shoved my hand into my purse and retrieved my notepad and pen. Pulling the cap off with my teeth, I spit it into my lap. "Thanks for calling me back."

"It's about her murder, the reason you called, isn't it?"

I appreciated Abby not wasting any time in dancing around what I knew was a sensitive subject. "I'm sorry about what happened to your friend."

"I still can't believe it," she stammered.

"I was hoping you could help me understand what kind of friend Mallory was and who might have done this to her."

"Mallory was a true unicorn. You know, a friend like no other." Abby spoke about loyalty and how funny Mallory was. Then she said, "She was my best friend."

Soft whimpers filled my earpiece as I jotted down my notes. As I listened to Abby speak so highly of her friend, it was easy to paint the picture of Mallory when thinking back to the photos I had seen of her on her Facebook profile.

"When was the last time you spoke to Mallory?" I asked.

"The night she died. I was supposed to meet her at a nightclub downtown, then, at the last minute she canceled."

"Did Mallory's cancelation surprise you?"

"It was unusual for her to do something like that," Abby said sincerely. "But I assumed she must have met a guy and they decided to do something together instead."

"Why did you assume that?"

"Mallory was having a bad week. She started the night early and, as far as I know, she was alone." Abby paused as if to collect her thoughts. "Men liked her. She was beautiful and she welcomed their attention."

"Any ideas who she might have gone off with?" Philip Price's name flashed bright like a neon sign behind my eyelids, but maybe only because I'd just come from his place. I held my breath and waited for his name to come through the phone.

"It wouldn't be safe for me to speculate because I really don't know. Mallory was a free-spirit because of her home-life growing up."

I stared over the hood of my car. "Did she have a rough childhood?"

"I didn't know her back then, but she told me about her mom being an addict and her absent father drifting in and out of her life. I think she sought stability in ways maybe I wouldn't. Do you know what I mean?"

"You mean Mallory was hoping these men would fill that void left inside of her by her parents."

"Exactly. She wasn't from around here but she fit into the scene right away."

"Did you two have a regular spot you would begin your nights out?"

"Violet's Place. Downtown. And 16th Street Tavern."

I jotted down the names and made a promise to find the time to check them out myself. "Does the name Darcy Jean mean anything to you?"

Abby sniffled. I heard her crying softly before she wiped her nose. "Only that I know she was murdered, too. Did the same person do this to her?"

"She wasn't a girl you and Mallory were friends with, was she?"

"I didn't know her. Maybe Mallory did, but probably not well. Like I said, we were best friends."

CHAPTER FOURTEEN

THE HOT SMELLS OF SPICES FILLED THE AIR WHEN I STEPPED inside the restaurant. But I wasn't in the mood for a fiesta.

With Abby's words still echoing in my ears, I dragged my feet across the floor and buried my hands inside my pockets. Did Mallory know the person who killed her or could it be a stranger she met that night? Statistics were against the idea of a random act of violence. But I didn't have enough to rule it out, either.

"Table for one?" the hostess greeted me.

I blinked and came out of my head. "I'm meeting friends."

The young woman turned her head and glanced to the far side of the restaurant near the bar. I followed her gaze and found my two besties, Susan and Allison, waving their fingers. "That them?"

"That's them." I smiled and made my way to my friends who were having their first round of margaritas. "Sorry I'm late," I said, climbing up on a stool. "Dawson changed my assignment and I interviewed Philip Price." Just saying his name put a sour taste in my mouth.

They both arched a perfect brow as they stared.

"What?" My gaze bounced between them.

"I never thought we'd have to have an intervention," Susan said seriously, "but I have to say it."

"Say what?" The cords in my neck stiffened.

They shared a concerned glance. Then Susan said, "You work way too much."

The girls burst out in laughter as Susan leaned into Allison's shoulder. We were all single, working professionals, ready to make a mark in our chosen professions. We also worked harder than anyone else we knew. I joined them in giggling our stresses away and Allison already had a drink coming for me. By the time it was pushed in front of me, we toasted to the afternoon and friendship and I couldn't wait to wrap my lips around the straw to decompress after my interview with Price.

Allison caught me spinning my wedding band around my finger. "Everything all right, Sam?"

I lifted my gaze, my heart heavy with guilt for what happened to Mallory and Darcy. "Not really."

"Gavin would want you to move on." Susan reached over and took my hand inside of hers.

My eyes began to water as we shared a knowing smile. "I know he would, but I'm not sure Mason will understand." After a quick hug from Susan, I opened up about the latest challenges with my son.

"A boy needs a father," they both agreed.

Swirling my straw around my frozen margarita, I knew Mason could benefit from having a father figure in his life. Without meaning to, I thought of King and how long Mason and I had both known him. He had always been like a father figure to Mason, an incredible shoulder to lean on when I needed one myself. He was protective, loving, and honest. King made complete sense. And I knew Gavin would agree with that assessment. Hell, he'd even asked King specifically to watch over me the year before Mason was born when he re-enlisted. Since Gavin's death, King was the closest thing Mason had to a father and I had to be open to letting their relationship grow.

I changed the subject, knowing I had bigger worries to share. "I can't worry about the lack of men in my life when I'm not even sure I'll have a job next week."

Susan nodded. "I heard the rumors."

"Can you imagine Denver without a newspaper?" Allison's head shook as her mouth slackened. "Who will be there to put checks and balances on the government if it closes?"

"Who will cover sports?" Susan huffed out a disbelieving laugh.

I pulled on my straw and said, "I can't worry about any of that right now, either."

"How is your blogging going?" Susan asked, with Allison equally as interested.

My website was a side project I had started when covering stories that didn't pass the editorial cut. It was still in its infancy but could turn into something fulltime if it had to. Both Allison and Susan were loyal readers and had been my number one fans since its conception. I felt my veins open and my head perk up when I thought about the current story I was working. "Can you two promise to keep a secret?"

Allison's eyes lit up. Susan scowled. "You know we can," she said defensively.

I twisted my spine toward them, lowered my voice, and told them about the murdered women.

"There's a serial killer roaming the streets of Denver?" Allison squealed.

"It's a little too early for that label," I said, knowing it took three murders for a serial killer to be born.

Susan narrowed her eyes. "Why were you interviewing

Philip Price?" She knew I usually worked crime and courts. "He didn't have anything to do with the murders, did he?"

"No. Well, maybe." I explained my sudden reassignment and the strange coincidence that the two stories seemed to be related. "The second victim, Darcy Jean, worked on his campaign."

Allison pushed her glass out in front of her. "My company is running his online political ad campaigns. And, believe me, that man is willing to say and do anything to get elected. But murder? I just don't see it."

"Price has his eye on the White House." Susan nodded.

"Wait, aren't you hosting his event tomorrow?" Allison asked Susan.

Susan flicked her eyes to me. "I can get you inside if you want?"

I chewed on the inside of my cheek, thinking about whether I wanted to be part of anything Price was affiliated with. But the more I thought back to earlier today, and how Christy came chasing after me to my car, I couldn't stop myself from thinking Price was the number one suspect in both these women's murders. At least with the little bit I knew about them. Maybe I could learn something by attending the party.

"So, what do you say?" Susan pressed.

I eyed her. "What time?"

She smirked as she stood and tossed her purse strap over her shoulder. "I'll message you the details."

"Where are you off to?" I asked.

Susan's eyes landed on the tall man with a full head of hair standing at the door. "Dinner, and then hopefully a romantic night wrapped in *his* arms."

Allison changed seats, scooting up next to me as we both watched Susan push her arm through the crook of her boyfriend's. Together, we watched Susan leave with Allison and me agreeing how perfect they were as a couple.

"I wish I had one of those," Allison said.

Spinning my head around, I asked, "I was thinking of going out tonight. You should come."

Allison frowned. "I would love to, but I have tons of work that needs to get finished before Monday." We both finished our drinks and Allison refused to let me pay. On our way out the door, she said, "I hope you find your story Sam, but please be careful. Some secrets just aren't worth getting killed over."

CHAPTER FIFTEEN

THE LADY KILLER STARED OUT THE WINDOW OF HIS DARK blue Toyota 4Runner. Overhead, thick clouds billowed in the cold gray sky. On the radio was candidate Philip Price discussing the economics of the oil and gas industry and its importance to the state. It was background noise to keep his mind focused.

He watched from afar as young couples moved up and down the sidewalk, acting as if they were safe. He stared, studied, and grew jealous of what he saw. Soon, loneliness swept over him, slicing his heart with a sharp pain of resentment.

He didn't know why he tortured himself the way he did. Why he liked to make himself jealous. Maybe it was his desire to live a life more complete than what he had. Or perhaps it was his sense of duty to work for something greater. Whatever the reason, he couldn't take his eyes off the happy couples marching up and down the streets, laughing and kissing the night away.

Price's voice faded into an ad for his opponent.

The Lady Killer glanced to the photo of the woman he

held inside the palm of his left hand. He brushed his thumb over her face, imagining the heat of what it would feel like to actually hold her face inside of his hand. He squeezed his aching erection with his free hand and didn't let go until his eyes drifted across the glossy image and landed on Philip Price.

His stomach clenched as he moved his hand from his groin to his thigh.

Price's arm was slung over the shoulder of the pretty young woman and his hand gripped her shoulder tight. It was an intimate hold—possessive and needy—a hold The Lady Killer believed could come back and bite him if he was not careful.

Adopting a sullen look, he turned off the radio having heard enough. He had heard more than enough—Price's voice constantly rattling around his head. Full of ego and machismo, Price's narcissism would be what got him elected.

Sliding the photo into the visor above him, The Lady Killer popped a breath mint into his mouth, smoothed out his hair in the mirror, and buttoned up his coat before finally leaving the warmth of his car.

He scampered across the busy street, a cloud of condensation forming with each breath he exhaled. The chilly breeze picked up and swirled around his ankles with threats of snow falling. He headed to the bar he knew would produce his next target.

The doorman greeted him and allowed him to enter without a hiccup.

Warmth swept over him as he stalked his prey like a lion. There were targets everywhere. Elegantly dressed women that elevated his mood—and his blood. He stepped toward the bar, hope filling his chest as he scanned each of the tables he passed. Men and women chatted, flirted, and laughed. His eyes continued to scan for his target, then, suddenly he stopped, feeling his breath leave his lungs.

She was here, just as he was told she would be.

Casually moving closer, he took an empty chair in the middle of the bar not far from her, making himself at home. He swore he could smell her perfume drifting toward him as he ordered a Tom Collins, watching his subject talking with a friend.

Soon, his drink came and he glanced at his watch. *Right on schedule.*

He sipped the sugary drink peacefully by himself, keeping her in his periphery the entire time. When he was finished with his first drink—his confidence building—he ordered another before finally turning to face her.

She was quick to catch his gaze. Her initial fear relaxed and subsided into a welcoming glimmer of flirtation. Together, they playfully glanced at each other, smiling, having fun until he knew she was talking about him to her friend. Her friend glanced over her shoulder and he put on the charm, playing the game he knew how to win. His heart sped faster when he watched her friend stand and head to the restrooms in the back, creating the opportunity he had been waiting for.

He wrapped his fingers around his Tom Collins, dropped his polished shoes to the floor, and made his move.

CHAPTER SIXTEEN

VIOLET'S PLACE WAS YOUNG, HIP, AND POPULAR. I FELT TOO old for the bar but knew I couldn't leave. I'd come here to make sense of Mallory's last night and was determined to ride it out until I found the answers to the questions I couldn't stop asking myself.

Sitting at the bar alone, I imagined Mallory doing the same. An attractive young woman, starting the night early while waiting for her friend to join her. It seemed so normal, simple, a night like any other.

I listened to the soft beats play through the speakers above while being constantly aware of the lack of experience that surrounded me. Mallory was probably no different than many of the women here tonight. Innocent and naïve, they shared hopeful eyes and bright faces. Nearly none of them had the lines that told a story of the ache that came with a broken heart.

Swirling the olive in my glass, I had barely drunk any of the martini I'd ordered when I first arrived.

I was nostalgic for the life I'd once had. The routine that seemed so long ago. Deep inside of me, there was a real part that wished I could go back. The times of my youth seemed easier, less real, and without the stress of knowing a single mistake could send ripples across my entire existence.

Taking a sip, the alcohol warmed my insides.

I was sure that Mallory Madison's thoughts weren't all that different from how I'd once approached life. There was something about being young that gave you a sense of invincibility. Sadly, that same naïveté was what got her killed.

After meeting my girls for drinks, I'd headed home with thoughts of Gavin. It was impossible not to imagine how different my life would be now if he was still here with us. I needed his support, but Mason needed his guidance. There was simply no replacing a father, no matter how close he could become with King.

As I got ready for tonight, a part of me was glad Mason decided to stay after school to work on a science project. That way I could let my emotions spill freely without having to maintain face in front of my son.

I glanced to my wedding band. Touching it, I spun it around my knuckle. The action had become second nature, each time reminding me of the day Gavin proposed. I could still feel the tears streaming down my face as he slid it on, saying that I was now officially his to have. I didn't want to take it off. Ever. Even if it was the reason men were quick to move on to the next woman after meeting me. I didn't know what to do. Gavin was gone. He was never coming back. Mason was without a father. *What was I holding on to?*

Slowly, I slid the ring over my knuckle, then pushed it back in place.

My reasons were entirely selfish. I feared that my decision to not let Gavin go was also what was keeping Mason from moving forward. I was insanely lonely but my heart was still clinging on to my one true love—Gavin Bell—as if he was always in the room with me.

My cellphone started ringing, thankfully bringing me back to the present just before the onslaught of tears arrived. I dug it out of my purse and answered. "It's about time you called back," I razzed King. His light chuckle filled my ear and put a smile on my face.

"I'm up to my neck in this investigation," he apologized. "How did the interview with Price go?"

I jumped off my stool and headed toward a quieter area of the bar as I shared how Price had been kept in the dark about Darcy's murder by his own campaign manager. "She says she doesn't want his thoughts to stray from the upcoming debate, but I think it's a cover for something Price knows."

"Nothing suggests Price had any connections to Mallory." King's playful tone dropped as he answered the question I'd left on his voicemail. "What did your gut tell you?"

Suddenly, my martini had me feeling lightheaded. Glancing over my shoulder, I had the suspicion I was being watched. I paused and stared but noticed nothing unusual. "That Price definitely knows something but doesn't want to speak out, afraid of the political consequences if he does."

"I guess that's where you come in."

"Dawson would never approve of me telling that story," I said, pausing mid-breath as I watched a well-dressed man staring. "If you discover anything else, call me."

"Where are you?"

"I wish I could say," I murmured as I watched my seat be purposely taken by a young man.

"Sam—"

I killed the call before King could finish. He was the type of detective—and friend—who was always on. I knew he would be listening for clues of where I was. I appreciated his wanting to be part of my life but not while I was working on finding the facts of Mallory's last moments.

The man who'd stolen my seat was still staring at me. He

had one arm perched on top of the bar counter, a deep dimpled smirk pulling his lips upward. My heart pounded against my ribs as I felt my legs begin to make their approach.

There was something about this man that made me want to speak with him. And it wasn't only because he had taken my seat. He was attractive and confident and I hoped that maybe he was a regular who might have known Mallory.

"Hi." His voice was surprisingly deep for his slender frame and it was clear he was intent on speaking with me. Maybe even had his eye on me for longer than I'd known. I wasn't the best choice in the bar but I was an easy approach. Single women without a friend to impress always were. I had nowhere to turn if things took a turn for the worse, and he knew that.

"Hi." My voice came out sounding surprisingly shy.

A glimmer sparkled in his eye as he continued to stare. He was no older than twenty-five, a full fourteen years younger than me, and had slender but muscular thighs and biceps that rounded his suit jacket.

I didn't know what I should do next so I said, "Is this how you normally pick up women?"

His scent drifted close and he was well groomed. He held his chin high as he grinned. "How would that be?"

"By taking their seat."

He cast his gaze down to his lap as if looking for a name associated with the stool. If I was younger, it would have been a well-played maneuver to get me to look at his crotch but he couldn't fool me. I didn't care how big or small his package was, I just wanted my seat back.

He leaned over to the person sitting next to him and whispered something in their ear. To my surprise, the person stood and left without protest. "There. A seat just opened up."

Smiling, I hated how I suddenly liked this guy. Sitting, I said, "What did you say to get that person to move?"

He took a pull from his dark amber drink and said, "Just that I wanted to speak with the most attractive lady here tonight."

My eyes narrowed as I shook my head. Bringing my hands to the counter, I gave him an arched look. "You're going to have to do better than that. I'm a tough nut to crack."

"Then I guess I was right about you." The light caught in his hazel eyes.

His confidence was attractive and I couldn't deny how great it felt to be noticed. Except I was here to work, not get picked up and let down by a kid fresh out of college. "You come here often?"

"Just about every weekend."

"You know a woman named Mallory Madison?"

His smile faded and his eyebrows pulled together. "Why do you ask?"

"She came here the night she was murdered."

"What makes you think I was here that night?"

"Maybe you saw something, or heard people talking? She was here alone."

"Look," he shook his head, "I don't know anything about that." He dropped his feet to the floor and was nearly sucked back into the swelling crowd behind us.

"I'm not saying you do," I reached for his arm and stopped him from swimming away too soon, "but maybe you could help us catch whoever killed her."

His round eyes swayed with mine. "Are you a cop?"

"Reporter with *The Colorado Times*."

"I have nothing to say." He turned and was finally swallowed into the crowd, never to be seen again.

I cursed under my breath, disappointed that I wasn't patient in my approach. It was a rookie mistake—a blunder that should have never happened. He was the perfect suspect. A charming young man who took advantage of a single woman at the bar alone. Maybe he was telling the truth, or maybe he was afraid of knowing too much.

Feeling like my night was over, I finished my drink, squared up my tab at the bar, and headed to the bathroom before making my way home.

Pushing my way through the crowd, I straight-armed the women's bathroom doors open. Out of nowhere, a silhouette came from the shadows and nudged me inside. Quick to shut the door behind us, my heart hammered in my chest as I scrambled away from reaching hands.

Backing away, I stared at the person, knowing I had seen them before. "Who are you?"

"A friend." When the jacket hood was removed, long blonde hair spilled out.

My eyes did a once-over of her. After a quick but thorough assessment, I wanted to tell her to dial her makeup back a notch—that she was beautiful without it—but instead I said, "You were there, at the motel, then again at the hotel."

Her lips curled at the corners.

I narrowed my eyes. Why was she at the motel? I'd been chasing my next story, desperate to bring Dawson something to make him keep me on board. But this chick? "What were you doing at the motel?"

She chuckled, like I'd told some joke. "I sleep with the police scanner on. It's safe to say that I haven't had a decent night's sleep in quite some time."

"And the hotel, too?" She nodded. "Why did you keep running away from me?"

"Maybe I was scared."

"Then why are you here now?"

She lowered her head and stepped forward. "Because I'm interested in who murdered those women, too."

CHAPTER SEVENTEEN

HER NAME WAS ERIN TATE AND SHE WAS A DOCUMENTARY film maker turned podcaster with years of experience in investigative journalism. I saw the potential immediately. We could be great together but I remained hesitant.

"And you've been following me?"

"I wouldn't say that," Erin said.

"Then how did you end up here?"

"Same way you did. It's where Mallory Madison started her evening on the night she was killed. The police aren't saying anything. Why is that?"

My thoughts immediately went to Darcy Jean and Philip Price. King was certain that Price didn't have a connection to Mallory, but I remained naturally skeptical. I'd seen enough political scandals uncovered to know that Price was likely hiding something.

"Who told you that Mallory's night began here?"

Erin gave me a knowing look. "A friend of hers." She paused, as if considering whether or not to open up. Then she said, "Abby Wales."

I gathered my hair up in my hands, turned toward the

sink, and blew out a sigh. My mind raced to decide if Erin would be a valuable asset or would just get in my way. Working alone had its advantages. It gave me room to pivot and change direction quickly. It was also dangerous. There were benefits to having a partner but, first, there was something I needed to know. "Am I your source to everything you know?"

Erin's shoulders fell as she tilted her head to the side.

"Or are you just one step behind?"

"It goes both ways, honey." Erin shifted her feet. "I had to know you could be trusted before I came to *you*."

"We must know the same things because we keep showing up at the same places."

"We both want the same end result." Erin folded her arms across her chest. "A murderer is still out there somewhere and, though the police are working the investigation to the best of their abilities, it's not doing this city any favors by keeping the public in the dark."

I stared without moving but I agreed with everything she said. "It appears you know an awful lot about Mallory but, tell me, what do you know about Darcy?"

"She came from a good family. Wasn't rich, but wasn't poor either. And, from what I've gathered, it seems she and Mallory weren't all that different when it came to opening their doors to unknown men."

It all lined up with what Christy had told me earlier about Darcy. Erin didn't say anything about a connection to Price, and I chose to keep that bit a secret. At least for the time being. I didn't need any more friction in an already complicated mystery, and wasn't going to shoot myself in the foot by revealing too much too soon, either.

The door to the bathroom swung open and nearly hit Erin between the shoulder blades. A woman walked in, gave us both a strange look, and disappeared into an empty stall.

"Here's my card." Erin handed me her information. "Give me a call if you're interested in working together."

I took the card between my fingers and watched Erin backpedal, reaching for the door. Before she left, she glanced back and said, "By the way, I love what you're doing with your website."

I held my eyes steady with hers. "Thanks."

"My only piece of advice," she said sincerely, "is to decide what you want more. Your job, or your website. In today's work environment, they won't let you have both."

After Erin disappeared, I sat on the toilet, thinking about her departing words. Dawson was aware of my website but, with a change of ownership, the future was yet to be written. Anything was possible, but I also knew I wasn't going to stop.

I stepped out of the bathroom with my eyes glued to Erin's business card. Slowly, I walked toward the front. Then, out of the blue, I accidently bumped a man's arm. Spilling his drink on his expensive suit, he cursed.

"I'm so sorry," I said.

"Jesus, look at you." His reptilian eyes pulsed. "Were you even watching where you were going?"

My heart hammered and my nostrils flared. Making a fist with one of my hands, a cold shiver zipped up my spine. He wasn't worth my time. "You know what, forget it," I said, pushing past him.

He slung curses at my back as I marched toward the exit.

A thick arm scooped me up at the waist. Instinctively, I pushed the man away. He stammered back with open eyes. "Alex?"

King smiled. "Sorry. I thought I would surprise you."

I tipped my head back and growled. Closing the gap between us, I asked, "Was this your plan all along?"

He lifted his gaze and looked around the bar. "I don't take my dates to dangerous places."

"Is that what you think this is, a date?" I folded my arms and smirked. "News to me."

"Let's discuss this over a drink." His eyes narrowed into sharp slits. "What do you say?"

My heartrate increased and I felt the arteries open up in my neck. I had always found King attractive but tonight he seemed irresistibly so. Maybe it was the margarita and martini talking. "I can't."

"You know, you make it hard to do my job when you're always one step ahead of me."

I smiled and said, "You're welcome."

He laughed. "You really should have been a detective."

I raised a brow. "I don't like guns."

King bent at the waist and put his mouth dangerously close to my face. "You and I both know that's a lie." We both laughed.

"All right, Detective. I'll stay," I said, looping my arm through the crook of his. "But only one drink."

"We'll see about that." King led me outside and to a bar more our style.

CHAPTER EIGHTEEN

ALLISON DOYLE'S COMPUTER MONITOR SHINED BRIGHT ON her face as she sat behind her work desk, searching the internet for images of Darcy Jean. She was alone, and all but the emergency lights in the hall were off. Since meeting with her friends earlier for margaritas, she couldn't stop thinking that a serial killer might be targeting women in her home city.

She scrolled through the images of Darcy that populated her screen. Each digital image came to life more than the last. Big smiles and a promising future in Darcy's eyes were what Allison kept noticing most about her. It was so sad, Allison thought, but it was Samantha's theory that really had her head spinning.

Allison tapped her mouse, closed a browser, and opened up her client's folder.

Philip Price was one of her digital software company's biggest clients and it destroyed her to think that she might be doing business with a man connected to these crimes. Diving deep into his vast chest of advertisements her company was managing for the gubernatorial candidate, Allison's team had ads spread across social media sites and search engines as far as the eye could see.

The hairs on the nape of her neck stood on end when Price's face popped up on her screen.

Allison paused to stare for a moment, searching his eyes for truth, before clicking away. She continued reading different ads, making notes of the message he wanted to convey to the people, looking for anything suspicious. When she found nothing, she opened up his official Facebook page and began scrolling.

Philip Price was a family man—a widower with grown children. He was also a patriot dedicated to honor and sacrifice and a call to serve the greater good. Allison was proud of her team for the image they had helped create for Price, but there was one question she kept asking herself over and over. *Who is paying for these ads?* She knew it wasn't Price himself, but a PAC.

Allison closed her browser, clicked on Price's client folder, and maneuvered to the invoices. The latest invoice was created only last week and addressed to *A Better Future for America.*

Allison sat back and nibbled her fingernails. She glanced to the clock and debated whether it was too late to call. It didn't take her long to make the decision. After all, she was the boss and this was her company—she had a reputation to maintain.

Reaching for her phone, Allison put a call in to her chief of operations, Patty O'Neil. "I apologize for calling so late, but I'm doing some work on our client, Philip Price, and couldn't find who his point of contact is."

"Hang on a minute," Patty said. Allison heard her close a door and boot up her computer. A minute later, she said, "It looks like we have a Mr. and Mrs. Eric Foster."

Allison scribbled down their email and phone number as

Patty rattled them off. She thanked Patty and wished her a good night before ending the call. Allison leaned back in her chair, staring at the name. She knew who Mr. and Mrs. Eric Foster were by only their reputation. What she didn't know was whether this would be of any help to Samantha.

CHAPTER NINETEEN

I STEPPED INTO MY HOUSE WITH BEER ON MY BREATH. KING left me feeling slightly buzzed but not dizzy enough to keep me from driving myself home. I couldn't be sure, but thought he might have hoped I would ask him to come home with me.

The car keys rattled into the clay bowl when I dropped them into it. Shedding my coat near the front door, Cooper barked once. He jumped off the living room couch and came scurrying to the front door with his tail wagging as soon as he knew it was only me.

"Hey boy," I said, flapping his ears around. He nudged my leg with his head and yawned. "Did Mason feed you?"

Cooper followed me to the kitchen. His food bowl was empty. Opening the closet, I scooped out a healthy portion of pebbles and told him to eat up. Walking to the back of the house, I cracked Mason's door open. He was sprawled out over his bed, fast asleep. I smiled and wished him good night before turning off the hall light and heading back to the kitchen.

I pulled out a cheap bottle of bourbon from above the

stove and allowed myself one last drink because it had been one hell of day. With drink in hand, I sat on the living room couch with Cooper resting his big head on my thigh.

My mind soon drifted back to Mallory and Darcy. And as I petted Cooper to sleep, I couldn't stop thinking how Violet's Place seemed to attract weak men and assholes. I didn't have the best experience, but surely it couldn't have been like that every night. And certainly not like that for everyone. Still, it left me with a bad impression and topped with Mallory's murder, it didn't get any better.

Cooper snored and I laughed.

I flirted with turning on the television to catch the evening news, but instead I lifted my gaze to an old family portrait hiding at the back of the mantel.

My pulse slowed as I felt my throat constrict.

Gavin held a two-year-old Mason upside down as I laughed hysterically. I could still hear Mason's giggle and his pleas for his daddy to do it again, and again, as if it had happened today.

The prickling of tears filled my eyes as I thought how fourteen years ago seemed like a lifetime. A lump formed in the back of my throat as my body crumbled.

"I'm still beautiful," I said to Gavin. Smiling, I curled my lips over the rim of my glass, deciding to tell him about getting hit on by a 25-year-old. He continued to smile as if thrilled to see me happy. "But he was too young for me so I decided to have drinks with someone closer to my age." I paused and smirked. Even with Gavin silent, I couldn't tell him that I'd gone for drinks with his best friend.

I blinked out the first tear. Its warmth streamed down my cheek, falling off my chin and onto my breast. With a hardened stomach, I dropped my head to my chest and felt my body go cold. I cried softly for several minutes before wiping my cheeks dry and giggling. "You never were the jealous type."

Gavin's eyes glimmered.

"I miss you, baby." My whispers filled the room. "It's not the same without you."

The room fell silent.

I knew Gavin would want me to move on but I didn't know if I had it in me to do so. It would feel too much like betraying the vows I'd made to my husband—and, frankly, I was afraid of forgetting what it felt like to be touched by him.

Finishing my drink, I pushed Cooper to the side and dove my hand inside my pants pocket. Fishing out Erin Tate's business card, I held it in my hands and stared at her web address for a minute before heading into my home office. Sitting behind the computer, I pulled up Erin's website, slid a pair of headphones over my ears, and began listening to her crime podcast. "Let's see what you got, girl."

CHAPTER TWENTY

My head pounded. It was safe to say that I regretted that last night cap. My tongue was sandpaper in my mouth. Even worse than the drink, though, was that I'd hardly slept. Plagued by thoughts of Mallory and Darcy, I'd woken early, anxious to get the day started.

Mason was off to school early. Things with him seemed to be getting back on track. He wasn't fighting me—or other kids at school—and he seemed really excited about his chemistry project. I watched him ride away on his bike and was happy for him—proud of the independence and responsibility he was creating for himself—but I was still worried that there was more going on that he wasn't telling me about.

By the time I found myself in the newsroom, I wanted to ignore the apprehension I could feel coming from nearly every single one of my colleagues I passed on my way to my desk. It proved to be a challenge. I rounded the corner and my stomach sank when I saw Trisha lock eyes with me.

"Great. Here comes bad news," I muttered under my breath.

Trisha hurried to me and I knew there was no escaping it.

"Did you hear?" she asked.

"I guess not." I shortened my stride but I didn't bother to stop. I was so close to my desk I could see it and hoped Trisha would catch on to my disinterest.

"Nearly thirty percent of the staff will be laid off in the coming weeks," she rambled, "and, even worse, this hedge fund that purchased the *Times* has a track record of eliminating every two out of three positions in the papers they've acquired."

"I can't worry about this now, Trisha," I said, dropping my bag on my desk.

I turned to look at her. Trisha nodded, pulled back slightly, and shuffled her feet. "Samantha, you're not immune from what is happening."

Of course she was right. I was as vulnerable as anybody. But I really didn't want it to get in the way of my work. I owed it to Mallory and Darcy to tell their stories. "Why are you telling me this?" I finally asked. "Are you purposely trying to ruin my day?"

Trisha gasped. "Sam," her long lashes fluttered over her eyes, "I'm telling you because I know you have a history with challenging authority."

I felt a grin pulling my lips tight. "Whatever this new owner decides to do isn't my fight."

"Perhaps not today, but maybe one day it will be." Trisha looked behind her in the direction of Dawson's desk. "Besides, I'm not the only one with one foot out the door."

I dropped my head into my hand as soon as Trisha left my desk. My fingers dug deep into my throbbing temples, providing little relief. I didn't care to know who had one foot out the door or who was worrying more about tomorrow than today. Trisha didn't have me spooked. Instead, I lowered my bottom into my chair, thinking about what I could do to prove I deserved to stay. I wasn't going to be like the others and start polishing up my résumé when pretending to work. Journalism was a dying breed, it was what I loved to do, and it would take a whole lot more ingenuity on all our parts if the industry were to survive the impending apocalypse.

Opening my shoulder bag, I pulled out my laptop and fired it up. The screen loaded and as soon as my files were synced, I clicked open and reread the article I'd pounded out after listening to a couple of Erin's shows last night.

Erin Tate was articulate and convincing. I'd quickly been sucked into her podcast. She had a great voice, which was essential for storytelling. When one show finished, I needed to listen to the next. It was that addicting.

I leaned back and threaded my hands behind my head.

I couldn't stop thinking about Erin. She was a woman who wasn't afraid to take action. I liked that, and it could prove useful when solving a case like the one we both found ourselves working. She'd also convinced me that she wasn't afraid to ask tough questions in her pursuit of finding the truth, which was important to me, too. But what really had my stomach tied in a knot was the fear that another woman would soon end up dead before any arrests were made. And that was what finally dropped my feet to the floor and got me to give her a call.

Erin answered immediately. "That didn't take long."

"I listened to a couple of your episodes last night," I said, bent over my desk with elbows perched on top.

"What did you think?"

"You have an addicting show."

She laughed and thanked me. "I'm just about to record this week's episode."

"What's the topic today?"

"You'll just have to listen when it becomes available." I could hear her smile crackle through the line. "So, why are you really calling, Samantha?"

My eyes swept up and landed on my computer screen. "There was something I wanted to share about the case."

"Are we working together?"

My brows slanted. "Did you want to hear what I have to say or not?"

"My apologies." Erin laughed. "Please, continue."

"Darcy Jean canvassed for gubernatorial candidate Philip Price." I paused, and I knew I had her full attention. The line went silent. Then, over the next several minutes, I told Erin about what happened yesterday during my interview at Price's house.

"What's his sex life like?" Erin asked, already knowing how the two victims had been found.

"I'm not sure, however, his wife passed suddenly about five years ago and I wasn't allowed to ask him about it yesterday."

"You think he did her in, too?" Erin's voice rose an octave.

"That's what I thought maybe you could find out." I heard Erin scribbling notes on a piece of paper. "I'm up to my neck in deadlines with the paper, but I think it could be an interesting angle to explore."

"I'd love it. Tell me what you need."

"I'd like to know if there are any similarities to his wife's death—what their sex life might have been like—and compare it to what we know about Mallory and Darcy." The line went quiet. "What do you say, think you can do that?"

"I thought you'd never ask." Erin was beyond excited, and so was I. Finally, I was working with another intelligent woman and someone who wasn't afraid of potentially losing their job.

"Sam, you got a minute?"

I spun around in my chair to find an unhappy Dawson staring down at me. "Is everything all right?"

He wagged his head. "Let's talk in my office."

CHAPTER TWENTY-ONE

I COULD FEEL MY COLLEAGUES' GLARING EYES ON ME AS I followed Dawson to his office. Hanging onto the column I'd written last night, I refused to stare back at the many faces hiding behind their screens, silently wondering if I was the beginning of the layoffs.

Dawson held his office door open for me. I thanked him as Erin's words echoed between my ears. Maybe she was right about having to decide between my website and the job. I knew I could do both—neither of them getting in the way of the other—but could I convince others of that?

Dawson closed the door and told me to take a seat. As soon as I was down, he stared at me from across his desk. "You look like hell."

"Have any Advil?" I asked.

He continued staring at me from under his brow before opening his desk drawer and tossing me a white bottle. "I would ask you how yesterday's interview went with Price, but I'm afraid he's already filled me in."

I popped the top of the Advil, more concerned with

getting rid of this aching headache than what Dawson had to say about Price.

"He was livid, Sam."

The pills caught in my throat as I swallowed them dry. Placing the bottle on Dawson's desk, I asked, "Price called you personally?"

Dawson answered me with a look. "He also said that if I ever sent you again, he'd personally make my life a living hell."

"The guy is such an asshole."

"That may be, but you weren't just representing the paper, Sam."

"Charlie should have gone himself if he's worried how I handled his interview."

Dawson furrowed his brow. "Why do you always make things harder than they need to be?"

My jaw cocked out to the side. "Admit it, you like it."

He stared with sealed lips for a moment before saying, "Do you purposely like to make my job harder than it has to be?"

"I asked tough, *relevant* questions. That's it."

Dawson leaned back in his chair, his unwavering gaze still staring with questioning eyes. "You do love to do the opposite of what you're told."

I exposed my neck as I felt my eyes glimmer with satisfaction. "I can tell you my side of the story whenever you're ready."

"This better be good." Dawson held his fist to his mouth as he listened.

I broke down my visit from the moment I arrived to make sure Dawson saw the complete picture of yesterday's event. I told him about Price's ill attempt at flirtation and how I completed the entire interview both he and Christy set out for me—always on point—before shifting the conversation to

Darcy's murder. "He claimed he didn't know anything about it. But she worked for his campaign."

Dawson twirled a pen between his fingers. Did he already know? "How did he react to your question?"

"I'm certain he's hiding something."

Dawson's eyes shined.

"His campaign manager, Christy Jones, stopped the interview before Price could answer. But, get this: On my way out the door, Christy caught up with me."

Dawson's body tipped forward in his chair. "What did she have to say?"

Now I knew I had Dawson's full attention. He wasn't mad, maybe even a little impressed. "It was like she needed to sell me on the idea that Price knew nothing about his own volunteer's death."

"So, what do you think they're hiding?"

I pushed my story across his desk. "Not exactly sure, but I do have a convincing theory that he might be hiding an affair with Darcy, or, perhaps Darcy discovered something about him that he didn't want the world to know."

Dawson slid his reading glasses over his nose and quickly read my story. He squinted and sighed his way through it. Then he lifted his head and said, "We need more."

A grin curled my lips. "I'll be attending his fundraiser tonight."

"Good." Dawson set the column down.

"As far as I know, no other reporters are on this story... at least not this deep. We're the first, Dawson. And if he had anything to do with Darcy's death, we'll link him to Mallory, too."

Dawson stared. "You have a good start, Sam, but it's not complete." Then he bounced his gaze between my story and me. "You need to get this right. If you don't—"

"Don't worry. I know. No mistakes." I stood and thanked

Dawson for being incredibly understanding and supporting my work with little resistance.

Before I was out the door, Dawson said, "Good work, Bell."

I left his office with my chin high. Price was definitely hiding something, and I was determined to find what that was. I hoped his secret didn't involve Darcy but, until proven otherwise, I kept assuming it did.

When I got back to my desk, my voicemail was blinking with a new message. I smiled and said, "Erin, you devil you. You sure do work fast." But before I could reach it, my cell rang on my belt.

I answered the call from King with a beating heart. "I have a killer headache but I got home safely."

"Sam," his voice was grim, "there's been another murder and it fits the profile of the first two."

I pressed my hand against my forehead, feeling my throat close up. How could this be? We were too late. Another daughter of Denver was dead. I asked King where, and after he told me, I said, "I'm on my way."

CHAPTER TWENTY-TWO

I ARRIVED ON SCENE SHORTLY AFTER THE CALL FROM Detective King.

This time the entire cavalry arrived to cover the show. Local news crews were lined up to the side, and even the first national coverage was here to let the nation know what was happening. This time the crime scene was chaotic and nearly impossible to maneuver.

I edged myself around the back of the swelling crowd of spectators before finding an opening. Wedging myself to the front of the line, I was quickly stopped by the uniformed officer. I asked him several questions but the cop's lips were sealed tight. "No comment," he kept saying.

"Who was murdered?" I asked. "What was her name?"

He glared. "No comment. Now move back."

It was clear by the looks in their eyes and their attitude that the cops were frustrated word had gotten out so quickly. It made their job more difficult, and national attention wouldn't make it any easier.

I caught sight of King near the entrance of the hotel. He gave a slight nod before heading back inside the building, choosing to keep his distance. It was for the best. Besides, I wasn't going to receive anything until the ME and CSI teams were finished combing the place for evidence.

I walked the police line, keeping my ears opened for clues. A part of me was tempted to duck the line and sneak my way inside but the odds for success were against me today. There were just too many cops—too many reporters. The only advantage I had was knowing this wasn't murder number one, but the third in a string of crimes targeting Denver's young women.

I spotted her yellow hair from across the way and raised my hand to catch her attention. Erin pushed her way through the crowd. "Thanks for giving me a call," she said.

"We're in this together, remember?" We shared a knowing smile, our bond and friendship starting off on the right foot.

"I was just able to speak with a hotel employee who was working last night," Erin said, stuffing her hands deep into her vest pockets.

My brows raised, impressed by her success. "What did they have to say?"

"According to her statement, it sounds like this woman was killed in a similar fashion as the last two." She paused and flicked her gaze to the entrance. "Tied to the bed, naked, and apparently strangled to death."

I wondered if there were any signs of intercourse, or just made to look that way. That was how Darcy and Mallory were found, so why would today be any different? "Any idea where Price was last night?"

"Funny you ask." Erin squared her shoulders.

I titled my head and arched a sharp brow.

"I was looking into his past like you asked, and happened to be checking his schedule when you called me about this. According to his schedule, he shouldn't have been anywhere near here. But his schedule and his actual whereabouts are two different things, and without a name to the third victim we can't tie her to anybody. Including Price."

"How was his relationship with his wife? Did you learn anything about that?"

"I wasn't able to find someone to speak on that yet." Erin rolled her neck to me. I hadn't exactly given her much time. "He wasn't in public office at the time of her death so his campaign members might not have been close to him back then but I'm sure those details will surface eventually. But, according to my source, Price is definitely sleeping with one of his staff members."

I held Erin's gaze. It was safe to say I'd liked her almost immediately. "Was it Darcy?"

She tucked her hair behind one ear and shook her head. "I'm still working to confirm this woman's identity, and if there is only one woman."

A chill caused me to shiver just thinking about Price. I wouldn't put it past him to be juggling several girlfriends at once. "If there is one thing I know for certain about Price, it's that he likes to get touchy."

"I should be hearing back from my source any minute." Erin pulled up her sleeve and glanced at her watch. "He has me convinced this woman is ready to go on record and speak about her relationship with Price."

Hooking my thumbs in my jeans pockets, I started scanning the crowd of pedestrians. "This crowd keeps growing."

"That's what live news coverage does."

I glanced to Erin. "Do you think the killer is here?"

"What? Now?"

I nodded and told her briefly about how serial killers often revisited the place of their crime. Erin furrowed her brow and kept her eyes peeled for anything unusual. "I have a friend in the police department who profiled this killer as being male."

"Half the faces gathering are male." Erin sighed. "Any other distinguishing features or characteristics I could look for?"

"A male who needs to demonstrate his dominance." Erin gave me a sideways look. I shrugged. "That's all I know." We didn't have ethnicity, height, weight, or age. We had nothing.

Erin's cell buzzed. We both held our breaths and stared at it. "It's him," she said. "And he has the woman who claims to be having an affair with Price." She lifted her head and looked up at me. "Should we take your car or mine?"

"Is that—" I spotted a familiar *male* face hiding in the crowd. My heart kicked into high gear and once he caught my gaze, he turned and ran.

CHAPTER TWENTY-THREE

MY EYES SPRANG WIDE OPEN.

He was running.

I couldn't believe what I was witnessing. My heart hammered in my chest as I scrambled into action. Digging my toes into the pavement, I couldn't let him get away. Not without finding out what he was doing here in the first place. This wasn't a place he should have seen me at, let alone, been at. Yet he was here, and was now trying to get away without speaking to me.

What was he thinking?

Erin called after me a split second before I broke into a full sprint. "Samantha, who is that? Wait!"

Settling into race pace, my arms pumped fast as I gave it my all. It didn't take me long to close the distance between us. "Stop." I held up my hand and raised my voice. "Mason, stop!"

The whites in Mason's eyes widened with fear when he glanced over his shoulder. He might have had a head start on me, and youth was certainly on his side, but I had the worry and anger of a mother ready to protect her kid.

Adrenaline flooded my veins as I collared him and yanked out his earbuds.

"Mom," he protested, juggling the white chords in his hands.

"Shouldn't you be in school?" I snapped.

His brow furrowed. "Mom, it's Saturday."

A blankness fell over me. "But you left for school this morning."

"I told you. Mr. Simmonds opened the chemistry lab early for a few hours so we could finish up our project. I'm done, and now I'm going home."

With my mind preoccupied with the murders, I must have missed those details. Placing my hand over my belly, I felt awful. "Then what are you doing here?"

"I was in the area, on my way home," he reiterated. "I saw the commotion and was curious to what was happening."

"Gosh, Mason." I shoved a hand through my hair. "You need to start telling me where you're at."

"I did." He glared from under his brow. "And I shouldn't have to update you every minute of my life."

"I just need to know that you're safe."

"What's going on, Mom? Is everything all right?"

I twisted my heel around and glanced back at the hotel. "This is an active crime scene. You shouldn't be here."

"Was someone killed?"

I couldn't look my boy in the eye. It was too much to imagine that on the other end of these murders was a family, devastated with the sudden loss of a loved one. None of us were immune. It could be me—could be Erin—maybe even Mason.

Erin caught up to us. She gave me a look after studying Mason. "Samantha, who is this?"

"This is my son, Mason." I turned back to Mason and introduced her to him.

"He looks like you," Erin said.

My gaze darted around, looking for Mason's bike. "Where's your bike?"

"I got a flat. It's locked up at school."

Mason looked so young in that moment. His round, innocent eyes shining back as if looking for answers to life's complicated questions. Heat bloomed across my chest and my heart swelled with love. I hated how I'd overreacted. Perhaps I was too quick to jump to conclusions before hearing him out. He had done nothing wrong but it sure felt like I had. "C'mon, let's get you home," I said.

Mason nodded. "Can we pick up my bike?"

I turned to Erin. "We better take my car," I said.

She grinned.

I slung my arm around Mason's neck and squeezed. "I'm sorry, kiddo, your mom's had a rough week."

The three of us loaded into my Outback and it didn't take us long to retrieve Mason's bike at the high school, load it into the back, and drop him off at home. Erin and I watched my son wheel his broken bike to the front door.

"He seems like a good kid," Erin said.

"He is," I said, thinking how Mason was growing up too quickly. Flicking my gaze to Erin, I asked, "Do you have kids?"

She shook her head. "Wasn't in my cards." No wonder she could chase stories in the middle of the night. At least she wasn't leaving a teenager at home alone all the time like I was.

"They can be a handful," I said, dropping the car into gear. Then I pointed the hood in the direction of where we were to meet Price's alleged mistress, knowing it was time to get back to work.

CHAPTER TWENTY-FOUR

"IF ALL PRICE WAS HIDING WAS A RELATIONSHIP, IT THROWS my entire theory out the window," I said, turning off I-70 and heading southbound on I-25. We merged into the river of traffic, glancing at the clock, knowing we were running late.

"Not if he was having an affair with more than one woman. Or with a married woman. Or with someone inappropriately young," Erin added.

Touché. "Price still claims to know nothing about Darcy. Why is that? He should have come out with a statement by now. There is no advantage to keeping him in the dark other than ensuring his denial if the authorities begin asking him questions."

"And maybe that is all it is."

His ignorance wouldn't last. Now that the murders were piling up, Mallory and Darcy were sure to be part of the top story all weekend. I turned and glanced out my window. "There has to be some connection to Darcy besides just the campaign."

"Hopefully this person we're about to meet has something to say about that."

"Price's campaign manager is clever and she made it clear to me that she intends to win this election." I rolled my neck to Erin. "Did I tell you that Price called my editor, threatening to retaliate against the paper if I interviewed him again?"

"The balls on that guy." Erin made a fist on her thigh. "If he's innocent of only having an affair, he sure is acting guilty of a crime."

"That's what I can't shake. His behavior is odd. Especially for someone running for office." My mind raced as I thought how the story of these murders had been exclusively ours when we woke. Now the entire city was on it and nothing was guaranteed. "Once the media learns these murders are linked, we're going to find ourselves scrambling to stay ahead of it."

Erin angled her body toward me and had a serious look on her face when she asked, "What are you doing with that website, Samantha?"

"What do you mean?" I said, noticing her one eyebrow lifting further on her head. "It's spill-over content for everything that doesn't make the editor's cut."

"I know that, but what are *your* plans for it?"

Pursing my lips, I gave Erin a questioning look.

"I've seen how popular it is."

"It's just a hobby. A way to make sense of my work."

"You're a natural. People respond to what you write."

"I can't write about Price. Not until I know more about what it is he's actually hiding."

"You can open up the conversation. Who knows, maybe it will lead to something that will actually give you what you're looking for." Erin's eyes glowed.

"Blowing up this story seems preemptive."

Erin grinned, a knowing glimmer flashing across her blue irises. "You and me, we're different. We don't have to answer to anybody but ourselves. We can publish and say whatever we want. Your editor wants more facts before he pushes your story to print, but what about until then? You have content. Put it out there."

I exited the highway and headed east on Alameda with my pulse throbbing. I knew what Erin was suggesting but I wasn't sure it was the right move. At least not now. "I don't want to influence an election based on a theory that can't be proven."

Erin stared ahead, her eyes on the brake lights on the car in front of us. She took a silent minute to think before responding. Then she turned her head and said, "And I don't want a no-name junior reporter making headlines for a story that should be ours."

My skin tingled as I let out a bark of laughter. Erin joined me and, together, we laughed as if we had been best friends our entire careers. Soon, we settled and sat in silence with thoughts spinning in the wind. Together, if combined, we had an incredibly large audience. My column at the paper would hit regional and with her podcast and my website, our audience ballooned beyond Colorado's borders into something larger I wasn't sure we could quite comprehend. What was I waiting for? And why hadn't I made a move to break out on my own? It was a risk, and I had to think about Mason. With Erin's help, I knew I could do it.

I glanced to Erin. She had her elbow propped up on the window ledge as she stared out her window. We were both determined to solve this case ourselves. Nobody could take that away from us. Erin was right. It was our duty to let the Mile High City finally know what was happening beneath their noses, and let the public be the ones to ask the tough questions about why the police wanted to jeopardize everyone's safety by keeping the murders quiet.

Erin glanced to the GPS on her cellphone. "Turn here. Her house is somewhere on this block."

I slowed the tires to a crawl and asked, "What's your story? How did you end up running a podcast?"

Without taking her eyes off her phone, she said, "It's the same story as every newspaper across America. Readership was declining, price was increasing, and everybody was turning to the internet for their news."

"So you quit?"

"I was laid off." Erin smiled and pointed to a driveway. "This is it."

"You seem proud that you got fired," I said, parking.

She raised her chin high and looked me in the eye while turning off her GPS. "It's the best thing that happened to me." A woman appeared at the front door of the house. She waved and Erin cracked open her door. "You better be ready for when your day comes, Sam. Because it's coming, and there is nothing you can do to stop it."

CHAPTER TWENTY-FIVE

PRICE'S MISTRESS WAS NAMED KIMBERLY BISHOP AND SHE
lived in an upscale neighborhood south of the city. She
welcomed us into her home. "I'm sorry for my appearance. I
got the call last minute and didn't have time to finish getting
ready."

"It's not a problem, Ms. Bishop," Erin said, thanking her
for meeting with us on such short notice.

I was last to enter the house. After wiping my sneakers
clean at the door, I floated behind Ms. Bishop and Erin with
my head swiveling back and forth on my shoulders. Her
house was immaculate. It had an open floor plan, modern
décor, earth tones matched against wall hangings of photos
taken in natural settings. But I hit the brakes when I came
face to face with a cougar stalking me from its high perch on
the wall.

"Isn't it an amazing creature?" Ms. Bishop said of the dead
animal.

"Do you hunt?" I asked.

"No. I prefer my modern conveniences to rustic living.
The outdoors was my husband's thing."

Erin shared a glance with me.

There was a bull elk head mounted above the stone fireplace and the furniture was made of leather. The house belonged in the west, no doubt, but seemed out of place here in the city. It would have been a better fit tucked somewhere in the mountains, I thought as I continued to peruse the walls.

"Please, follow me to the back. I must finish getting ready." Ms. Bishop smiled, turned on a heel, and clacked her way down the hall. "Philip has a fundraiser tonight and I must look my best."

Since I was planning to attend the same party, I glanced to my watch. The party didn't begin for several more hours and I found it unusually early to be acting as if time was running out. I asked her about it. "What times does the party begin?"

She rolled her friendly eyes to me. "This conversation is off the record." She paused until Erin and I had both confirmed our understanding. "Philip asked me to come early." Then she turned back to the mirror, stabbing her ears with a pair of dangling diamond earrings. "If you know anything about Philip, he doesn't like it when you're late." She laughed gently.

Erin and I stood awkwardly behind her, unsure how we'd found ourselves in her master bath, watching her put on her face.

The bathroom was as immaculate as the rest of her house and larger than my own bedroom. It had white walls, lots of lights, padded chairs, and gold trimmed mirrors everywhere. There was a soaking tub and a shower fit for royalty.

"Maybe we can talk about that," Erin said. "The reason we're here—"

"I know why you're here, honey." Ms. Bishop finished putting on her lipstick.

Erin wasn't deterred by the otherwise odd behavior we were witnessing. "So, how do you know Philip Price?"

A yearning look formed in Ms. Bishop's eyes as she wet her lips with her tongue. She began walking and motioned for us to follow along. "I met him at one of his original campaign fundraisers."

"So you two haven't been dating for very long?" I said as we found ourselves back in the living room being stalked by the stuffed cougar.

"I think it's a bit preemptive to be calling what we're doing *dating*." She pulled her gold bangles down on her wrist and touched all half-dozen of her rings.

Everything she wore glittered, meant to please the eye. She clearly ran in a different social circle than I did but I wasn't going to ask about it unless it proved relevant. "And now you work for him?"

"That's right, sweetheart." Her red lips curved upward as her gaze bore deep inside of mine. "He asked me to come on to his campaign after the night we met," she said, flicking her gaze over to Erin.

"Did you know Darcy Jean?" Erin asked.

"It's a tragedy what happened to Darcy." Ms. Bishop glided into the kitchen. We followed like little chicks following their mother to the hen house. "From what I understand, she was a real go-getter."

"What was Philip's relationship with her like?" I asked.

Ms. Bishop paused and cast her gaze down to the island's marble countertop. "There wasn't much of one." Her eyes lifted and landed on mine. "Darcy was low on the totem pole. She worked the street, canvassing door-to-door, so didn't cross paths much when Philip was around."

"Did Philip know about her murder?"

Her eyes narrowed. "Not until you told him yesterday."

Erin looked at me, then asked Ms. Bishop, "What about

Christy Jones, would she have any reason to be upset with Darcy?"

"Christy Jones runs a tight ship but she has Philip's best interests at heart."

Erin stepped to the counter. "Any guesses to who might have killed Darcy?"

"Darcy had such a contagious positivity about her, I can't imagine anybody wanting to kill her."

I floated around the kitchen, rolling my eyes at the China I was certain were reserved for dinner parties only. Pictures of Ms. Bishop's grown children were everywhere but I never saw any signs of a man of the house. "Do you live in this big house all by yourself?"

Ms. Bishop took her eyes off Erin and rolled her head to me. "I do." Then she corrected herself. "Well, sometimes my youngest daughter comes home for the weekend."

"Does she live nearby?"

"She attends Denver University. A junior this semester."

"And you, do you have any siblings?"

"Two older brothers."

"Are you parents still alive?"

"Sadly, both have passed."

"Are you from Denver?"

"My family is originally from St. Louis. I moved here in '92 and have been here since."

"You said you and Philip's relationship took off immediately." Ms. Bishop nodded and smiled. "Does he talk much about his wife?"

"He doesn't."

"Any guesses why that might be?"

"I imagine it hurts too much. We were both married before. This isn't our first rodeo." She cackled. "We know what we're doing."

"Is your husband deceased?"

"Divorced." Ms. Bishop frowned. "I wouldn't be sleeping with Philip if I wasn't. Though, I suppose even marriage doesn't stop everyone from having an affair these days."

"Are you the only woman Price is currently seeing?" Erin shot me a look. "I don't mean to sound rude, Ms. Bishop, but if he was seeing anyone else, it would be nice to know."

"Price is a good man. A family man with integrity. If he was seeing another woman, I can assure you that I would be the first to know about it."

"Ms. Bishop," Erin stepped forward, "would you be jealous if it did come out that he was seeing another woman?"

"Why?" Her head bobbed. "Do you know something that I don't?"

"When was the last time you saw Philip?"

She straightened. "Last night."

"Here?"

Ms. Bishop shook her head. "We have to be discreet with him running for office. You know what the opposition would say about two consenting, non-married adults sleeping together. Never mind the media's spin on it. Nights we share a bed, we have to meet at hotels, arrive and leave at different times. It's a game I prefer not to play, but I understand what is at stake for him."

"Mind sharing what hotel you two met at last night?"

She lowered her brow. "I do mind." Her pupils shrank into tiny beads as she stared. Then she perked up and said, "Not that I don't trust you, but reporters are known to twist the truth."

"Why are you willing to speak with us now?" I asked after Ms. Bishop assured us she was with him until early this morning.

"Because he didn't kill Darcy. It's unfortunate what has happened but I saw the news and know that Darcy wasn't the only victim." Her expression grew serious. "I can assure you that he has nothing to do with her death."

Erin and I finished our interview and Ms. Bishop walked us to the door. She wished us well with our investigation and told us she would call if anything came her way. My cell started ringing as soon as I was alone with Erin.

"Alex, hey," I answered. "Sorry I couldn't stick around earlier."

"You wouldn't have gotten far if you had." He sighed. "I thought you'd like to know the ME has ruled a time of death for the third victim."

"That was quick."

"Her name was Jamie Lambert and she died between the hours of 11PM and 2AM. Strangulation. No initial signs of sexual intercourse."

Just like the others. "Thanks, Alex. I owe you one."

"How's your investigation going?"

Opening up my car door, I looked over the roof and met Erin's gaze. "The further down this rabbit hole I go, the more lost I get."

"Tell me about it."

King promised to call me later and as soon as I pulled my phone away from my ear, Erin asked, "Was that your contact at the station?"

I nodded and shared what King said about the time of death. "That means, if what Ms. Bishop said today was true—"

"Philip Price has an alibi that clears him from the murder of victim number three." We both shared a knowing glance.

I felt the blood leave my cheeks. "Unless they were at the same hotel as Jamie and are both in on the murders together?"

Erin swallowed hard. "God help us all if that is the case."

CHAPTER TWENTY-SIX

Susan Young scrambled beneath the vaulted ceilings to make sure everything was perfect for tonight. It wasn't just to please her client, Philip Price. Her reputation as an event planner was on the line, too.

She rolled her shoulders and bounced a foot. Regretting that afternoon cup of coffee, she fingered the necklace dangling in the dip of her collarbone, looking for imperfection everywhere.

Her employees hustled between dinner tables. She could hear the sounds of utensils clicking in the back, near the kitchen. Massive tiered crystal chandeliers glittered in the soft light as Susan sighed. One quick glance to her check list told her nothing had changed since the last time she'd looked at it.

Susan's head popped up when the heard the echo of a microphone. Her eyes swept to the front of the room. "Excellent," she said to herself before beginning to thread her way between the dozens of round tables. When she noticed even just the slightest wrinkle, she stopped and ironed it out, knowing that if she didn't do it now, she would forget to come back.

Deep inside, Susan held a real fear that even after spending tons of money and booking A-list talent for tonight's entertainment, no one would show. That kept her insides knotted as she knew better than anybody that tonight's major donor fundraising event was perhaps the biggest event of her career.

Soon, she found herself at the front of the room standing behind the podium. The sound engineers assured her all was good and offered for her to sound-check herself.

She stepped behind the microphone with a silly grin of embarrassment twitching her lips sideways. She imagined the soon-to-be crowd sitting at their tables—faces who came because they believed Philip Price's leadership skills—giving her their undivided attention as she welcomed them to tonight's event with open arms.

Susan inhaled a deep breath, cast her gaze down, and tapped the microphone with her index finger. A loud thump crackled through the speakers. Bending closer, she said, "Sound check."

The sound engine laughed and nodded his approval.

Susan smiled when she noticed her staff had stopped to listen. Not wanting to waste the moment, she said into the microphone, "Thank you all for your tremendous work. I couldn't have done this without you. We're one hour away from showtime. Let's make sure people know why we're the best."

Her staff clapped and cheered as she backed away from the podium. Clapping along with her employees, she then turned to the long table behind her where Philip Price would be seated. She straightened his name tag and arranged everything to perfection.

A smile was permanently stamped on her face. She had

been waiting for tonight, preparing for it for so long, and couldn't wait to begin.

Secretly, Susan believed in Philip Price and wanted to see him become the next governor of Colorado. She liked his message, his plan for the future. And though she would never express those thoughts out loud—wanting to keep things professional—she had to admit that her conversation with her best friend, Samantha Bell, left her feeling a bit queasy.

Susan closed her eyes. The floor seemed to have fallen out from beneath her feet. Her head spun uncontrollably. Having seen Susan nearly tip over and collapse, her assistant rushed over to keep her from falling. "Ms. Young, are you all right?"

"A glass of water, please," Susan said as she lowered herself gently into a nearby chair. Her assistant rushed to fill Susan's request.

Samantha wouldn't have mentioned it to her if she didn't think Price was somehow involved. Susan knew how thorough Samantha was when deciding what stories to tell—never making decisions based on her own political affiliations, rather what she believed the public had a right to know.

Susan's assistant was back seconds later with a full glass of cold water. Susan washed down her thoughts and could only hope that Darcy's death didn't stop people from attending her event tonight.

"Now is probably not the best time, but..." her assistant began.

"No. I'm fine." Susan reached for her assistant's arm. Looking her in the eye, she asked, "What is it?"

With wide unwavering eyes, her assistant said, "Senator McKinney called and his flight has been delayed but promises to get here ASAP."

It was a loss but not something that would ruin the event. "As long as we have the Fosters in attendance, we'll be just fine," she said, standing and handing back her empty glass.

"Yes." Her assistant nodded. "I spoke with Mrs. Foster myself. They will be here shortly."

"Good." Susan was feeling better, a sense of pride beginning to replace her initial anxiety. She continued her rounds, double checking everything with her mind drifting to tonight's sponsors.

Mr. and Mrs. Eric Foster were wealthy investors and major funders of candidates and causes that often seemed to be long shots. It didn't matter which side of the aisle the candidates fell on, the Fosters liked unique brands and lofty visions above anything else. This year, that was Philip Price.

"Excuse me, Ms. Young?"

"Yes." Susan turned to her staff.

"There is a man in the lobby requesting to speak with you."

Susan's eyebrows knitted.

"I checked. He's not on the list."

"Did he say what he wants?" Susan kept a watchful eye on the man, pacing back and forth with his gaze glued to the floor. There was something off about him, she thought.

"Just that he needs to speak with you."

Susan thanked her employee, tipped her chin up a notch, and made her way to the tall and evenly built man hiding beneath a tan brimmed hat. "You requested to speak with me?"

The man stopped pacing. He picked his head up and stared. "Are you Susan Young?"

Susan's muscles flexed as an uncomfortable feeling rolled through her. "I'm sorry, who did you say you were?"

He took one step forward. "I need to speak with your friend, Samantha Bell. Do you know where I can find her?"

CHAPTER TWENTY-SEVEN

I DROPPED ERIN BACK AT HER CAR. AFTER WE CAME TO THE realization that Kimberly Bishop and Philip Price might have been at the same hotel as Jamie Lambert, we fell into a deep silence. Sure, it was a long shot, but certainly worth hiding if it was the truth.

Our minds were swirling with possibility. The investigation had taken a sudden and unexpected turn. I kept asking myself the same questions over and over: Did Kimberly Bishop give Philip Price an alibi? Or did she mistakenly drop us a clue to where we should start digging next? I didn't know. But what didn't make any sense to me was why did Kimberly call for the interview in the first place? Simply asserting Price's innocence didn't seem like enough.

I drove instinctively without thinking about what I was doing or where I was going.

My stomach squeezed and I was surely going to give myself another headache if I didn't relax my face from the building tension. The lines on my forehead were permanently twisted the more I thought about Ms. Bishop and our new victim, Jamie Lambert.

Before I knew it, I was parked at the curb outside my house. Once through the front door, I called out to Mason. "Mason, are you home?"

Cooper came trotting from the back with his tail wagging.

"Hey, boy," I bent in half—giving my hamstrings the much-needed stretch they deserved—scratching behind Cooper's ears. He flopped to the ground, groaned, and rolled over. I laughed and scratched his belly. "It sure is great to see you." I smiled, feeling my shoulders relax.

There was still no sign of Mason when I moved to the kitchen. I wondered where he could have gone and why he hadn't bothered to inform me of his departure. Cooper's bowl was empty and I headed to the pantry, Cooper wagging his tail behind me as I said, "You hungry, boy?"

Cooper inhaled his food and I continued calling out to Mason. There was still no response, and my frustration with him only grew before I forced myself to relax. Mason was old enough to make decisions for himself. I had to allow him to grow up—be the man I knew he was on track to become. And I had to get ready for tonight.

On my way to my bedroom, I heard a *clanking* out back. I peeked past the curtains and saw Mason in the garage by the alley working on his bike. I smiled, nearly laughing at how close I was to letting my anger ruin my evening.

"Hey," I said, walking up to him. "Did you get it fixed?"

"The air seems to be holding. Must have run over a nail or something." He cranked the pedals and the tires spun.

"I have a fundraiser I have to attend tonight."

"Is it for work?" he asked without looking.

"It is." I nodded, feeling guilty about constantly working. I hadn't told Mason about the possibility of losing my job— didn't want him to worry. Mason kept working at his bike and a part of me swore I saw resentment cross his face. "There are frozen dinners in the freezer when you get hungry."

"I know." He stood and flipped his bike over.

"I shouldn't be home too late." I followed his movements with my eyes. "If you leave the house, will you let me know?"

"I don't have any plans." He squeezed and tested his brakes. "Probably just play some video games or something."

I wrapped my arm around him. "I love you."

"I love you, too, Mom."

My eyes closed when I pressed my lips to his forehead.

Back inside the house, I closed my bedroom door and stripped my clothes off for the shower. I was working too much, I knew that, but I was doing the best I could. And Mason knew it. At least, I hoped he did. I promised myself that when this story was finished, I would take a weekend off so the two of us could get away. But, with no arrests made, there wasn't a moment to rest.

Standing beneath the steaming stream of water, I thought again about Christy Jones and Kimberly Bishop. I knew they had talked before Erin and I arrived to Ms. Bishop's house today. But was it a conspiracy to cover for Philip and what he might have known about Darcy? Or to give him an alibi for Jamie? I didn't know, other than it all seemed too convenient for me to not be suspicious.

I toweled myself dry, asking myself if we might be missing something by spending so much of our efforts on Darcy while neglecting Mallory, and now Jamie.

After blow-drying my hair, I slid my slender frame into a jet-black cocktail dress questioning why I was attending tonight's party at all, other than I'd promised Susan I would.

We had few leads to go on, but learning what hotel Ms. Bishop and Price were at last night was definitely at the top of my list of information to find out.

Then, all my immediate plans went out the window when I received a call from Susan.

CHAPTER TWENTY-EIGHT

SUSAN SOUNDED SHAKEN UP. AS SOON AS MY EYEBROWS pulled together, the tension in my neck was back. At first, I thought it was nerves I heard in my friend's voice, but it was too much to be just pre-party jitters. Something had her worried, and when she told me how a man came to her requesting to speak to me personally, I was left standing breathless as well.

"Where is he now?" I asked.

"He said he would wait in the lobby." Susan inhaled a deep breath. "I left him there. Sitting by himself."

"Why did he come to you?"

"Maybe he knows you're coming tonight?"

"Did you put my name on the register?"

"No one has that information but my staff."

I didn't want to offend Susan by asking if she could trust everyone on her staff. Her business was her baby and she took hiring seriously. Instead, I asked, "Well, what does he look like?"

"He's not a bad looking man, just kind of strange."

I rolled my eyes, annoyed by the lack of details, and felt my body temperature rise. "Did you get his name at least?"

"I have my hands full here, Sam," Susan said in a sharp tone. "Guests are beginning to arrive and it's not like this is high on my list of priorities."

I closed my eyes and sighed. Susan was right. She had more important things to worry about than having to deal with the details surrounding my life. "Would he be willing to speak to me on the phone?"

"Hang on one second." I heard Susan begin walking. "Let me ask him."

Mason came back inside the house and decided to wash his greasy hands at the kitchen sink. "Mason, please," I covered the mouth piece on my phone with my hand. "Can you wash your hands in the bathroom? We eat in here."

He showed me his dirty palms and trudged his way to the half-bath in the front of the house. I heard the faucet turn on when I moved to the kitchen sink and stared out over our neighbor's yard. An empty raised garden bed had just been planted with garlic bulbs and a strong breeze lifted the fallen leaves off the grass. It was dusk and soon it would be dark.

Cooper nudged my leg and demanded I rub his head.

"Sam, are you there?"

"I'm here." *Why doesn't this man want to speak to me on the phone?*

Susan paused for a moment. Silence hung on the line. The sound of my heart thrashed in my ears. "I can't find him," Susan said. "He's gone."

"Are you sure? I mean, maybe he had to take a leak?" I flipped around, leaned my tailbone against the counter edge, and stared at the empty fruit bowl on the kitchen table.

"Hang on," Susan said. The line ruffled and the clack of her heels had me imagining Susan running across the ballroom floors. "My assistant is calling me over. Maybe she knows something."

I squinted and perked up my ears. I heard Susan ask her assistant if they knew where the man had gone. "I told you to keep an eye on this guy." Susan's voice found its way into my ear.

My heart hammered hard inside my chest. Susan's tone had changed and suddenly I felt like this might have been a bigger deal than I'd initially thought. "What's going on?"

"He's not here."

"It's okay. I'll be there soon. Maybe he'll be back?"

"I don't feel good about this, Sam. I'm telling you, something about this man wasn't right."

I gathered my keys and took my clutch between my fingers. Mason was on the couch watching TV when I passed through the living room. "I'll be back in a couple of hours. Remember, if you leave, text me."

Mason barely nodded as I scampered to my car. "If he really wanted to speak with me, he's not going to go far," I said to Susan.

"Wait one second." Susan was talking to someone. "Sam, someone on my team just informed me that the man knows you from your website." Another woman was still talking to Susan. "Made it sound like you two had met before."

Feeling my ribs squeeze my lungs tight, I tried to recall anything that might spark my memory. Nothing came to mind. I pushed the key into the ignition but didn't turn it. "I'm on my way now."

"Here, just speak with my assistant." Susan handed her phone over.

"Sam, this man wouldn't shut up about you. Says he has information about the murders you're investigating and said that you would be the one to solve the case."

My heart stopped.

Sweat poured from my palms and time seemed to freeze.

Who was this guy and why was he coming to me with supposed information related to the murders instead of going the police? How did he even know I was working this investigation? I hadn't posted anything.

I swallowed past the growing ache in my throat. Susan's assistant was breathless when she said, "But that's not all. He left me with an envelope and it has *your* name on it."

CHAPTER TWENTY-NINE

I ENDED MY CALL, PROMISING I WOULD GET TO THE fundraiser as soon as I could. Then my gaze clouded as my thoughts seemed to freeze.

Susan was right; something about this man wasn't adding up. I didn't understand why this man left without first getting what he'd come for—me. I wouldn't have been long. Maybe with guests beginning to arrive he wasn't comfortable showing his face, waiting around for me to show.

My skin prickled with goosebumps as I shivered. Turning the car on, I let the engine warm before cranking on the heat.

Swiping to King's phone number, I kept wondering what was inside the envelope Mystery Man had left for me. I hadn't written anything publicly about this case, only Dawson knew I was working it at the paper. Yet this stranger knew I was working on the investigation and even went as far as saying I would be the one to solve it. It didn't make any sense. But anybody who read the *Times* knew my columns were from the crime desk. *Could that be enough to personally seek me out?*

King finally answered. "Hey, did you happen to retrieve

the surveillance video from the hotel where Jamie Lambert was killed?"

"What's going on Sam? What are you up to?"

"Did you, or didn't you?"

"We did."

"Have you reviewed it yet?"

"Sam, cut to the chase, will you?"

"I had a meeting with a woman who claims to be having an affair with Philip Price."

"You still think Price has something to do with these murders?"

"Either him or someone from his campaign. I'm not sure." I turned the knob and cranked the heat. "This woman also claimed to be with Price last night but wouldn't tell me which hotel they met at."

"And you think they might have been at the same hotel as Jamie?"

"It's a possibility." *A slim one.*

King sighed. "I'm losing confidence, Sam. I could maybe believe a political candidate being involved in the cover-up of one murder, but not three. Forensics is too good for someone with his ambition to risk getting caught. And do you know how many hotels are in Denver? Or even the Denver area?"

King had points I didn't want to admit. There was too much on the line for Price to be personally committing these crimes. "Maybe Price isn't directly involved, but someone in his campaign could be."

"What's this woman's name?" King asked. "I'll run her name through our database."

"Kimberly Bishop." I heard King scratching the tip of his pen over a piece of paper. "I'd also like to know the names of the men Mallory, Darcy, and Jamie were sleeping with. It's possible that Kimberly learned she wasn't Price's only mistress and got jealous."

"I'll see what I can find."

I ended my call with King and caught a flash of movement out of the corner of my eye. I jerked my head and felt my heart leap into my throat. Mason came running to the car at the speed of light. Immediately, I thought something was wrong.

"Mason, what's wrong?" I rolled down the passenger side window. Cold air came rushing inside.

"Mom, Nolan just texted. He asked if I could stay over tonight."

My mind scrambled to remember who Nolan was. Then I remembered, knowing Nolan was a good one—someone I trusted Mason hanging around with.

"He asked everyone to come. Please, Mom. Can I go?" Mason bounced on his toes with excitement.

"When are you going to start bringing friends over to our house?"

"Next time, Mom."

I rocked my eyes back and forth between his. It was always *next time*, or *I don't know*, and *why so many questions, Mom*? But the truth was, with me working so much, I didn't blame Mason's friends' parents for not wanting their child here without adult supervision. Too much could go wrong but, ironically, I asked Mason the same question his friends' parents probably asked of him. "Will Nolan's parents be there?"

"They're home."

One eyebrow arched. "You asked?"

"They're always home." Mason gripped the window sill tight. "You like Nolan's mom. Remember? She made the stand at the PTA meeting you couldn't stop talking about for, like, a month."

I smiled. "It wasn't a month."

"So, can I go?"

"Will you eat before you leave?"

"Thank you, Mom." Mason dove inside the car and gave me a hug. Retracting back out of the window, he said, "I'll eat at Nolan's."

"Text me Nolan's house number," I called out to Mason as he hurried back inside, "and charge your cellphone before you leave."

"I will," he called back.

Suddenly, it seemed like we were turning a corner and our worst days were behind us. But then Mason surprised me by turning back and coming to the window once again. "I forgot to tell you, I just saw the news about what happened at that hotel earlier today."

My stomach sank.

"A girl was murdered?" Fear flashed over his innocent eyes.

"Sadly, she was." I frowned.

"Mom, are you in danger?"

I felt the backs of my eyes swell. "No, honey. Mom is not in any danger." I wasn't certain of it.

CHAPTER THIRTY

KIMBERLY BISHOP DID A GOOD JOB HIDING HER SECRET relationship. I watched her move effortlessly through the party, mingling and charming the guests. People responded to her well, and not once did I see her interact with Philip Price himself.

Musical instruments harmonized in the background to the soft murmur coming from the crowd of people. Leftover scents of dinner hung in the air and my impatience was grating on my nerves.

I still wanted to get my hands on this mysterious envelope. I hadn't arrived quickly enough and knew it wouldn't be right to pull Susan away, not with how hard she'd worked to make tonight's event a success.

Susan floated around the room, making sure every transition was natural. I busied myself by taking my time with my first glass of champagne before switching to sparkling cider. I small-talked with eagerness keeping my belly knotted.

Philip Price caught me staring and I held my breath when I watched him excuse himself and begin making his way over to me.

My skin crawled and I could still feel his hands touching my arm. I purposely wrapped my shawl around my shoulders tighter, keeping my eyes sharp and my mind even sharper.

"I didn't know you would be here tonight." He stood next to me and turned to face the room.

Keeping my spine straight, I watched as Christy Jones stared like a hawk from the other side of the room. "I thought you'd be getting used to all the press you've been receiving."

He chuckled. "Kimberly mentioned your visit with her today."

"Don't worry, I neglected to mention you hitting on me."

Price barely reacted. "Sweetheart, if that's what you call flirting, you and I live in two different worlds."

He was right about that. "Kimberly had some interesting things to say about the two of you."

Price rubbed his chin. "How did you find out about us?"

"So you *are* admitting it's true?" He answered with a look. "I'm just that good, Price." I couldn't hold back the smile.

He turned his attention back to the party. "Then I hope you're just as good at keeping secrets."

"That depends." I took my eyes off Christy and looked at a wide-eyed Price.

He quirked a brow and wrapped his lips around his flute of champagne. "Are you about to blackmail me?"

"Don't be so dramatic." I angled my body toward him, my confidence building. "I'll keep your affair with Kimberly safe so long as you make me your exclusive reporter."

Price stared, his face void of expression. It was a lofty request, especially knowing that Price had personally told Dawson to never send me to interview him again. But I knew that if I could get Price to agree, it would settle things down with Dawson and maybe even give me a few stories to keep our paper from expiring before this thing was all over. "I cover everything campaign-related."

A waiter passed and Price set his empty glass on his silver tray. "Let's walk."

I emptied my own hands and followed Price out of the ballroom and into the hall. He smiled and greeted guests along the way. Here, it was quieter with fewer people around and gave Price an opportunity to speak freely without worrying about others' ears.

"I apologize for coming across as insensitive yesterday." His voice was low, his eyes sincere.

Naturally, I remained skeptical, wondering if Kimberly influenced this discussion. "You weren't even sorry for Darcy's death. She was a member of your own team." My arms swiped through the air as I talked. "The least you could do was say something nice. Instead, you just sat there." I grinded my teeth, unable to stop my muscles from quivering. But I was so mad.

Price stared dumbfounded with parted lips. I gave him a moment to respond before I started up again. Then he swallowed and said, "You're right. Darcy was such an incredible talent. No one had anything bad to say about her." He lifted his head and swiped his hand over his mouth. "I can't believe it happened. But I couldn't speak about it until I knew for sure her family had been properly notified."

Though his words were something we could both agree on, Price was a politician. Everything was calculated. His words were carefully crafted tonight, just like his response to every issue. Nothing came out of his mouth without first being rehearsed. I didn't know if I could believe him or if his view would change tomorrow.

"My editor won't always be able to control what I write," I said, threatening him with what little power I held.

Price dropped his chin. "I know about your website."

I swallowed down my sudden surprise. I hadn't published anything about Price, even if Erin wished I had. "It's nice to know I have at least one reader," I said sarcastically.

Price chuckled. "I'm as determined as you are to catch the person who is killing these women."

I searched deep inside his eyes. He stared back, his thoughts swirling in his irises. Unable to hold myself back, I asked, "Where were you last night?"

Price's smile faded as his spine straightened. He flicked his eyes through the door and I followed his gaze to Kimberly. Then he turned his head back to me and said, "You already know."

"Then be honest with me." I tilted my head to the side. "I know you were with Kimberly last night, but *where?*"

"You wouldn't believe me even if I told you." His dark eyebrows raised.

"Try me, Future Governor."

He smirked, liking my compliment. "Denver International."

"The airport?" I took a step back.

"See?" He wagged his finger. "I told you, you wouldn't believe me."

"Mr. Price," Christy stood under the threshold of the ball-room entrance, "we'd like to get a photo when you have a minute." Her eyes flicked to me.

"I'm on my way," Price responded. As soon as Christy left, he turned to me and said, "I heard about Jamie Lambert. It was all over the news. I want whoever is killing these women —whoever murdered Darcy—caught."

"So you'll accept my offer?"

"I can't make you exclusive but I'll make sure you're one of the first to know when anything happens."

I narrowed my eyes.

"That's the best I can do." He held his hand out and we

shook. "Now, I believe I'm about to have my photo taken with tonight's sponsors. What do you say we make this an exclusive image reserved specifically for *The Colorado Times*?"

"I think this new partnership is going to work out swell," I said, and together we headed back into the ballroom with Price laughing.

CHAPTER THIRTY-ONE

SUSAN FOUND ME SOON AFTER I TOOK PRICE'S PHOTO. "I'M so sorry, Sam. I told you to hurry and then things quickly got away from me. Now look, the night's nearly over and we've barely talked."

"Don't worry about it." I glanced at Susan—my friend who stood tall and looked like a million dollars. It was impossible not to smile and be proud of her.

"Except I *will* worry about it because I hate letting my friends down."

"If that's all you're worrying about, I'd say you just pulled off an incredible event."

Susan's cheeks ripened like apples as she leaned her shoulder against mine. I wrapped my arms around her and squeezed her tight. "I'm happy for you."

"Thank you, Sam. Really." She squeezed the air out of me. "Even if I didn't get to speak with you much tonight, just knowing you were in the room gave me the confidence I needed to pull this off."

"That's what friends are for," I said. Together we watched her client, Philip Price, schmooze his way around the room. A part of me regretted our rough start, but another part knew that I needed to keep an open mind and not let personal feelings get in the way of facts.

"I can't stop thinking about what you said about Price the other night." Susan sighed. "It's so sad to think he might be involved in that young woman's death."

"Price is guilty of having an affair, but I'm starting to doubt he's the killer," I murmured into my friend's ear.

Trust was hard to come by and if it weren't for my phone call with King earlier, I wasn't sure that my conversation with Price would have gone quite as well tonight. We might have had a different outcome, one where I was pushed to the sidelines instead of brought into the fold. King was right, though. There was too much on the line for Price to risk involving himself in something as horrific as murder.

"Are you all right?" Susan asked me.

"I'm exhausted."

"Is it Mason or the case?"

I flicked my gaze to her. "A little of both, but mostly this investigation."

Susan gave me a knowing look, reaching for my hand.

"It's been nonstop and I've barely slept."

Holding my hand, Susan insisted, "Sam, you didn't have to come tonight. If there was something more important you should be doing, I would have understood."

I felt my spine collapse as I gave her a look. "You know I had to come."

"Oh. Right." Susan's eyes perked up. "I nearly forgot." She reached inside her dress and pulled out the envelope she had stashed inside her bra.

"You kept that thing there all night?" I laughed.

"I didn't want to lose it." She handed it over like it was no big deal.

Feeling breathless, I stared at the small white rectangle,

damp with Susan's sweat, for a minute before finally taking it between my fingers. It was surprisingly light and felt empty. "It's still sealed shut?"

"What did you think, that I would open it?" Susan's head wagged.

"Did you ever see that man again?"

"Completely disappeared," Susan said with round eyes.

We still didn't know why he had come to her rather than to me. I was easily accessible and could be reached about a dozen different ways—email, social media sites, work, phone —yet he chose to go to straight to Susan.

"This is so weird," I muttered, flipping the envelope around between my fingers just as the well-dressed couple Price had his photo taken with strolled up on us.

"Mr. and Mrs. Foster, please meet Samantha Bell." Susan introduced me to the couple who had paid for tonight.

"Please, it's Eric and Camille." Eric smiled.

"Pleasure meeting you both," I said, shaking both their hands.

"Eric and Camille are philanthropists, too." Susan highlighted the Fosters' résumé, clearly to their approval.

I smiled and nodded, acting as if I cared more than I did. I could interview anybody—dig deep into people's lives without a second thought—but flattery was by far the hardest skill I had yet to master. Even before the photo op with Price, I knew of the Fosters but had never personally met them.

"Are you a donor?" Eric asked me.

"Reporter," I said proudly.

His thin eyebrows pulled together. "With who?"

"*The Colorado Times*."

Eric glanced to Susan. "Not much of a future in print, is there?"

He laughed, but I didn't find it funny. "There will always be news as long as someone is there to report it."

A stunned look crossed over Eric's face. My stomach tied itself into a knot and I immediately regretted turning things awkward in front of Susan. But I could see a sparkle in Camille's eyes that told me she approved of me standing up to her husband's silly jokes.

"I suppose you're right," Eric said before changing the subject. The three of them discussed the late arrival of Senator McKinney, Philip Price's poll numbers, and I stood there pretending to care while secretly itching to finally open this envelope.

Camille made her way over to me. "I've read your column." Eric and Susan were still lost in their own conversation when I turned my attention to Camille. "I'm a fan." She smiled.

"Thank you."

"Were you there today?" Excitement filled her eyes.

I gave her a questioning look, unsure what exactly she was referring to.

"I saw the news breaking this morning. Is it true?"

"Is what true?"

"Another woman killed." She stepped up to my ear and lowered her voice. "I heard these women are being bound to the beds they are killed on."

Tucking my chin into my chest, I considered how best to respond to her strange sense of excitement. Was she a closet sleuth getting off on true crime stories? Or just digging for what it was like to see death first-hand?

"This fetish stuff would have never happened if that book hadn't been published." Camille rubbed her wrists as if speaking from experience. "Though, I must admit, I read every single page. *Twice*." She laughed.

"Perhaps," I said.

"Women must be careful." A serious look tightened her face. "Asking a man to get aggressive in bed is one thing, but being choked while seeking orgasm?" Camille tilted her head while lightly touching her neck and adopting a faraway look. "Seems a bit much. Then again," she flicked her eyes to her husband, "some men get off on submissive women."

I stared at Eric, wondering if I was overthinking what Camille was trying to tell me or if she was trying to tell me anything at all. The conversation was bizarre. She must have seen the appalled look tighten my jaw because she quickly apologized.

"I'm sorry," she said. "This isn't the setting to be discussing such gruesome details."

"No, it's okay," I assured her as I kept one eye on her husband.

As my gaze drifted over Eric's tuxedo, my eyes landed on his gold Rolex watch. Suddenly, I realized who the real alpha in the room was, and it wasn't Price. It was Eric Foster. Everything about him screamed dominance. He controlled the conversation with whomever he was talking to. It was clear he wanted everyone to know he wielded the power, had the money, and was the first to recognize the strength in endorsing Philip Price's candidacy for governor.

Pulling his hand away from Susan's shoulder, Eric turned to me and snaked his arm around his wife's waist. His fingers dug deep into her hip, gluing her to him. Camille submitted to his will and melted into him.

"It was wonderful meeting you, Samantha." Camille smiled.

Eric and Camille shared a glance. "If you'll excuse us, there are many more people we've yet to pass our greetings to." Eric winked at me. "Great meeting you, Samantha, and I wish you luck with your reporting."

When Susan excused herself, I couldn't stop staring at Eric and Camille thinking there was a strange familiarity

Camille shared with the victims. Almost *too familiar* for me to ignore what she'd said.

CHAPTER THIRTY-TWO

I DARTED STRAIGHT FOR THE BACK WALL. IN THE DARK corner of the room, I dug out my phone from inside my clutch, needing to be sure that I wasn't just making this up.

My heart knocked as I pulled up the images I had of both Mallory and Darcy.

I held my breath and waited as the screen populated with their beautiful faces. Thoughts swirled between my ears— assumptions coming faster than I could keep up with. I couldn't escape the glaringly obvious similarities both Mallory and Darcy shared with Camille. There they were, staring back at me, telling me my gut feeling was right.

I swiped my thumb back and forth. Mallory to Darcy, Darcy to Mallory. Then I swept my gaze across the room with a gaping mouth and quickly found Camille.

My veins opened up and I could feel my pulse throbbing hard and fast in my neck.

Camille filled her husband's shadow perfectly. Laughed when he laughed, nodded along as he spoke. She was the definition of submissive, but there was something odd about their relationship that made me think it wasn't as great as they let on.

Together, they glided across the floor as I looked for hints into their private lives. Camille's soft features and wavy long blonde hair was nearly identical to the victims'. Each of the three women had plump lips, cute little button noses, and sharp eyebrows above almond brown eyes.

It couldn't be coincidence.

As I stared, I began to wonder what Jamie Lambert looked like. I suspected I could describe her face without knowing the details. She probably had the face of an angel—the face these three women shared that easily attracted men. Maybe even men like Eric Foster.

I startled when I accidently dropped the envelope to the floor. It dropped like a small stone, landing with a thump. I blinked and stared as the room suddenly felt much smaller than before.

Bending at the knees I plucked it from the floor, turned to face the wall, and finally ripped it open.

Inside, a key slid to one corner. Fishing it out, I flipped it over in my palm. On the other side of the key was #67 sketched on the back of what I assumed to be athletic tape.

With a pinched expression, I searched to find meaning. It gave me nothing. No note to go along with it. Just a key. No instructions for what to do with it or what came next. And, worst of all, Mystery Man left without giving us his name.

I felt my body cool with sudden sweat.

This one wasn't going to be easy to figure out without further clues and, by the time I turned back around, I found Eric staring from across the room.

I froze. My eyes locked with his. Fisting the key inside my hand, I wondered if he'd known this key was coming for me. His wife left me beyond suspicious of what they were up to and, though I couldn't stop staring, I knew he was on my list to research next.

Finally, Eric grinned and turned his attention back to the conversation swirling around him.

Samantha Bell will solve this case. Mystery Man's words echoed between my ears and followed me wherever I went. I felt helpless and was once again asking myself what I was doing here instead of working on my story—finding the facts Dawson insisted I uncover.

Escaping to the powder room, I sat on the toilet, dropped my face into my hands, and took a moment to collect my thoughts. I needed time alone, to not be seen. There were too many eyes and it felt as if they were all on me.

Eric and Camille were the perfect couple, but my conversation with Camille had me thinking there was more to it than what was on the surface. I couldn't shake the thought. And, if that was the case, that meant they had secrets. Stories I wanted to hear. A past I needed to know. Finally, I had to call it a night, knowing I still had a story to write.

I found Susan outside the ballroom, wishing her guests well as they began filing out the door. She hurried over to me. "Did you open the envelope?"

I held up the key. "This was inside."

"Any ideas what it goes to?"

"Your guess is as good as mine."

Susan took it to examine herself. She brushed her finger over the #67 and murmured, "This is strange, Sam. Something about this doesn't feel right."

I took the key back, wondering where it would lead me next. "I know what you mean." We shared a knowing glance. "Are you going to be all right?"

"Look around." Susan raised her brows. "I'm surrounded by power. It's you I'm worried about."

I swallowed a constricted breath. "I'll be fine."

"Call me when you get home," Susan said as she walked me to the exit.

"I will." We said our goodbyes and, on my way to the car, I stopped dead in my tracks as I caught sight of Eric Foster leaving the building. He scampered down the front steps and into the back of a waiting limousine. Not a second later, the wheels were set in motion and he was gone, without Camille.

CHAPTER THIRTY-THREE

ERIN TATE WAS BUSY PUTTING THE FINISHING TOUCHES ON this week's podcast episode when she stopped to consider how best to open this case up for debate with her listeners.

It was a question she kept asking herself since putting Samantha on the spot when discussing the plans she had for her crime website.

Erin stared out the window, both hands wrapped around the hot mug of green tea she was drinking, allowing her thoughts to get away from her. Her reflection shined back on the glass but, when she looked past it, the warm glow of street lights illuminated the dark night, tempting her to take a night off.

When other women were busy managing families or enjoying a night out on the town, Erin found herself with her legs tucked beneath her, sitting behind her desk, following leads, looking for clues. There was nothing she'd rather be doing, even if she had a reputation for being a workaholic.

Erin was proud of the work she was doing. Her subscriber numbers were going up but she knew she could do even better. There was always room for improvement. And she wanted to be the best.

Covering this investigation in real time was risky. She couldn't predict the outcome—or know how many episodes it would take to complete. Inside her mind, Erin trusted the process and relied on her skills. She would do anything to make sure she didn't let her listeners down.

That was what she loved about podcasting. The storytelling, bringing the news to life. Having complete strangers from across the country tune in and hear what she had to say filled her heart with purpose. But these murders were chilling. The fact that the death toll continued to climb with no arrests had Erin constantly doubting her own safety.

She turned back to her computer screen.

Once this newest episode was published, her listeners would know everything she did—including how Darcy Jean worked for gubernatorial candidate Philip Price. A sense of excitement rushed through her when she thought about exposing the secrets of someone like Price. Then, something inside made her stop and consider a new angle: The murderer might also be tuning in and listening to her show.

Erin placed her mug on a coaster and landed her eyes on the notes from her interview with Kimberly Bishop. She and Samantha had formed the same opinion about Ms. Bishop and Erin couldn't wait to hear back from Sam on how Philip Price's campaign fundraiser went. That gave Erin reason to pause before conviction.

If the murderer was a listener, would she be giving too much away? Would releasing her podcast cause the killer to slip up? Or set his sights on someone else? Someone too close to finding out their identity?

Erin knew just what she had to do.

She glanced to the clock. It was still early enough for her to visit another of the bars Mallory was known to have been the night she were murdered. She'd already been to Violet's Place—one of Mallory's final watering holes. Erin wanted to see another for herself, talk around, feel what the women felt. It was all about the vibe and, without knowing the atmosphere of a place, it was impossible to completely understand.

As Erin got ready, she decided she would ask her listeners to bring their tips, theories, and questions to her on a message board. She hoped that it could be done on Samantha's website since she already had the infrastructure in place to make that happen.

Erin stood in front of the wall mirror and smoothed her hands over the suede lace jacket. She turned and checked herself out. Her skinny jeans and knee-high boots made her feel sexy and she laughed when flinging her long blonde hair over her shoulder.

She drove to the heart of the city, determined to find the answers to her many questions that kept her awake at night. Erin decided to visit 16th Street Tavern first since both she and Samantha had visited Violet's Place.

She parked a block away and walked the streets alone. It was a quiet night considering what Erin thought it should have been for the weekend. Men smoked in dark corners. Women laughed somewhere she couldn't see. The trolley rolled by and, when she stepped inside the tavern, the warm smells of food made her stomach grumble.

"Just you tonight?" the hostess greeted her.

Erin stepped forward. "Actually, I was hoping to talk with the owner."

The hostess's smile faded as she swung her head around in confusion. "Uh, sure. Let me see if I can find him."

Erin made friendly eye contact. "Thank you."

While waiting, she moved near the entrance, scanning the fliers stapled to the wall. It was full of events, concert promotions, and art happenings throughout the month. Then she turned back around to study the environment. What brought Mallory here in the first place?

Tonight, there were enough empty tables to take notice, but the murmur of conversation still managed to drown out much of any other noise. Sports played on the television, and Erin's imagination took her away to the night of the murders.

A man sitting at the bar locked eyes with her.

He stared and she stared back.

Then he smiled and Erin looked away as the hostess came back. Towing a tall man wearing a sports jacket close behind, Erin was introduced to the owner.

"Jack Olson," he said, extending his hand to Erin. "You requested to speak with me?"

Erin introduced herself, mentioned her podcast and how she was investigating the murders of Mallory Madison, Darcy Jean, and Jamie Lambert. "I'd like to ask you a few questions, if that's okay."

Jack held her stare and sighed. Then he glanced at his watch and said, "Let's take a table in the back."

"That would be great."

"Can I get you something to drink? Or perhaps you're hungry?" Jack asked Erin as they meandered past the bar and into the back corner where an empty table waited.

Sitting, Erin declined. "That's all right. Maybe after we're finished I'll relax with a drink."

Jack grabbed the attention of a nearby waitress and requested a bottle of water and two glasses. Then he took a seat, saying, "The detectives were here the day after they found Mallory's body." He frowned with heavy eyes. "I told them I didn't see anything out of place and, truthfully, I couldn't place her if you asked me to."

Erin glanced around. "Popular place."

"We get a lot of traffic in and out of here. Especially on

weekends. But, I must say, when word spread that the murderer may have picked Mallory up in my bar," he jabbed his finger in his chest as if feeling personally insulted, "people started going elsewhere."

"How did people connect those dots?" Erin's brows knitted. "It's not like the police are saying more than their investigation 'is ongoing.'"

Jack shook his head and sighed. "I don't know. Maybe they saw the detectives arrive and put two and two together."

A bottled water arrived and Jack filled Erin's glass half-full at her request.

"Do you have security tape from that night?"

"I already gave it to the police. If you want it, you'll have to go through them."

"Did you review it before you handed it over?"

He shook his head. "There wasn't any need to. No crime was committed here. In fact, we had a great night. Hardly any trouble."

"Who was behind the bar that night?" Erin glanced to the bartender. Jack's eyes glimmered when he followed her gaze. "Can I speak with him?" she asked.

Jack reluctantly agreed. Standing, he said, "I hope you're able to help find whoever did this. The public deserves to know what's happening in their city. But, please, keep the name of my bar out of your story." His eyes pleaded with Erin. "I can't afford to lose any more business. I have a family to support."

Erin couldn't make any promises to Jack. So much of Mallory's story began here, and it needed to be told to give a complete picture. Instead, she stared back, allowing him to assume her silence was her way of promising him something she couldn't.

Erin barely sipped her water—her bladder full from the pot of tea she'd drank earlier—by the time the bartender arrived to her table. He came with a curious look twisting his brow and his thick arms stretched his button-up shirt. With his hair slicked to the side, he wore a neatly trimmed beard well. Erin introduced herself.

"Jack told me," he said, nodding.

"Do you remember seeing this woman that night?" Erin reminded him the date she was referring to, turning a picture of Mallory around so he could take a good look.

The bartender took a moment to study the photo of Mallory. "Yeah. I remember her."

"And do you remember who she was with?"

"She was alone for a while. Much too long if you ask me."

"Why do you say that?"

"Look at her. She should have been picked up as soon as she walked into the place. She's beautiful." They both stared at Mallory's perfect smile.

"Do you know who she eventually left with?"

He shook his head and glanced to the bar as if looking to spark his memory. "I didn't catch his name." Then his eyes were back on Erin. "But she must have trusted him enough to leave here with him."

"What did he look like?" Erin asked, hoping to get a description since seeing the actual security footage would be damn near impossible.

"Tall. Over six feet. Well built. Just like many of our clientele. Any one of these men could have been him. She was just the unlucky one. Shame, too, because she had the best laugh." The big man slumped over. "I'll never forget it."

Erin's phone chimed with a message from her Facebook app. "Anything else you can remember that might help find who did this to her?"

The bartender's eyes squinted for a quick pause. Then he said, "He was drinking a Tom Collins."

Erin thanked the man for his time and, as soon as he left, she opened her message.

Use the key and Samantha Bell will solve this case.

Erin's pulse raced. She glanced around but no one was paying any attention to her.

Erin read the message again. She didn't know what it meant or who it was from.

What key? she messaged back but it was too late. The person was gone, the account disabled.

CHAPTER THIRTY-FOUR

THE LADY KILLER STARED INTO THE BRIGHT HUE OF HIS cellphone's screen.

His breathing was labored, his blood running cold. Again, he reread the message he'd just received as if needing to dissect each word for its proper meaning.

You're a great man. Even if they can't see it now, they will see it soon.

He loved her. She was the only honest woman in the world. Even if he sometimes hated her, she was his everything. No matter what he did, she forgave and provided a clear path forward. Mistakes were never dwelled on. Together, they were on a mission that was far from complete.

The Lady Killer pressed his index finger into the pad of his thumb. His pulse throbbed hard as he sniffed and wiped his nose. He finished reading the message in its entirety, refusing to let go of the one person who believed in him completely.

Do what you have to do. Your secret is safe with me.

He took one last glance at the photo of the woman that

was attached to the WhatsApp message and closed his browser. His heart swelled. He loved her more than anything.

Tucking his phone away inside the front of his suit jacket, he let his head fall back against the seat's headrest. Sitting in the dark with his eyes closed, he breathed deeply.

What to do? He kept asking himself this same question like an ancient mantra channeling his spirit to the gods. *What to do?*

He was restless. Nothing calmed him. The answer to his question was easy, but he hesitated as if wanting to believe there was some way around it. He knew there wasn't. They had been here before. He had needs and she understood that.

Sitting still proved to be impossible. He wasn't meant to be tied down.

His knee bounced and his fingers drummed. When his eyes shot wide open, he shook his head and growled out all the frustration building inside of him.

A rush of life shot through his core like a spike of adrenaline.

Despite feeling trapped—acting as if there was no way out —he knew what he needed to do and it had to happen tonight. He reached to his neck, his collar feeling more like a noose than anything else. He tugged and fumbled his buttons until they popped open. Then he gasped for air, suddenly feeling the freedom he was after.

He leaned forward and gripped the key dangling from the car's ignition. The sight out his window gave him reason to pause and reflect.

He watched the rivers of traffic flow opposite each other. Safely perched high in a nearby parking lot, The Lady Killer stared without blinking at the red taillights snaking south. Then he flicked his eyes to the white headlights heading north.

He stared with a childlike gaze as if reading the metaphor, understanding it for the first time.

The river's relentless current proved difficult to peel his eyes away from. Good versus evil. Heaven and Hell. Black and white. Right and wrong. The two forces constantly in friction with each other. It could have represented now or when his journey began. The darkness living inside of him and the white purity of heaven he longed to get back. It was the story of his life—a legacy he was born to fulfill. There was no escaping it. This was what he was meant to do.

His hand tightened its grip on the steering wheel, the blood leaving the tips of his fingers. A second later, he fired up the engine and popped the clutch. The tires squealed over the pavement as he raced between an opening in traffic and onto the highway below.

The taillights in front of him illuminated his skin. He followed the familiar red glow, slowly easing his foot down harder on the accelerator. Shifting into fifth gear, he couldn't get away fast enough.

Tonight, he'd met his match. He wasn't the only man of power in the room. There were others challenging him for his spot on the pyramid.

But, now that he was gone, he was thrilled to have escaped the stuffy event. He'd had to leave his true love there, but he'd see her again. It was the people that always ruined good meals, fun times. Everything had to be taken so seriously. He hated the hierarchy, putting on face to impress strangers and people who pretended to be friends.

His chest tightened as anger seethed inside of him. The more he replayed the night's events inside his head, the more frustrated he became.

Lowering his chin, he glared.

No one listened. They seemed to ignore what he had to say. But what they didn't understand was that he knew best. It was the world that refused to believe the truth of what was coming. The future, he saw crystal clear. It was an ugly sight if put in the hands of the wrong people—something which he promised himself he wouldn't let happen.

He zipped around a city bus, cursing the driver for driving slow in the left lane.

The Lady Killer couldn't allow the children of this state to grow up to a future where men peacocked their blood money and women swooned at those same assholes he despised.

A sour taste dried his tongue as his bitter thoughts grew.

When he reached his exit, he pulled off the highway and headed toward the place he knew would be filled with young naïve women who would listen to his words.

An erection swelled in his pants with thoughts straying to the bedroom. He would assert his dominance, reclaim the strong man he knew he was inside. He'd make the woman submit and he'd get off in the process.

The sign flashed bright as he pulled into the parking lot.

He could see the crowd through the windows. A grin pulled at his lips. Circling the building, he stared, finding several beautiful faces he would target—women who would soon learn who was boss.

After parking, he entered the building and headed straight for the bar.

"What can I get you, Chief?" the bartender asked before The Lady Killer had time to sit down.

"Tom Collins."

The bartender knocked the countertop with his knuckles. "You got it."

A minute later, a Tom Collins appeared and The Lady Killer had his lips wrapped around the rim of his glass. One sip and he felt his chest loosen up. He turned and glanced over his shoulder. Immediately, she locked eyes with him from across the room.

They stared and the room spun.

Then he called her in with his dimpled smile he knew she couldn't resist.

She had long blonde hair with stunning brown piercing eyes. She had more weight on her bones than what he preferred, but she would have to make do. She was his target tonight.

"Hi," she said. "Is that seat taken?"

"Saving it for you." He smiled.

The blonde beauty sat next to him, not knowing that tonight would be her last.

CHAPTER THIRTY-FIVE

MY DRIVE HOME WAS QUICK. I COULDN'T STOP THINKING about the Fosters and why Eric might have left the fundraiser alone. Where was he going without Camille? They were sponsoring the event; wouldn't they stay until the very end?

As soon as my foot hit the curb, a cold wind shot up my dress. I shivered with shifty eyes darting into the pitch-black night.

The wind howled as the streetlight flickered above before going out again.

Leaves rustled beneath my parked car, gathering against the tires. The neighbor's dog barked and made me jump. With one hand over my beating heart, I glanced toward my house. It was as dark as the night but I could see Cooper's light fur in the window, accompanied by his bark.

"Easy boy," I said. "It's just me."

Cooper kept barking as I walked to the front door, trying to find the right key. It wasn't like him to bark once he knew it was me. Something wasn't right.

"Coop, quiet," I snapped when I finally found the house key. Then, when I glanced to the window to tell Cooper to quiet down, I caught movement in the window's reflection of a man's silhouette heading directly for me.

I spun around as fast as a tornado, the whites of my eyes bugging out of my head. I gripped my keys, knowing I had the house key pointing out. I pulled my hand back, ready to stab my attacker's eye. Instead, my feet left the ground as I yelped. "One day I'm going to draw a gun on you." I struggled to catch my breath and slow my beating heart.

Alex King showed me his palms. "Not funny?"

"Not funny at all." I swung my clutch at him and hit him in the shoulder.

He took my beating like a gentleman.

"What are you doing here?" I turned the door handle, surprised to find it unlocked.

King's brow furrowed. "You always leave your house unlocked?"

Cooper stopped barking as soon as we stepped inside. I was quick to flip on the lights, knowing it had been left unlocked by accident. "Mason is at a friend's house. He must have forgotten to lock up before he left."

Naturally, King swept my house just to make sure it hadn't been broken into. I appreciated the gesture even if I thought it was a bit overkill. But my nerves were jittery since receiving this mysterious key and I wasn't going to stop him. His mere presence was enough to calm me tonight.

"I'm going to have some tea, you want some?" I asked, putting the kettle over a blue flame.

King nodded and sat at the kitchen table. He had a dark shadow of facial hair filling his face, and his piercing eyes sent my heart fluttering with the way he stared. I pretended like I didn't notice a handsome man was sitting in my house—pretended like my kid wasn't away for the night—but it proved to be impossible when I joined him at the table.

"You look tired," I said.

"So do you."

I shook my head. "I'm exhausted."

He chuckled. "If that's your exhausted look, you're doing all right for yourself."

Feeling heat gloss my cheeks, I swept my eyes up and asked, "Did you run Kimberly Bishop's name through the database?"

"She doesn't have a record." King then confirmed everything Kimberly already had told me.

"Thanks for doing that, but I spoke with Price himself tonight and he confirmed his affair with Kimberly."

"Is that all you think he's hiding?"

"All that's important to me." I shrugged.

"If it will make you sleep easier, I'm certain, Sam, that Philip Price is not the man killing these women." King gave me a knowing look. "The evidence confirms it."

"Care to share what evidence that is, Detective?"

"Keep glancing at me like that and you might just get me to tell you everything."

I laid on the seduction, felt my eyes sparkle. King laughed. He didn't bother telling me to keep this conversation off record when he did a deep dive into all three investigations, and I wasn't going to remind him, either.

"The medical examiner came back with Mallory and Darcy's toxicology reports."

I pulled my lips off my mug. "And?"

"GHB was present in both victims." His voice was once again heavy with guilt.

"The date rape drug," I muttered into my tea.

King sighed. "We don't have shit, Sam." He stood and walked to the sink. He stared out the window for a moment before turning back around. "We have a glass at the first scene with fingerprints but we don't have a match. It's not in the system. If it was Price, we'd know it was him."

"Then the killer doesn't have a criminal record." I cast my gaze down to the table in thought. "Were they raped?" I swiveled in my chair and faced King.

"No signs of intercourse." King strode back to the table, falling heavily into his chair. The joints creaked under the pressure of his over six-foot-tall frame. "Drugged, stripped, and tied up to die."

An ill feeling twisted my stomach. "But you have security tape; you must have someone you've identified as possibly being your suspect?"

"We've reviewed everything." His eyes hooded. "From the hotels to the bars and the streets between."

"And you have nothing?" My brows knitted with disbelief.

"There are a few people we're speaking with, but nothing that would convince the district attorney to file charges."

I silently went through the list of details King shared, trying to make sense of the unexplainable. There had to be something. We couldn't let another woman die. "These murders have to be linked."

"It certainly seems that way." King smoothed his hands over his thighs.

After finishing our tea, we moved to the living room and sat on the couch, Gavin's smiling face looking down on us from multiple photos on the wall. Tucking my feet beneath me, King slung his arm around the back, inserting his large frame into the opposite corner. We stared for a long while without saying a word. I could see his eyes travel from one family photo to the next, looking at the man we both dearly missed.

Finally, I asked, "Why are you telling me this?"

He flicked his gaze down to me. King must have known I would write about what he shared somewhere—either for the paper or on my blog, or perhaps both. "You're smart, Sam."

I held his eyes inside of mine. My heart begged me to

reach out and touch him. Instead, I said, "I found my next lead tonight."

King lifted a perfectly arched brow. "Oh?"

I told King about Mr. and Mrs. Foster and Camille's strange story. "It led me to an epiphany." King pulled his eyebrows together. "Let me guess, Jamie Lambert had blonde hair and brown eyes."

"Did I show you her photo?"

I shook my head. Silence hung between us. "Am I right?" I asked.

King dove his hand inside his jacket and pulled out a photo of Jamie. "Right on the money."

I took the photo and brought it close to my face. Jamie's bright eyes shined back and I could easily place all three women's faces inside of hers.

"Our perp has a type." King stared up at the ceiling.

"All three women are nearly identical to Camille Foster."

King rolled his head and locked his eyes on mine. "And plenty of other women. Don't tell me, you have Eric Foster in your crosshairs."

"I wish you could have seen him tonight." I briefly cast my gaze down, searching for the right word to describe what I felt when in Eric's presence. Instead, I said, "Can I show you something?"

King cocked his head to the side.

Reaching for my clutch on the coffee table, I revealed the key from Mystery Man. "Any ideas what it might go to?"

King pinched the key between his fingers and inspected it. "My guess would be it goes to a padlock." He handed it back. "Why? Whose key is it?"

His guess was as good as mine. I chose not to tell him how I'd acquired it but King was smart, always noticing the clues that surrounded him.

"Sam, if there is something you're not telling me..."

I listened to my heart as I debated telling King more. Instead, I glanced to the clock and said, "It's getting late and Dawson is expecting a story from me by morning."

King nodded and stood. "If that key has anything to do with these murders, you should tell me now, Sam."

"I don't know what it is," I said honestly.

I walked him to the door. But, before leaving, he turned and stared. A sharp intake of breath had my head spinning. I watched his blue eyes sway with mine, and my gaze drifted to his very kissable lips. The door creaked open and the cold fall air pulled my feet back down to Earth. "Thanks for the tea," King said, stepping out.

Weak in the knees, I could only nod as I shut the door behind him.

I followed him with my eyes all the way to his car. I knew he wanted to kiss me goodbye, and a part of me wished that he had.

"Thanks for the information," I whispered to an empty house.

CHAPTER THIRTY-SIX

ALEX KING KNEW HE SHOULD HAVE KISSED SAMANTHA. Last night was his chance. Now he struggled through the regret. It was all he could think about on his drive into the station.

He wiped his tired eyes while listening to the morning news. All night, he'd tossed and turned, stared up at the ceiling, beating himself up about not making a move on the woman he had it bad for.

They were alone, and the way Samantha kept looking at him didn't leave room for second guessing. He could see the longing in her eyes, the hooded gaze of seduction calling him in. Her scent still lingered strong, like flowers blooming in a mountain field after a summer's rain. It had his head spinning and he damn near lost it when he thought about how Samantha's stallion black dress accentuated the curves he couldn't stop dreaming about.

He should have kissed her.

Alex knew he might have missed his chance. But, the truth was, Alex was afraid that even a simple innocent kiss could be the ingredient that would ruin their friendship forever. His best friend had always made him promise to take care of Sam and Mason if something happened to him, but Alex was sure Gavin hadn't meant like *that*.

Pulling his car into the police station, he parked in his usual spot. Stepping out beneath the morning sunshine, Alex was determined to shake off last night. He strode to the entrance with his colleague rushing toward him.

"Taking the morning off, Detective?" Alex's colleague teased him.

"Just hoping to avoid having to speak to you."

"Well, you'll be glad you did, because it appears our killer was out last night."

Alex dug his heels into the pavement. He stopped breathing and turned to his partner. His stomach clenched and he feared the news he was about to hear. "Another girl?"

His colleague nodded. "Except this time, the victim got away."

Alex's chest expanded as his heartrate increased. "Is she here?"

"Came in early this morning. Alvarez is taking her statement now."

"You should have called me." Alex hurried to the door, his colleague chasing behind him.

"I expected you at work earlier. Just like every other day."

Alex's stride lengthened as he weaved his way through the halls and to the belly of the station. "What has she said so far?"

"She's shook up but is speaking. You better get in there before Lieutenant sends her off for a medical evaluation."

Alex shoved a hand through his hair, excited by their luck. This was the break he had been waiting for. A witness—someone who saw the killer with their own eyes. One foot inside the interview room and Lieutenant Baker held up his hand to slow Alex down.

Lieutenant turned his attention back to the glass, crossing his arms as he listened with an intent look on his face. Alex stood beside him and listened as Detective Alvarez asked the victim if she'd caught the perp's name.

"David," she said.

Someone behind Alex handed him a sheet of paper. A quick glance at it caught him up on the victim's name and what they had learned so far.

Her name was Kristin Newsome, age 24, and was picked up at the Brews Brothers just west of downtown. Alex knew the establishment, had once had a drink there himself.

"No last name?" Alvarez asked Kristin.

Kristin's head hung low as she shook it. Her blonde hair draped over her slumped shoulders. Her spine collapsed in the chair and Alex thought she looked absolutely broken.

Alex pinched his throat as it suddenly felt sore.

"Did you exchange phone numbers?" Alvarez's empathetic voice came through the speakers.

Kristin whispered, "No."

"Friend each other on Facebook? Any other social media accounts?"

Again, Kristin said, "No."

Then Alvarez asked Kristin to describe what David looked like. "Tall. Lean. Good looking. A full head of dark hair."

Kristin went on to provide a few more minute details before Alex said, "Great. No distinguishing features. We're looking for an average built Joe who fits the description of half the city."

Then he heard Kristin say, "His shoes. He had really expensive shoes. I remember because I knew how much they cost."

"What were his shoes?" Alvarez asked.

"Neiman Marcus dress shoes. The Tom Ford edition. You know, the ones with the Edgar Medallion Cap-Toe?"

Lieutenant rolled his eyes to Alex. "I guess you'll have to round up some perps with expensive shoe purchasing habits and see if we can't get our vic to single one out."

And, just like that, Alex King was back on duty.

CHAPTER THIRTY-SEVEN

I SLEPT LIKE A BABY AND WOKE EARLY. WITH MASON AWAY, I took Cooper for a quick run and left the house just as the sun was rising over the eastern horizon.

It felt great to have that time to myself because, as soon as I stepped into the newsroom, it vanished.

My phone was off the hook with calls and my email was blowing up. It seemed suddenly everyone knew something about these murders and wanted to come to us first, hoping for their two minutes of fame.

The collective energy buzzed and, for the first time in a long time, no one was worried about their jobs. That put a smile on my face. We were all playing catch up, going after the same goal, doing the work we loved.

I marched straight to Dawson's office. His door was open and, though I knocked, I didn't wait for him to invite me inside. "It's crazy out there."

Dawson stared at his TV screens, the local news covering the story we were after ourselves. "With three women dead, the entire city is on edge."

Suddenly, my chest squeezed, almost afraid to ask if he'd

received the story I'd sent him last night. Dawson must have seen my hesitation because he leaned back in his chair and raised both his eyebrows.

"Did you get my story?"

"Loved it." His smile stretched to his ears. "Good work, Bell. Luckily I checked my phone before going to bed because I was able to okay it for print."

"You what?" I dropped my head into my hand, not wanting to make this as dramatic as it sounded but I couldn't help myself.

"Is something wrong?" Confusion lined Dawson's face.

"You ran it?" My voice cracked and terror filled my eyes.

"I had no choice but to run it." He laced his fingers on his stomach and stared. "It was some of your best work."

"It was preemptive."

"The angle was perfect. I couldn't have done it better myself."

I masterfully deflected each of his compliments before falling into the chair opposite Dawson. He stared proudly but all I wanted to do was cry. I regretted the angle and regretted my words even more. Though it was all true based on the facts I currently had to work with, I thought maybe I should have been more tightlipped than I was.

Dawson said, "Don't beat yourself up. If I didn't approve of it, I wouldn't have run it."

I blamed it on my one drink from the fundraiser, the frustration of not being forthcoming with my crush on King, but mostly it was the exhaustion and lack of evidence I knew the police had in this case that got me to spill the words onto the page. These women deserved justice and I could no longer sit on the sidelines and wait for another woman to get killed. I had to do something, but it shouldn't have been this, not after talking with King.

Dawson pulled his desk drawer open and handed me today's issue.

I held my breath and cast my gaze to the headline.

THE CAMPAIGN GOES ON, NO TIME TO MOURNE

Below was the photo I'd snapped of Price standing with Eric and Camille Foster. The three of them smiled like a million dollars, and, next to them in a separate photograph, was an innocent looking Darcy Jean.

"The truth hurts," Dawson reminded me. "Maybe now Philip Price will come out and finally give his staff member the condolences she deserves."

"Cross our fingers," I murmured as I stood and left Dawson's office, taking today's headlines with me. All the trust I had built with Price last night would be gone once he got hold of this. Now, all I could hope for was that this wasn't all done in vain.

CHAPTER THIRTY-EIGHT

THE MOMENT I SAT BEHIND MY DESK, MY CELLPHONE RANG.

I didn't flinch. Didn't bother to answer. My eyes were glued to today's paper, paralyzing me.

It was strange to actually feel like I had let Price down by writing an article about his campaign's lack of interest in the death of his own political canvasser, Darcy Jean. But I did.

My relationship with Price was going to be critical when digging deeper into the life of Eric Foster, and I should have waited to tell my story. Now, best case scenario was for Christy Jones to take the article for what it was and start plugging more empathy into Price's campaign messaging. Then again, she could just point her muzzle at me and blame me for trying to sabotage his campaign.

My cell continued to ring until finally clicking over to voicemail.

Pressure built behind my eyes.

I wanted to get this right. Going after an individual as powerful as Eric Foster was no easy task. He had resources to refute claims—whether real or not—and with the paper's future in jeopardy, this theory might have to go straight to my website until it grew into something that was supported with more than just circumstantial evidence.

There was a brief pause before my cell started up again.

Sensing the urgency behind whoever was calling me, I swiped my belt and pulled my phone from its clip, answering with a sharp tone.

"Screening your calls now?" King said.

A sense of calm fell over me at the mere sound of his voice. "Is this a personal call? If not, you can hang up and call back on my work line."

King chuckled but I could hear that something weighed heavily on his mind. "Would you like to have coffee?"

"You haven't answered my question. Is your call personal or business related?" I grinned.

Erin arrived and sat on my desk. Her feet swung through the air as she stared and listened.

"Can't it be both?" I imagined King leaning back in his chair with the corners of his eyes locked in a playful smirk.

"Depends." I wagged my brows at Erin. She had her hair pulled back into a ponytail and wore a fleece jacket with jeans that let me know she was here to work.

"I need your help, Samantha." King's tone dropped considerably, and I knew then that his call was only business.

"Sure, coffee sounds great." King told me where to meet him and I could be there in fifteen minutes or less. When I pulled my phone away from my ear, I said to Erin, "Want to meet my source at the station?"

Excitement flashed over her eyes. She slid off the edge of my desk and let her feet plant heavily onto the carpeted floor. "Is there something I should know about you two before I meet him?"

"Like what?" I asked, gathering my things.

"You know..." A knowing glimmer caught her eye.

"There is nothing worth reporting," I said, giggling my way out the door.

I didn't want to discuss the complicated path my relationship with Alex might be heading down. There was too much history, too many times we could have crossed over into making our relationship something more than friends. But we hadn't. And the longer it went on, the less I believed it ever would.

"Is it always like that inside?" Erin asked the moment we got to my car.

I knew she was referring to the chaos of the newsroom, the loud murmur making it impossible to think. "News has caught on about the murders, and tips are coming in hot and fast."

"That reminds me," Erin said. "I've been considering making my podcast interactive."

"What do you mean, like a tip line?"

We both were inside the car, buckling up.

"Yes," Erin said. "Except keep it online in the form of a message board."

I started the car.

"What do you think?" she asked.

"I think it sounds brilliant." Thinking of all the tips coming in just this morning, I knew regular people were more than willing to put their ideas out there. "What do you need to make that happen?"

Erin glanced out her window as we drove. Then she turned to me and said, "I was hoping we could team up together and use your website."

I held her gaze, thinking over the logistics of making it possible. I had the domain and I was sure my webmaster could incorporate an open forum as long as the hosting could keep up with the traffic.

"What do you say? Combine forces and receive information pertaining to our investigation in real time? I think it might prove to be useful, Samantha."

I looked over at my new friend. "Is this your way of pulling me away from my column?"

Erin's eyes glimmered. "Maybe just a little. But just imagine," Erin rested her hand on my arm, and I could feel the excitement coursing through her, "if we told the public about our theory on Kimberly Bishop, witnesses could message, maybe even with photos, proving whether her alibi checked out or not."

My nose scrunched and Erin reeled her arm back in.

"What is it, Sam?" she asked with a wrinkled brow.

I swept my gaze off the road and flicked my eyes back to her. "I've moved on from Price."

"What? Why?" Erin tipped forward in her seat and touched the dash. "When were you going to tell me? Your article certainly didn't make it sound like you had."

I flinched, only confirming that I should have waited to go through with last night's story. "Things are happening faster than I can keep up with," I apologized. Then I told her about the party and how Price admitted to his affair with Kimberly and how I turned my focus on Eric Foster. "But, before any of that, a man came to my friend Susan who was organizing the event and gave her an envelope to give to me."

Erin opened her mouth, then quickly shut it.

"A key was inside."

"A key to what?"

"A padlock maybe?" I shrugged.

"Holy shit," Erin cursed. She dove for her phone, her thumbs swiping fast over the screen. "That's what it meant," she mumbled while staring at her screen.

"That's what what meant?" I tried to focus on my driving but it was proving to be more difficult by the second. I wanted to see what she was looking at. "Is there something you want to show me?"

"I got a strange message last night. I'd show you but it's gone." She lifted her head. "I guess the person's Facebook account has to be activated in order for it show."

"Well, what did it say?" My heart drummed.

"Um..." Erin squinted through the windshield. "Use the key and Samantha Bell will solve this case."

I slammed on the brakes and cranked the wheel. The tires squealed and I parked beneath a large cottonwood, reaching for Erin's phone.

"It's not there," Erin said, telling me how the person deactivated their account after sending her the message.

Her story was as strange as my own and I didn't know what to make of it. But something told me that whoever dropped the envelope off with Susan might also be the one to have sent Erin the message.

"Someone knows we're investigating the murder, but how?" I asked.

Erin held my stare. "Yesterday, when I was finishing up my next episode, I kept thinking, what if the killer is a listener?"

"But you haven't released it, have you? Nothing about this investigation yet, right? And, besides, this sounds like someone who might know who the killer is but doesn't want to be the rat."

"Can I see the key?"

I fished it out and showed Erin. She inspected it, quick to have theories about what it might go with. "#67," I said. "That's our only clue."

Erin gave me a look and told me she visited the 16th Street Tavern.

"Where Mallory was last seen."

Erin gave me a knowing glance. "The bartender described the man she left with, too."

My head swung to her. "And?"

"Besides the fact that he looks like every other man in the city, I did learn he was drinking Tom Collins."

I put the car in gear and made a mental note to ask Susan what Eric was drinking at the fundraiser. Tom Collins wasn't your typical drink among people Mallory's age, but it was common enough to not get too excited about, either. At least we had something.

By the time we arrived to the coffee shop, King had his hands tightly wrapped around his mug and was staring blankly at the empty table in front of him. He looked distraught with his head hung low. I wanted to throw my arm around him and let him know that everything was going to be all right.

King perked up when he saw us coming. Sitting, I said, "I hope you don't mind I brought my friend, Erin." He barely acknowledged her. "She's the one behind the soon-to-be podcast everyone in American will listen to." King flashed a weak smile. "We've teamed up on the case so anything you tell me you can tell her."

King sat back and reached to his side. He then dropped a photo of a woman on the table and spun it around to face both Erin and me. Together, we shared a glance before tipping forward and having a closer look.

She looked just like the others. Blonde hair, brown doe eyes, absolutely gorgeous. My stomach dropped and I felt the tips of my fingers go cold. I was afraid to ask, already feeling my stomach clench with what I suspected the answer would be. "Who is she?"

King swallowed. "The woman who got away."

Erin and I glanced at each other again. King told us everything Kristin shared this morning, including what the man looked like. His words sent a chilling wave under my collar and I knew I needed to get the girls together.

CHAPTER THIRTY-NINE

ERIN AND I SAT QUIETLY AS WE WAITED FOR ALLISON AND Susan to arrive. We dipped our plastic straws deep into our water glasses and watched them pop back up. My mind floated between Eric Foster and Kristin Newsome.

I couldn't shake the sight of Eric leaving alone last night. Where did he go? Could he have been the man named David that Kristin escaped from? Camille certainly gave me enough reason to suspect her husband.

"Neiman Marcus shoes, who buys these things?" Erin scrolled on her phone, searching for the dress shoes King said Kristin described as David's. "Almost $2,000." She swept her gaze up and looked at me. "That's one grand for each shoe."

It was the kind of money I could only dream of having—the kind of money I knew Eric Foster had. "People with more money than they know what to do with, I guess."

"What kind of shoes was Eric wearing last night?"

I shrugged and glanced to the front entrance, anticipating the girls' arrival. "I wish I'd paid closer attention."

Erin said, "I like him."

"Who?" My brows knitted.

"Alex King," she sang.

"Really?" I thought about the way Alex was acting. He wasn't himself. His charm drowned out by this emotional investigation. "He can be a lot friendlier than he was today."

"I think he likes you."

I laughed. "And you're basing that off of what exactly? The conversation about Kristin?"

"Have you two ever dated?"

Erin still gripped her phone between both hands. I could tell she wasn't going to let this go. "It's complicated."

I glanced back to the entrance with one knee bouncing. King left the coffee shop promising to call me and, though I looked forward to it, I wasn't going to fool myself into believing it was anything other than business.

There was a burger joint across the street from where we'd left King, and Erin offered to buy me lunch. I couldn't refuse but if Susan and Allison didn't get here quick, I would come to regret it. Especially if Erin kept pressing me for more information about why I wasn't dating Alex King.

I rolled my head back to Erin. "What about you, is there a man in your life?"

Erin barked out a laugh. "Honey, I'm months away from turning forty. There aren't too many men glancing in my direction."

My gaze fell over her soft features. "I don't believe that. Look at you, you're gorgeous."

"I've chosen to marry my work." The crown of Erin's skull pulled to the ceiling.

"And so have I." My eyes flicked back to the front.

"Not saying that if the right man came along I wouldn't make room for him, because I certainly would." Erin closed her lips around her straw. "And you should, too."

"What are you suggesting?"

"Nothing."

"Really? Because it sounds like you are."

"Alex would look good on you. That's all I'm saying."

"Noted. Now, can we please move on?" I looked down to my wedding band. I still couldn't take it off. Gavin may have been gone for years, but he was still my one love. I wasn't ready to share all of that with Erin, though, and thankfully she didn't ask.

"Fine." Erin tossed her hands up. "It was really generous of him to share so much information with us."

"King is a good one when he has your trust."

Erin's eyes bounced around the restaurant before blowing out a heavy sigh. "I just wish we had more to go on. I mean, the perp's appearance matches every other male face I see."

I knew exactly what Erin was saying. There were half a dozen men here right now who could be rounded up based solely on the physical appearance we were given. But, without closer inspection, I couldn't spot a Neiman Marcus shoe.

I glanced to the entrance again. Still no sign of my friends. Checking the time, I said, "I wonder what's taking them so long."

I needed to hear again what the man who'd come to Susan looked like. There was still this key, waiting to be placed in a lock. It wasn't like I had all the time in the world to work with.

The bells on the door jingled. In came my friends. They were laughing into each other's ears when they spotted me from across the room. I waved and watched their smiles fade. Both mine and Erin's faces were stone compared to theirs and, when they approached the table, I introduced them to Erin.

Erin stood and shook their hands.

"I've heard about the podcasts," Allison said. "Subscribed but haven't found the time to sit down and listen."

Erin mentioned a little bit more about her work before

we were greeted by the waitress. We ordered our burgers and settled in. I switched from water and ordered a Coke, needing the caffeine boost, knowing it was probably going to be another long day.

Susan met my eye. "Have you learned any more about the key?"

Allison tipped forward, her brow twisted with confusion. "What key? What have I missed?"

We quickly filled her in, telling her the story of Mystery Man and the delivered key.

"No note?" Allison asked. "What's it for?"

Erin leaned in and told her story about the disappearing message on Facebook. The girls listened intently and something about sitting around a table surrounded by my best friends brought a smile to my face, despite the somber reason we were all together. It was clear Allison and Susan liked Erin as much as I did. Erin fit naturally into our tight click of intelligent professional women carving out a future for ourselves and I could definitely see her sticking around for a while.

"That's what Mystery Man said." Susan's eyes rounded. *"Samantha Bell will solve this case."*

They all rolled their eyes on me. Then, Erin said, "Sam has a new suspect in her crosshairs."

All eyes once again shifted to me.

I hesitated, afraid to mention Eric Foster's name in Susan's presence. I didn't want her to think I was jumping to conclusions without having convincing evidence to base my theory on. "Who is it?" Allison asked.

I flicked my gaze to Susan. Lowering my brow, I murmured, "Eric Foster."

"Sam." Susan sounded disappointed. She cocked her head to the side and glared. "Really?"

Every muscle in my body froze. My stomach sank with

the look my friend was giving me. Though I didn't regret revealing the truth, I was disappointed with Susan's reaction. I had Eric Foster targeted.

"Oh, Sam, I've been meaning to tell you," Allison jumped in before Susan could say anything else. "After our last meetup, I went back to the office and dug deeper into who is paying for Philip Price's political campaigns. Lo and behold it's the Fosters." Allison's head nodded as she bounced her gaze to each and every one of us.

Susan was still glaring at me when I said, "There was another victim last night."

"What is that, three, four?" Allison pondered.

"Four," I said.

"And you think Eric Foster was the one to do it?" Susan directed her question at me, her tone slightly less than friendly.

"Erin and I have been investigating, and we are learning more about the person the cops think is behind this." I paused and wet my lips. "Susan, I need you to tell me more about what you remember about Mystery Man." I desperately wanted to know how he fit into all of this.

She inhaled a deep breath. "Well... just that I didn't get a good feeling about him and that he was tall, handsome, and—oh, I don't know, Sam. He was there before the party. I wasn't paying too much attention to him, to tell you the truth."

Erin folded her hands on top of the table. "Then maybe you can tell us what you know about Eric's relationship with Camille."

Susan admitted she didn't know much about their private lives. "Can you blame them? Everyone wants their money. When you're living life in the spotlight, they deserve to keep some things private. Don't you think?"

No one disagreed.

"Do you think he's the one killing these women?" Allison

held her stomach as if sickened by the thought of working with a murderer.

"What shoes was Eric wearing last night?" I flicked my gaze to Susan. "Do you remember?"

Susan's brows pinched.

"Neiman Marcus?"

"I don't know, Sam."

"Any idea what he was drinking?"

"What does this have to do with anything?"

"Because we know that the person who is going after these women has a taste for Tom Collins and wears Neiman Marcus dress shoes." Then I pulled out the photos I had of Mallory, Darcy, Jamie, and Kristin. "Do you see what I see?"

Allison leaned over the table alongside Susan. "They all look the same."

"That they do." I nodded. "But you know who else they all look like?"

Susan hugged her stomach as her posture sagged. "I wish I didn't."

Allison snapped her head to Susan. "Who?"

Susan leaned back, dragging her palms down her thighs, and muttered, "Camille Foster."

CHAPTER FORTY

"ERIC WOULD HAVE PERSONALLY KNOWN DARCY." SUSAN'S voice was thick with disgust.

Erin nodded. "If he is the one targeting these women, he clearly has a type."

My chest expanded as I sighed. "This has to stay between us."

"Of course," everyone agreed.

"I can't let what happened with Price happen here. I was wrong about him—"

"Not entirely, Sam." Erin's chin lifted, quick to come to my defense. "Price was having an affair and he was keeping a secret when you interviewed him."

"I was wrong about Price being involved," I continued. "And I can't afford to be wrong again."

A somber silence fell over the table. Excellent timing, too, because our food arrived. The delicious smells of hamburgers swirled in front of our faces but no one seemed to care. We couldn't peel our eyes off the victims' faces—now perfectly framed by our plates of food. It was like we'd known them personally—each day learning something new about the women they'd once been.

Susan laid one hand against her breastbone. "I'm sorry that I didn't make the connection sooner."

"It's not your fault."

"I should have seen it." Susan frowned. "I thought the Fosters were good people."

Susan was clearly in denial. "I'm only trying to connect the dots," I assured her. "Right now, until we now more, I'm not accusing anybody of anything."

I shared a glance with Erin. She nodded and I finally took my first bite of food. The girls followed my lead. We ate slowly, still trying to make sense of this puzzle we were struggling to piece together.

"You know what I think?" Susan perked up, a mischievous gleam in her eye. "I think whoever wanted you to have that key is the killer."

"Like a cat and mouse game?" I questioned, skeptical that the guilty party would be sending clues.

"Sick, I know." Susan brought her hamburger close to her mouth but didn't take a bite. "But it might be worth looking into."

I wasn't sold, and called her on it. "Of course I want to find who sent me the key. They're obviously following me. And Susan, too, to know that she would deliver the key to me. And if the same person sent Erin the Facebook message, they're following her, too. They know we've been talking and they know we're looking for the murderer. Why would the killer try to put us on their trail?"

No one responded. There was no good answer. Susan's theory was just that—a theory.

"Why wouldn't they go to the cops, then?" Susan asked, fear starting to creep into her words. I didn't want to scare my friends, but their lives could be in just as much danger as my own.

Erin jumped in before I even had a chance to open my mouth. "Plenty of reasons. They know the murderer and don't want to rat out their friend. They have a criminal history and the cops wouldn't take them seriously." She paused, making eye contact with each one of us before turning our blood cold with her next statement. "Or because they know it would put their life in danger, and they'd rather we did that instead."

Another silence filled the air while we sat back and considered our mortality. Suddenly, the burger in front of me was less than appetizing.

"How well do you really know the Fosters?" Erin finally asked Susan, getting us back on track. "And is Price blindly accepting campaign contributions? If Eric Foster is the one terrorizing these women, it would be devastating to Price's campaign if he were caught."

The questions were piling up, but answers were not forthcoming.

"Without an active Facebook account, we'll never find out who sent me the message," Erin said, returning to our best lead for more clues so far.

"You know," a glimmer of excitement flashed over Allison's eye, "I can help hack the account and see who this person is."

"You can?" My voice rose like a breath of fresh air.

Allison nodded. "Wouldn't be too hard."

"Even with the account disabled?"

"It will only work if the account ever comes back online, but we could have traps waiting for if or when it becomes live."

"That would be amazing." Erin's eyes sparkled.

"I don't believe last night was a random act of violence," I said. "There's a connection to the previous murders. If we could get that link—"

A woman I didn't recognize stepped up to the table, interrupting me mid-sentence.

"You're Samantha Bell, right?"

My brows knitted as I wondered who this woman was. "I am."

"Can I speak with you?" Her eyes rounded the table. "It's about the girls being murdered. The ones you're writing about."

"Do you know them?" I asked.

"No." She shook her head. "But I think I might know who's doing it."

CHAPTER FORTY-ONE

FOUR PAIRS OF EYES STARED. JAWS DANGLED ON THEIR hinges. I was out of breath. My heart raced with anxiety and the restaurant seemed to go quiet.

Standing, I swallowed back the parched feeling tickling my throat. "Let's talk in private."

The woman's eyes drifted to the victims' photos still on display in the center of the table. Erin was quick to act. She swiped them up and hid them inside her palm. I could tell our new informant wanted to say something but not with everyone staring or listening with the same attentive ears I had.

"C'mon, let's step outside." I angled my body and took a step forward.

The woman nodded and followed me through the doors.

It was another Indian Summer kind of day. Temperatures in the mid-70s and comfortable. The sun was shining but there was a storm brewing inside of this woman's eyes and I feared what I was about to learn next.

"Tell me more about what you know."

Her name was Tamara Chase and she'd read my story on today's front page. "I'm scared."

"Me, too," I admitted.

"I've drank at many of these bars. Often alone." She glanced around but there was nothing to worry about here. We were safe. Plenty of pedestrians going about their days. "And to think that trusting the wrong man could have led to my own death."

My eyes drifted over her shiny brunette, shoulder-length hair. She was pretty, too, but didn't fit the profile of the victims.

"Did you meet somebody at one of these bars that scared you?" I lifted my hand and let it grip her upper arm. I needed her to feel comfortable, let her know that I could be trusted with whatever it was she had come to me to say.

Tamara stared at me out of the corner of her eye. "The story you wrote in today's paper, it was mostly correct."

"About Darcy?" I inquired.

Tamara nodded. "But there was one glaring omission I couldn't get past."

I felt my brows pinch.

"Something so obvious, I knew it as soon as I saw it." She paused and held my stare. "I had to tell somebody and I can't believe I saw you here." She flicked her gaze to the restaurant's entrance. "It was like it was meant to be."

I reeled my hand back to my side. "You said you think you might know who is killing these women?"

Tamara's eyes darted around, across the street, back to the restaurant's windows. She blew out a heavy breath and said, "Yeah. I'm afraid I might."

"Do you want to tell me who?"

She clutched her arms and held herself tight. "I'm scared to say."

"Have you gone to the police?" I wanted her to tell me what she knew, but I wanted her to feel safe, too.

She shook her head. "I wouldn't have even come to you if you weren't in this restaurant." She rubbed her arms. "I don't know who to trust. I know who this man is. He's wealthy and holds tremendous influence and I know he's friends with people in powerful positions."

"Like candidate Philip Price?" I speculated. He was all over today's story. He was a natural fit even if I no longer thought he was guilty.

She nodded and her eyes watered.

"I can keep your name anonymous," I whispered. "That isn't a problem. And if your story checks out, I know people in the police department you can trust to keep you safe."

Tamara tugged at her clothes.

"They can protect you if that's what is needed."

"Shit." She sighed and tucked a loose strand of brown hair behind her ear. "I wish I never went out that night."

Tamara didn't like the position she was in. I understood that. It was a frightening place to be. Having to stand up and do what her heart knew was right. "Like you said, you were meant to be there," I looked her straight in the eye, "just like you were meant to find me today."

Tamara held my gaze and she finally reached for her phone.

Did she send Erin the message? Did she send me the key? My mind jumped ahead with questions that wouldn't stop. But when I watched Tamara open her phone and navigate to her images, I knew not only did she have an idea of who might be killing these women, but she might actually have proof to back up her theory.

"I didn't make the connection until today." She lifted her head and looked up at me. "Despite the news cycle's relentless talk."

"Can I see?" I asked, extending my fingers toward her phone with weak knees.

Tamara flipped her screen around for me to see.

I squinted at the image. It was of her and her friends out on the town, drinking at a bar. A selfie like any other.

"Do you see it?"

A breeze blew my hair into my face. I didn't know what she was referring to or what I was supposed to be looking for. "Was this at a bar one of the women was last seen?"

"The 16th Street Tavern." Tamara angled the screen so that she could see. "He was in the photo with Price in your article." She pointed her painted nail to the upper corner of the photo. There, caught in the back of the image, sitting behind Tamara's group selfie, was Eric Foster whispering in the ear of a beautiful blonde woman.

I gasped and shared a knowing look with Tamara.

"Wasn't that the first girl killed?" Tamara's brows raised.

"Yeah," I breathed past the ache closing my throat. "That's Eric Foster talking to Mallory Madison."

CHAPTER FORTY-TWO

THE LADY KILLER CLOSED THE DOOR BEHIND HIM AND turned the deadbolt until he heard it click. Holding his breath, he paused to listen, hoping he was alone.

His eyes traveled across the walls of simple decor, studying the furniture leading into the depths of the apartment.

After what happened, he didn't want to face anybody. He didn't have the confidence to hide the emotions of inadequacy throughout his body. It happened too fast. Even after driving in circles throughout the early morning hours, his regret only deepened.

With one raised brow he cocked his head, straining his ears to detect even the slightest of sounds.

Complete silence.

Not a rustle or hum to be heard.

He remained frozen with his back pressed against the door as he continued to look around. The rooms were bright —the sun's rays breaking through the curtains. Finally convinced no one was here, he wiped his shoes and moved to the living room. It smelled like home, even felt like it despite his mood.

Falling heavily onto the couch, he rubbed the stiff hair on the nape of his neck. No matter how hard he pushed, his hair refused to go down. His bones trembled, the quake moving from inside out.

Exhaustion swept over him.

Terror pumped his blood hard and fast.

Planting his sharp elbows into his knees, he buried his hands in his hair. He knew he'd made a mistake. His confidence had got the best of him. Letting her get away was a mistake that should have never happened. He'd let his guard down and would pay the price. It was an error built on frustration, a need to prove he didn't answer to anybody but himself. Always a need to prove he was strong and worthy.

What was he thinking?

His teeth grinded and he clenched his jaw like a vice. He wasn't sure if he wanted to cry or punch out a wall. This time, his ego got the best of him.

It wasn't about money or prestige. This was a deeper urge. Something unsolicited and completely guided by his own free will. A need to prove he was great, independent. A way to begin carving out a lasting legacy all on his own.

Now, he just thought he was a moron.

It was never a good idea to go it alone.

Springing to his feet, he kicked off his shoes and tore off his clothes. Dropping each item to the floor, he left a path to the bathroom sink. Turning the water to hot, he scrubbed his hands with soap. The suds, a thick melon-scented white, turned into a lather that he used to scrub his skin raw.

His eyes swept up and he caught his reflection in the mirror.

The sight made him pause. He stared into the eyes of a person who looked absolutely terrified. His skin was pale white. Dark bags hung like hammocks beneath his eyes. His hair was disheveled and his chest muscles sagged beneath the weight of stress. It was too much to bear. He hadn't seen that look in his eyes since he was a little boy, the day he got lost and separated from his mother at the state carnival.

Pushing his hands back under the water, he rinsed the soap, watching it swirl down the drain while thinking about his own future. His muscles flexed as he turned to look at the clothes in a neat path behind him.

Panic tightened his chest.

His heart pounded, an intense pain growing by the second.

Looking at everything that could be traced back to him, The Lady Killer knew he was exposed. The woman, Kristin, knew what he looked like, knew the name he'd given to her, even if it wasn't his real one. She also knew the clothes he wore, including his shoes—the same pair he was too afraid to retrieve from inside the hotel room in case things got messy. This was all information the previous victims knew but never had a chance to share.

Sensing the trouble he was in, he hurried to scoop up his clothes. Gathering them in his arms, he imagined the gorgeous, free-spirited Kristin telling her story to the cops.

His adrenaline picked up again.

The Lady Killer raced to the kitchen, yanked open the cabinet beneath the sink and shook open a large black plastic trash bag. Tossing his clothes inside, he tied it up, set it near the trash, and rooted his hands on his hips.

Standing in nothing more than his boxer briefs, his chest rose in shallow breaths as he scrambled with thoughts of what to do next. He closed his eyes and she was there, waiting, inside his mind.

Kristin.

The one that got away.

She was so beautiful. The way she tossed her head back and laughed. How she moved closer to him the longer they talked. Reaching out and touching his arm, falling into his snare, the pickup was executed masterfully. Then leaving together just past midnight.

The Lady Killer startled when she choked on her own words.

He could still feel her hand slip away as she made an excuse to leave. They hadn't even gotten inside before her eyes widened with terror. The sight of the hotel gave it all away. There was too much talk in the news. He knew she was following the stories of the other women and, this time, she connected the dots before he even had her clothes off.

His chin smacked his chest.

He would never be able to forgive himself for the mistake he made last night.

He should have drugged her. It was his ego speaking—thinking he could convince her to fully trust him without it. It was a risk, a stupid risk, and something he should have never done. But he had, and now he feared the consequences of his mistake.

He breathed harder, his nostrils flaring with hot air.

That woman should have listened. Didn't she know who he was?

The Lady Killer spun around on a heel, slamming his knuckles into the kitchen table. The crack echoed off the walls, the sound splintering in his ears. "Fuck!" he growled.

He had a choice to make. Make up for last night, blend in and lay low, and hope that his mistake wouldn't get him caught.

A knock on his front door sent his heart racing.

Sucking back his last breath, he stared in its direction. Whoever was here would have to leave. He wasn't in the mood. Wasn't prepared for visitors.

Another knock.

The ticking in his pulse throbbed in his neck as he squeezed both hands into fists.

His next decision would determine his fate. There was no room for another mistake. Not if he wanted to survive.

CHAPTER FORTY-THREE

I'D KNOWN IT IN MY GUT BUT, NOW, THANKS TO TAMARA, I had the proof I needed to go after Eric Foster.

"What now?" Tamara asked.

I thought about Camille Foster and the subtle way she seemed to have reached out. A sinking feeling in my gut had me worried for her—deathly afraid to know what her husband might do to her if he ever found out about her turning on him. "Send me a copy of that photo."

Tamara took a step back. "You're not going to publish it, are you?"

"No. Of course not." My eyebrows scrunched.

"I don't want my face or name associated with this." Her voice rose and I could feel the fear heating her core.

"There is nothing for you to worry about. You can trust me." Tamara seemed skeptical so I told her what my next steps were. "When you send me that photo, I'll share it with my colleagues. We will then use it to convince law enforcement officials that Eric Foster was with Mallory the night she died. But, if you ever change your mind and allow me to publish it, this image could convince more people to come forward with information that could eventually lead to an arrest."

Tamara swiped a nervous hand over her head.

It was brave of her to come to me; her actions could be the difference between saving a life or ending one. Tamara knew it, too, whether it was on her mind now or not.

A minute passed before Tamara nodded. "Where should I send it?"

We exchanged contact details and my phone dinged with her message. I checked the quality, needing to make sure everything was perfect before she left. I couldn't afford to make a mistake and let this break in the case get away from me. We were close to nailing this S.O.B. Something told me this photo might be the piece that did it.

"You need to take your story to the police."

Tamara bit the inside of her cheek, giving me a sideways glance.

"You have to, Tamara," I said, even though I suspected the police already had the tavern's security tapes in their possession. Tamara's photo and eyewitness account could be the nail in Eric's coffin. What was stopping her from going directly to the police rather than coming to me?

As if she could read my mind, she said, "I don't want to be a part of this investigation."

I nodded my understanding. "I'll tell you what. Let me arrange to meet a detective away from the station. He's a friend. He'll protect your privacy. You can trust him."

Tamara nodded hesitantly.

I swiped my smartphone alive and called Detective King before she could change her mind.

CHAPTER FORTY-FOUR

KING WAS ON THE OTHER SIDE OF TOWN WHEN I CALLED. He agreed to meet us if we came to him. It wasn't a tough sell.

Keeping Tamara close, I said goodbye to my crime-solving friends, leaving them free to do their own investigating. Erin wished she could have come along, but I couldn't risk having Tamara clam up any more than I felt she already was.

Even Susan was coming around to wanting to get this right—opening her mind to seeing past who she thought Eric Foster was. I didn't mention anything about the photo Tamara shared with me, but I did say it had something to do with our suspicion of Mr. Foster.

I led Tamara to my parked car.

A renewed enthusiasm rushed through me as I thought about how we were now working two solid leads. Eric Foster was the first, but we also had the questions swirling around this key I still held and the enigmatic Mystery Man who'd delivered it.

Tamara rode shotgun as I drove. We didn't say much and, luckily, we didn't have far to go. King was already waiting at the underpass I'd asked him to meet at. Parking the car across from his, Tamara's slender fingers gripped her thighs tight as she stared at King.

"There is nothing to worry about," I said. "We can trust him."

Tamara was quiet as she stared ahead. Following her gaze, I looked at King as if seeing him for the first time. He was intimidatingly tall, broad shoulders, and a strong jawline that made him the imposing man many people labeled him as. Unfortunately for him, today he had the rare appearance of also looking like your stereotypical dick detective whose path you never wanted to cross.

"You know him well?" Tamara licked her lips and asked.

"No one knows me better." I glanced in her direction. "We've been working together for a long time. He's like a father to my son." Those words stabbed straight to my heart, but it seemed to do the trick.

"There is no turning back, is there?"

I reached for Tamara's hand and squeezed. She locked eyes with me. "There is no shame in sharing what you know. You've done nothing wrong."

Tamara bowed her head and tucked her hair behind her ear before we exited the car together. King was leaning against the hood of his vehicle with his hands buried deep in his coat pockets. As I approached, it was clear that this case was breaking the man down. He looked worn as old leather. I wished I could take his face inside my hands and smooth his wrinkles out. Instead, I said, "Thanks for meeting again."

"Not a problem." He flicked his gaze to Tamara. "It sounded urgent."

I introduced them both. Not wanting to waste any more time, I pulled up the image Tamara had sent to my phone. Handing it to King, he palmed the device and squinted his eyes. "You see it?" I asked.

Nodding, he handed the phone back and turned to Tamara. "Did you interact with Mr. Foster that night?"

Tamara clasped her hands by her waist and glanced to me. Then she shook her head.

"What night was that?"

Tamara answered King, confirming it was the night Mallory died.

"Did you see anything unusual?"

Tamara told King what she'd told me. That it was just coincidence that Eric Foster and Mallory Madison found their way into her photo. If it weren't for the news, she would have never even thought twice about it.

"Would you mind giving me a moment with Ms. Bell?" King politely asked Tamara.

Tamara shuffled her feet and looked to me for reassurance. I nodded, telling her to turn on the car if she got cold. King and I watched Tamara walk back to the car and close herself inside.

"We have the images in the security tapes," King said. "This isn't the first time I'm seeing Eric get close to Mallory."

My breath caught as I gave him a surprised look. "Have you questioned Mr. Foster?"

King kept his eyes on mine. "It's not as black and white as it might seem, Sam."

"But he's clearly talking with Mallory." I lifted my cellphone and glanced to it. "This isn't just hearsay."

"I'm glad you brought her to me." King jutted his jaw to my car. "She could be a valuable witness. How did you find her?"

I told him about meeting with the girls after having coffee with him. Then I said, "She came to me. I promised you'd keep her name out of it. She's afraid for what she knows." King nodded. He'd worked with plenty of skittish witnesses before—having valuable information often meant jeopardizing your safety. "The girls and I noticed that Mrs. Foster shares many similarities to each of our victims."

"That doesn't make Mr. Foster guilty," he said.

That was when I knew it: The department had already connected Mr. Foster to these women, noticed the pattern themselves. *Why hadn't he told me?*

"Have you cleared Eric Foster?" My tongue jabbed my cheek.

King sighed. "He lawyered up. As you would expect when dealing with somebody in his position." He rolled his gaze back to Tamara. "Mr. Foster hasn't been cleared, but there isn't enough evidence to charge him, either."

"But Mr. Foster *is* connected to the other victims?" I needed his verbal confirmation. He must have known Darcy, both of them working with Philip Price. But Jamie? Kristin? King was generous with what information he had shared, but I was more than a little frustrated with him for not telling me he had already zeroed in on Eric Foster.

King stared, then nodded. "Jamie and Darcy, yes. Unclear on Kristin."

"Shit, Alex." I pushed both of my hands through my hair, gripping my locks tight until they pulled at the roots.

"We're doing our job. Just like you." His eyes pleaded with me to understand that he was telling me everything he could. "The Fosters are well-known. It's not as easy as just linking them to the victims and charging them with the crime. The DA needs persuasive evidence just to charge him, never mind to convince a jury."

Tell me something I don't know. I rolled my eyes. "And you have nothing?"

"We're working on it," he said.

"Any chance your witnesses have been tampered with?" The Fosters' connections stretched far and wide, not to mention their access to money—dollars that could be used to influence a witness's judgement.

"Mr. Foster wasn't anywhere near Darcy or Jamie the nights they died." King lowered his head and rubbed his brow. "He had an alibi for Mallory's murder, too. His night ended early. It checks out."

"But what about last night? Have you asked him about last night? Maybe he was with Kristin?"

King frowned and gave me another look, silently telling me, *I'm working on it.*

"Care to share what his alibi was?"

"Lieutenant is one day away from handing this investigation over to the FBI."

"So you can't tell me or you won't tell me?"

"I want to find the killer as badly as you do. I'm this close," his index finger and thumb nearly touched, "to losing this case by speaking to you without approval from my superiors."

I flipped around and stared at my car. Secretly, I wished I had another source to turn to. Even as frustrating as all this was, I understood the predicament King was in. Then my heart leapt out of my chest when he surprised me with a question.

"You still have that key?"

"I do." I blinked, wondering why he was bringing it up. I hadn't told him where it had come from last night, and now I was a little disappointed I'd withheld that information. The more I'd talked about the case with the girls, the more I'd started fearing for my safety. And it wasn't just *my* life on the line. I had to think of my friends' lives and safety, too. And Mason's.

"There was more to it than you told me, wasn't there?"

I nodded and reached into my pocket. "I wasn't lying when I said I don't know what it's for. Your guess is as good as mine there. But it came into my possession via some random guy giving it to Susan before the fundraiser last night. He came to Susan to give it to me."

King held out his hand. His silence was louder than any scolding for keeping that secret last night. I already knew it was stupid. If we were going to work together, that meant sharing what we knew to bring down this serial killer. And that went both ways. "Maybe I can talk to forensics and learn more about where we might find the lock that goes with it."

I started to hand it over but hesitated. "There's more," I continued, knowing that he would only be able to put all the pieces together if I gave him everything I knew. "Erin received a message via Facebook telling her that if I used the key, I would solve this case."

King was speechless. I could read the disappointment written all over his face. "I know, I should have told you sooner. Whoever brought Susan the key obviously knows I'm close to both Susan and Erin. Alex, they might know that I'm close to you."

"Sam, you don't have to worry about me."

I nodded and handed him the key. But, before I released it, I looked him directly in the eye and said, "Anything you discover, you *have* to tell me first."

CHAPTER FORTY-FIVE

I DROPPED OUR NEW STAR WITNESS, TAMARA, OFF AT THE burger joint she'd found me at. Our ride back, like our ride to meet King, was mostly silent. My mind wouldn't settle but I couldn't tell her what I was thinking. Instead, I promised I'd keep in touch.

Tamara paused with one foot out the door.

Extending my arm, I said, "Here's my business card. My personal cell is on the back. You can call me about anything, even if it doesn't feel case-related."

Tamara took my business card and asked, "What happens next?"

Her eyes didn't blink as she waited for me to answer. "If Detective King has more questions, he'll be in contact. Otherwise, nothing." I paused to make sure I wasn't leaving anything else on the table. There was nothing I could come up with. "Your job here is finished."

Tamara's chest expanded as she nodded. "Thank you, Samantha."

As soon as she shut the door, I blew out my own hot air. I watched Tamara tie her brown hair back and get inside her car. It was important to me to see her drive away safely. There were too many unknowns and I couldn't be certain that I wasn't being watched. In fact, I was nearly certain that I *was* being watched.

Glancing all around, I scanned the sidelines. Nothing stood out but that didn't stop me from wiping my sweaty palms on my thighs.

My heart pumped fast with ideas about how to go after Eric Foster. Tamara confirmed my theory with what she'd captured in her photo and, for that, I would be forever thankful. It had come at the right time—the perfect time—like a divine gift from above. My thoughts soon turned back to King and what he might discover by asking his colleagues in forensics about that key.

That key held the answer to something big. Would it connect me to Eric Foster? I hoped King could answer that for me, and I was glad he'd asked about it. Even if his secrets were forcing me to question what else he might not be telling me.

Tamara's car started and we shared one last glance—our final smile goodbye.

It was important I stayed optimistic, trusted the process. It was all I had. But, most importantly, I had to keep that same faith in my good friend, Alex King. He was doing the best he could. His hands were tied, and with each new murder the pressure weighed heavily on all of us who cared.

Tamara backed out of her parking space and drove away.

I kept my car off, needing a moment alone to think. It was courageous of her to come forward, taking advantage of the opportunity when we crossed paths. But I couldn't reveal my cards—the real emotions playing out inside of me. She was already afraid, and if she would have seen what was going on inside my own head, Tamara would have run and never come back.

Now it was time for us to do our jobs. Time to use the new information from Tamara to find the killer so the police could make an arrest. But, before I could make a move on that, I had to first check up on my son.

Calling Mason's cell, I grew more and more impatient as it rang and rang before clicking over to voicemail. Then I tried the house. Still no answer.

A quiver of unease gripped my stomach.

"Where are you, Mason?" I asked as I scrolled through my messages, bringing up the last text I'd received from him. Mason had sent me Nolan's house number last night just as I'd requested. It was a last resort—something I didn't want to do—but I dialed it.

Heat rose behind my eyelids as I waited for someone to answer. With each ring, doubt dripped into my head. Suddenly, it clicked over. "Hello."

"Mrs. Dreiss. This is Mason's mother, Samantha Bell."

"Hey Samantha."

Mrs. Dreiss was a charming woman who worked as a dental assistant. She was also a proud mother, active in her children's lives more than my current situation allowed. When I let myself, she made me feel inadequate about my own parenting. Regardless, our boys had known each other for about a year, now, and I was thankful that Mason had found a friend in Nolan. "Thanks for having the boys over for a sleepover last night," I said.

"It's a pleasure. Mason is a wonderful boy. He's welcome here any time."

I stared at my kneecaps, smiling. After the stunts Mason had pulled, it was music to my ears. "And we would love to have Nolan over sometime, too."

There was an awkward silence that caused my mouth to pinch. I didn't know what to make of it. But I assumed there was a lack of trusting me as a parent. Again, the long hours I worked were causing me to doubt myself.

"There is something you should know..." Mrs. Dreiss's voice broke the silence.

I pushed myself up in my seat. "Did Mason do something?"

I could hear Mrs. Dreiss breathing, and I imagined her closing her eyes as she chose her next words carefully. "The boys wanted to see a movie last night."

"Okay."

"So I let them go after discussing what film they were interested in." She sighed. "But when I picked them up, I found them roaming outside of Brews Brothers."

"Near Sloan's Lake?" I held my breath and focused on her words.

"That's the one."

I pulled the phone away from my ear and cursed. My fingers pinched the bridge of my nose the moment my head fell into my hand. "What were they doing?"

"They didn't have alcohol on their breath. I don't know if they were trying to score beer or what, but I thought it was worth mentioning that they weren't where they said they would be."

My head lifted. I didn't like thinking about my teenage son drinking alcohol, but that wasn't even the worst of it. What had me most concerned was them being outside the same bar I knew Kristin Newsome was picked up at last night by our serial killer. "Is Mason still at your house?"

"He left nearly two hours ago." Mrs. Dreiss sounded surprised. Then her tone fell to a whisper. "I thought you knew."

Tightness squinted my eyes. I thanked her again and said, "I must have missed his call. I'm sure he's home by now. Work has been insanely busy for me." I was rambling.

"Yes, I've heard."

"Anyway, thanks for letting me know." Mrs. Dreiss was glad to help and, as soon as I ended the call, I released the muscles in my neck and sighed, feeling like I was losing control.

CHAPTER FORTY-SIX

SUSAN YOUNG COULDN'T GET ERIC FOSTER OUT OF HER mind. Erin and Sam had her questioning everything. What did she know about the Fosters' relationship? Only what they made public. Which told her absolutely nothing. But did having a private life mean they were hiding something?

After saying goodbye to Allison and Erin, Susan set out to find those answers herself. She drove to her office—preferring to work there instead of home—wondering what exactly that woman in the restaurant told Sam. It seemed big, even urgent, and Susan wanted to help.

Heading into an empty office, she flicked the overhead lights on and booted up her computer. Next, Susan called the hotel where she'd held Philip Price's event last night.

"Hi. This is Susan Young," she introduced herself to the head of security who immediately recognized her. He had been heavily involved in last night's event. "I was hoping I could review the security tapes from last night."

"Is something wrong, Ms. Young?"

"No," Susan said evenly. "I just like to see who crossed paths."

"I have them here. We can setup a time for you to come and review them, or I could arrange to have them sent over to you. Whichever you prefer."

Susan could hear clacking on a keyboard through the phone line. "Can you send them via email?"

"Sure can." A brief pause. "The files are quite large, but they should be to you within the next half hour."

"That would be great." She smiled and told him where to send them.

Dropping the phone back inside its cradle, Susan was determined to put a name to Mystery Man and set to work. Not surprising, the email she most wanted still hadn't come through by the time she was back on her computer, but she did have one waiting from the photographer she'd hired to cover the event.

She clicked through her email, scanning the text before clicking the link. It took her to a website. Susan typed in the password, and soon her computer screen populated with images from last night.

Susan's chest filled with pride. She'd pulled off an incredible event without major glitches. It was a success all around, except for maybe Samantha. Clicking through the images, she searched the faces. Susan knew many of them—had certainly talked to the majority of them. They were all friendly, having a good time, and she found nothing on Mystery Man. He'd left before the cameras' shutters started clicking.

She pulled up her browser. Checked her email. Still nothing from the hotel.

Swiping her mouse back to the photographer's website, she continued scrolling through the pictures. This time, she made sure to check in areas easily overlooked.

Eric Foster was everywhere. He worked the room like a magician. Popping up here, squeezing in there. Remembering that Samantha had said the killer had a taste for Tom Collins, Susan studied his hand closely.

Tipping forward in her chair, she put her nose to the monitor.

Eric was drinking, but seemed to only enjoy champagne like the majority of last night's guests.

"Oh, Sam, why do you do this to me?" Susan said to herself.

Even if Susan could see a different drink in his hand, she didn't know her drinks well enough to differentiate between a gin and tonic and a Tom Collins. To her, they all looked the same. But then there were the Neiman Marcus dress shoes to consider. "Now, shoes I can do."

A quick internet search allowed her to familiarize herself with the brand. She was surprised at their cost. Their price alone would cross a lot of names off the list of who could afford them and who couldn't. But she knew for certain that Eric was someone who could afford them.

Susan searched for photos where Eric's feet were captured. There weren't many—and none that were clear enough to be sure of what he was wearing. They were all just black shoes to go with the black-tie event.

Susan leaned back in her chair, clasped her hands behind her head, and sighed through her lips. They vibrated like a horse and the sound made Susan laugh. She reached for her cell and checked for messages. Nothing.

Finally, when she glanced back to her computer a new email had arrived.

Susan's heart skipped a beat as she opened it. Her pulse ticked in her neck as she moved the mouse cursor to the attached folder. It downloaded quickly and Susan opened it up, saying, "Let's see what we can find."

She scanned the first video file, rewound and fast-forwarded. Fifteen minutes passed as she searched for the man hiding behind the brimmed hat she told Sam was handsome. It made her sick to think that was how she decided to describe Mystery Man.

Her finger tapped the mouse.

The video paused.

Susan stopped where she was introducing Sam to the Fosters. Everything seemed cordial. Nothing out of place except for Sam's anxiety to know what hid inside the envelope.

Susan let the video play again.

Hitting pause, she stopped on an image of Camille and Sam talking. Susan had been preoccupied with Eric and hadn't caught it at the time, but now she could see the look on Sam's face. A look that said she was surprised by what she was hearing.

What were they talking about?

Susan watched it again. Camille stepping forward. Sam's eyes drifting to Eric.

She clicked the mouse and zoomed in as far as the video allowed.

Susan's eyes widened when she realized that Camille must be sharing something about her husband that made Sam question him. *What did Camille say? Was that the reason Sam shifted her focus to Eric so suddenly? If so, why didn't Sam mention this?*

Susan fast-forwarded the video, following Sam around, tracking her movements until finally leaving for the night. Susan thought she had nothing when suddenly she saw something on the video that made her gasp.

Feeling her face pinch, she replayed the scene to confirm that her eyes were not playing a trick on her.

Eric and Camille were in some kind of private, heated exchange. Susan watched as their faces twisted with restrained frustration, thinking again that the victims all looked like Camille. It was impossible for Susan to know what was being said, but she kept watching, hoping for a clue. With a clear expression of irritation, Eric stormed away from his wife and headed for the front doors to the hotel.

Susan closed the video and searched for the camera outside. After a few tries, she pulled it up. She fast-forwarded to the same time stamp from the previous video. A limo arrived. Shortly after, Sam exited the building, followed by Eric, who had composed himself. He scampered down the steps, tucking himself into the back of the limo.

Susan rewound the tape. She stopped on the limo and paused. Zooming in, Susan couldn't believe her eyes. There, driving the limo, was a man hiding behind the same wide brimmed hat as what Mystery Man was wearing.

Without hesitating, Susan reached for her desk phone and called the hotel again. The head of security answered. "Is it possible for you to send me the video of the hour before the event started?" Susan asked.

"Give me ten minutes."

Susan thanked the man, ended the call, and knew she had to share her revelation with Samantha Bell.

CHAPTER FORTY-SEVEN

MY KNUCKLES WENT GHOST WHITE AS THEY GRIPPED THE steering wheel.

One coincidence was believable for Mason to find himself at the scene of a crime, but not two. Going to Brews Brothers last night wasn't just irresponsible, it was dangerous. Could he have known that Kristin would be there? That she would be an attempted victim in Denver's string of murders? That was what I couldn't get past. It didn't make sense. Mason was smart and curious, but was he able to predict something even I hadn't seen?

Stomping on the brakes, I swung the tires into the curb and killed the engine. "That boy better be home," I muttered as I kicked my car door open.

I marched into our small house and immediately stopped to stare. My teeth clenched as I followed a trail of wet grass clippings straight to Mason's room.

Blowing out a hot breath of air, I shook my head and headed for his room. The dirty floor was my last straw and I could feel my chest ballooning with frustration as I pushed open his bedroom door.

I opened, then shut my mouth.

Mason was lying on his bed, looking exhausted. His music blared from his headphones and he had his eyes closed. I stepped into his room, pressing the corner of his bed with the tips of my fingers. He lifted his head, removed his headphones, and paused his music.

"Want to tell me about last night?" I asked, rooting my hands firmly into my hips.

"I told you." Mason's eyes blinked. "I was at Nolan's." He propped himself up on his elbows. "What's this about, Mom?"

My eyebrows pinched. "You boys went to a *bar*?"

Mason turned his head away. "Mom, it wasn't like that."

I struggled through heavy breaths, willing myself to stay calm. There was a real danger roaming the streets. The city wasn't as innocent as Mason might have believed. I didn't want him to have to live that truth; it was soul-crushing.

"I need to be able to trust you, Mason."

"Two more years and I'll be 18."

"But you're not an adult yet." I ran my fingers through my hair. "What is going on with you?"

Mason swung his legs to the edge of the bed and dropped his feet to the floor. Standing, he moved to the closet. He didn't look at me when he said, "What am I supposed to do when all you do is work?"

The walls closed in on me and shattered my heart into a million sharp pieces. I didn't know what to say. As bad as it hurt to hear, I respected Mason for calling me out on the truth of our current situation.

"The paper isn't doing well financially," I said. "I'm working a very important case to secure my job."

"Seems like an excuse." Mason pushed past me, stomping out of the room.

Suddenly, I found myself staring wide-eyed at what I

assumed to be the cause of Mason's acting out. There, near his pillow, lay a picture of Mason and his dad.

Gavin called me in with his eyes and I moved to him. When I picked up the photo of my two boys, my eyes prickled with tears. Sadness draped over me and I wanted to cry.

I didn't have the luxury of time on my side. My cell rang, Susan's name appearing on the screen, tearing me away from the past and back to the present.

CHAPTER FORTY-EIGHT

"It's a downloadable archive file that details your entire history of interactions with the network." Allison Doyle was getting nerdy while explaining the backend of her hack to Erin Tate.

Erin listened intently with a pinched brow. She followed along as best she could, asking questions when appropriate, only hoping they made sense. Allison did her best to explain what she was doing, using the simplest of lingo as her fingers tapped the keyboard.

The bright LED iMac monitor lit up their faces. Erin asked, "Can you access the account data now?"

Allison tapped her finger over the mouse. The cursor clicked a few times before more code was written. "Unfortunately not. But I'll have everything in place for if the account ever comes back online."

"Will we need to be present when that happens?"

Allison glanced and smirked. "It's kind of like house security. An intruder enters the house and a message is sent to your provider without you having to activate the call yourself." Allison kept typing. "Once the software receives the message the account has been activated, a trigger will begin scraping the account's information and send it to me personally."

"And what information will it give us?"

Allison's eyes sparkled. "Everything. In a matter of seconds, we'll have the account's entire history including GPS coordinates, photo meta-data, and IP addresses of logins."

"Incredible," Erin muttered.

"Want to see it in action?" Allison asked excitedly.

Erin moved her bottom to the edge of her chair and nodded.

"I need an account."

"Use mine," Erin said.

Allison rubbed her hands together and curled her fingers over the keyboard. She paused and turned her head to Erin. "Any secrets you want to share with me before I print them off?"

Erin's breath hitched.

"I'm just kidding." Allison giggled. "Well, sort of."

Erin sat in amazement as she watched how quickly Allison was able to scrape her Facebook account. The printer began spitting out her account network data and Erin wasn't all that surprised to see her entire digital history condensed into less than a dozen pages. The ease of Allison accessing it was what scared her most.

"That's it." Allison sat back and smiled. "Pretty cool, huh?"

Erin was still sitting in amazement with her head down, reading through her own personal account data.

"Now all we need is to find a way to bait this mysterious account holder into re-activating the profile."

Without letting fear take root, Erin lifted her head and said, "I think I might know how we could do that."

Allison slowly turned her head with parted lips.

Erin shared her idea, talking more about her podcast and the episode she was working on. "This person messaged me. They knew Sam had a key. They're watching what we've been doing, where we've been going, who we've been talking to."

Allison shivered. "So, they're a creeper. How is that going to help?"

Erin's grin reached her ears. "I'm working on my next podcast. I'll mention the message I received and request that the person contact me again to tell me more about this key."

Allison raised both her eyebrows and crossed her fingers.

Erin said, "It will work. It has to." Her cellphone rang. She answered and looked Allison in the eye. "Hey, Sam."

"Tamara is on her way home."

Erin could hear that something wasn't right in Sam's voice. "Are you okay?"

A pause. Erin could hear Sam breathing so she waited patiently for her response. "Mason was near Brews Brothers last night."

Erin stood and moved to the back of the room. "What was he doing there?"

"A movie theatre is nearby. He went with friends and, when I asked about it, he insisted it was nothing."

"Does he know about Kristin Newsome?" Erin speculated.

"If he does, he hasn't shared it with me." Sam let out an audible sigh. "This is the second time he has visited a place near an investigation."

Erin remembered the first. She would never forget seeing Sam go from zero to sixty in a matter of seconds. "Maybe he's trying to connect with you, Sam?"

"Yeah, maybe."

When Samantha didn't add anything more, Erin moved on. "Did you speak with King?"

"Where are you?" Samantha asked.

"I'm with Allison. We're at her office." Erin glanced to Allison, busy at the computer. "Allison worked her magic and we're all set up to capture the person who sent me the message. You should see it, Sam, it's incredible what we'll know if the account is ever reactivated."

"Stay there," Samantha said. "I'm coming to you. Susan found something that I think might take us on our next journey."

Erin's entire body froze. "Can you provide a sneak peek to what's coming?"

"King had already linked Eric Foster to all three victims."

"So our new revelation is old news?" Erin crossed one arm over her belly.

"Basically."

"Well, since Eric isn't in jail, I assume he's been cleared?"

"At least for the time being. But I think we need to at least see what Camille thinks about all this." Samantha paused. "Ask her what she knows about her husband's contact with these women."

"Sounds reasonable to me." Erin rolled her shoulders back.

"And maybe even warn her that she might be sleeping with the killer."

CHAPTER FORTY-NINE

GUADALUPE HERNANDEZ WAS BUSY MAKING HER ROUNDS.

She was working as fast as possible without compromising quality, considering she was the only maid assigned to the west wing. Normally, she would be with a team doing the rounds. Today, with two people out, they were forced to split up and Guadalupe was picking up the slack.

She yanked the sheets off the hotel bed and tossed them into the hamper on her cart. Her feet hurt but she didn't complain. She did what she did most days when her bones were achy and her legs tired. She sang songs inside her head, busied herself with conversation when she could, and kept working until it was time to knock off.

A few guests would stop to chat after requesting extra towels, but most acted as if she were invisible, thinking that she only spoke Spanish. Guadalupe didn't mind. It allowed her to stay focused on her work, which always received high praise from her boss.

Next on her list was the bathroom. She scrubbed and sprayed, replacing the used bars of soap with new ones. Not long after, it was sparkling fresh. Satisfied with her work, she closed up the hotel room and pushed her cart toward the elevator.

Waiting for the next available cart to arrive, she smiled and hummed. A minute later, the doors opened and she stepped inside. Riding the elevator to the fifth floor by herself—just her and her cart—she closed her eyes for a brief moment of rest.

She thought about her children, couldn't wait to see her husband late tonight after he was finished with his own work. They were her pride and joy, the reason she worked so hard.

Her eyes opened and she braced herself by reaching for the cart when the ride slowed to a stop. The doors dinged open and she steered her hefty cart down the hall. A tall man wearing a nice suit smiled and nodded as he let her pass. Guadalupe didn't think anything of it, always appreciating the simple gestures of strangers.

Putting on the brakes, she stopped in front of her first room on the floor. Knocking, she called, "Housekeeping."

Getting her supplies ready, there wasn't a response.

The sounds of a television playing down the hall carried through the walls.

She reached to her side and swiped her universal key at the door. The light on the lockbox flashed green and the lock clicked over. Guadalupe pushed the door open and kicked the door holder down, propping it open. Glancing over her shoulder, she noticed a travel bag open on the bed.

Guadalupe paused when she realized her mistake. "Housekeeping."

Again, nothing.

She glanced to the door handle. The "Do Not Disturb" sign was still hanging on the inside. Her brow furrowed as she tip-toed further into the room. She could hear her heart knocking against her chest and, when she turned the corner and glanced to the bed again, she let out a piercing scream that the entire hotel could hear.

CHAPTER FIFTY

ALLISON HAD A SPECTACULAR OFFICE ON THE NORTH SIDE of downtown Denver.

The redbrick Tudor building was a refurbished house which Allison had converted for her small team of software professionals shortly after starting her own company.

I left Mason at home, wishing I could stay and talk about last night and the photo of him and Gavin. Maybe Erin was right. Maybe he was reaching out to me by going to these crime scenes. I kept my work life private—for good reason—and this could be Mason's way of looking to connect. I'd have to make a point of bringing it up with him. Susan's call had ended the chance to do so right now.

As I drove to Allison's office, the photo of Mason with Gavin kept flashing across my vision. I hadn't seen that picture in a very long time and I had a feeling I knew the reason Mason had pulled it out. My gut twisted with memories of our intact family and wishes for what we could have been.

Allison met me at the door. "Can't wait to hear what you

found." We hugged and I followed her into her personal office. "Erin told me Susan discovered something."

I felt my ribs squeeze my lungs. "Yeah. Things are moving fast."

"Check this out." Erin stepped into the office and quickly handed me the printout of her profile history.

I took it between my fingers and scanned the data. "You can get that from any profile?"

"Only if the account is live," Allison said, explaining the system she'd set up with Erin. The trap was set and all we needed now was for Erin to be contacted by the same person again.

"Good work," I said, giving Erin the printouts. "But we can't just sit and hope to be contacted."

A knowing grin crossed Erin's face. "That's why I'm going to publicly ask the person to contact me again on my next podcast."

Our eyes met and Erin saw mine sparkle. "Brilliant."

"Whoever this is," she flapped the printed papers through the air, "knows both of us—and Susan, and probably Allison, too—and now it's time that we know who they are." I looked to Allison, who was listening intently.

Pushing my hands inside my vest pockets, I said, "I'll push a blog post toward your episode as well. If this is going to work, we need to act fast." I pulled up my sleeve and glanced to the time. "We better get going."

Erin nodded.

"Wait." Allison held up a hand. "You can't drop those teasers and then not tell me what you found."

"Sorry, babe. I'm already running late. We'll catch you up later." I glanced to Erin and wagged my head toward the door.

Allison tossed up her hands. "At least tell me where you're going?"

"To visit with Camille Foster."

"I'll be here." Allison's spine bowed when she sat on the edge of her desk.

I rested my hand on her shoulder and said, "Susan swears she has video of Camille speaking with Mystery Man before Philip Price's fundraiser."

Erin stopped what she was doing and snapped her head in my direction.

"Whoa... that's heavy stuff." Allison's lips parted. "You two go. Find out who is doing this to these women."

I held Allison's eyes inside of mine for a moment before jutting my jaw once again to the door. Erin grabbed her purse and coat and together we hurried to my car with her pushing her arms through her coat sleeves.

"Do you think they are in on this together—Camille and Eric?" Erin asked as she opened the passenger side door.

"Get inside. I have to show you something first." I had never seen Erin move so quickly. Once we were both buckled in our seats, I pulled up the still image Susan had sent me on my phone and handed it over to Erin. Erin pulled the screen close to her face. "Susan emailed the best image she could capture. It's not the clearest but, if Mrs. Foster spoke with him—"

Erin turned her neck and looked at me. "We could get her to tell us what he looked like."

I nodded, started the car, and set the wheels in motion. It was nice knowing Erin could finish my thoughts without me having to explain. I liked that we were always on the same page. For as little as we actually knew about each other, she felt more like the twin I never had than someone I'd met only days ago.

"Does Camille even know we're coming?" Erin's fingers couldn't stop drumming on her knee.

"I called her earlier."

"What did you say?"

"That I wanted to follow up with our conversation from last night." With one hand on the wheel and the other on the gear shifter, I shared a quick glance at Erin. "Truthfully, I'm surprised she accepted my request."

"Because of the article you wrote about Price?"

Turning my attention forward, I murmured, "Yeah."

"But Camille doesn't know me. Are you sure she's going to be cool with me showing up with you?"

"We're in this together, right?"

Erin nodded. "Totally."

"Then that's all Camille has to know."

Driving south, we soon drifted into our own thoughts. Erin was excited to meet this person who shared similarities with the victims, and I couldn't stop replaying the first conversation I'd had with Camille. I had to tell Erin about it.

"At Price's event, Camille brought up the book that got everyone talking about sexual fetishes and domination."

"I read it," Erin admitted.

"What did you think?"

"You haven't read it?" Erin's eyes widened with surprise when I shook my head. "Be prepared to get hot and bothered." Erin giggled.

"Did you want to read it?"

"After so much news coverage, I got curious." Erin shrugged, no big deal. "Though I hope that book isn't the reason why these women are being killed."

"Camille made it seem like she was into that stuff." I drove with a pinched brow. "Always rubbing her wrists and glancing to her husband like he was the inspiration behind their experimentation."

Erin pushed herself up in her seat. "Which is what made you think maybe she was telling you her husband was the one behind these killings?"

"Exactly." My grip tightened on the wheel, knowing I didn't have any evidence to prove my theory. "I don't know that for sure, but we know Eric was not only with Mallory the night she died, she was also found tied to the bed."

"The hero in the book was a billionaire—"

"And so is Eric Foster," I said, hearing the tires roll to a stop at the gated entrance that welcomed us to the Fosters' neighborhood.

My name was on the list and, after talking with security, we were quickly ushered through. I drove slowly as our jaws dropped at the sizes of these houses. Erin's nose was pressed up against her window and we were both quiet. The Fosters lived in Cherry Hills Village, a suburb of Denver clearly reserved for the ultra-wealthy.

Turning into the concrete driveway, beautiful manicured lawns lined the path leading up to the house Erin called a mansion. And a mansion it was. It reminded me a little bit of Philip Price's place but without the view. I assumed this wasn't the Fosters' only house and maybe another had a magnificent view.

"You could live two separate lives in a place like this," Erin said, peering out the windshield.

It must have been close to seven thousand square feet of living space. The castle-like design was wrapped in a land-scaped oasis and I couldn't stop staring at the four-car garage. This kind of wealth wasn't relatable. I just wanted to get out as quick as possible.

"C'mon, let's get this over with," I said.

We walked quietly to the front door, rang the bell, and were soon greeted by Mrs. Foster's butler. "Samantha Bell, I presume?"

I nodded, staring into a cleanly shaven face. "And this is my colleague, Erin Tate."

His dark eyes moved to Erin. Hovering above, he held her

in his sights for an uncomfortable moment as if assessing her trustworthiness. "Mrs. Foster is expecting you." He rolled his eyes back to me. "Please, come inside."

My head tipped back on my shoulders the moment we stepped inside. I stared up at the soaring ceilings and let my gaze drift over the gorgeous hardwoods. Natural light perfectly filtered into the building and we passed the chef's kitchen before being told to make ourselves at home in the living room. "Mrs. Foster will join you shortly. Please help yourself to some tea."

"Thank you," I said, lowering myself onto one of the sofa couches.

Erin and I stared at each other, in total awe of the grandiosity. Then my eyes landed on the wet bar. "Hey, look," I whispered.

Erin followed my gaze.

"You know what ingredients are needed to make a Tom Collins?"

Erin's knee stopped bouncing. Her brow furrowed and she said, "Gin, sugar, lemon juice, and carbonated water."

Standing, I moved to the small bar. "I see gin."

"Everything else could be in the kitchen," Erin mused. "Then again, maybe not."

Looking back toward the kitchen, not another person was in sight. I took the opportunity to dig a little deeper. Stepping behind the wet bar, I crouched down and peered inside the small refrigerator. Inside were a bottle of carbonated water and a few fresh lemons. The only ingredient missing was sugar. Pushing myself back up, I returned to Erin.

"Everything was there except for sugar." I poured a cup of tea for Erin before making one for myself.

"Oh good." Camille entered the room, her long flowing dress trailing behind her.

The sound of my thrashing heart pounded in my ears as I

slowly turned to face our hostess. Afraid that Camille had seen me snooping behind the bar had me fearing I'd given one of our best clues away to who was behind these murders. And when she looked me directly in the eye, my entire body froze.

"I like a guest who isn't afraid to help herself." She smiled and sat on the sofa chair adjacent to the grand piano. "Did you have any trouble finding the place?"

"Excellent directions," I said before introducing Erin. "Camille, this is my colleague Erin Tate. She is the producer behind the popular crime podcast, *Real Crime News*, you may have heard about."

Camille folded her diamond studded fingers on her thigh and chuckled. "Can't say I have caught on to the podcast craze." She smiled. "It's a pleasure meeting you, Erin."

"The feeling is mutual," Erin said.

"Samantha, I didn't expect to see you again so soon." Camille's bright eyes shined. "And certainly not so soon after the story you published about Price."

I felt my grip weaken when lowering my tea cup onto a nearby coaster. "We're just trying to find out who is killing these women," I said.

"And you think, what?" Camille's mouth pinched. "That I did it?" She paused and glared at both Erin and me. "I assume that is why you're here." If she had been forthcoming with me last night, she had certainly changed her tune today. Though I couldn't say I blamed her; my article did nothing to help her candidate's chances of election.

Leaning forward, I rested my sharp elbows on the tips of my knees.

"I know you were only invited to Price's gala because your friend was hosting the event."

Camille's hostility felt like more than just lashing out about the article. It felt personal. "Actually, we're here because it has come to our attention that your husband might have been with Mallory Madison the night she was murdered."

There was only the slightest movement at my news. Camille was trained at appearing stoic and hiding her emotions. "Mallory Madison?"

I nodded and glanced at Erin. Erin dove her hand inside her handbag and retrieved an image of Mallory. Standing, Erin walked it over to Camille. Camille eyed Erin with suspicion as she took the photograph for herself.

I watched Camille study the image. She didn't give any indication that she saw Eric in the photo. "Can you see your husband in the photograph?"

"Yes, I see him." Her tone hardened as she pulled the image away from her face, arching one eyebrow.

I couldn't tell if she was learning of her husband's tendency to stray off the reservation for the first time, or if she was just angry that he had been so careless when doing it. But what really had my stomach tied into a knot was whether Camille was even aware who Mallory Madison was or that she had been murdered.

"She's one of the women you were talking about last night," I said. "Who was tied to the bed and murdered."

Camille did an amazing job at keeping face. The best I'd seen. She gave nothing away. "This conversation is off record."

The mood in the room suddenly changed. We agreed, tucking our devices away.

Erin took a sip of tea before asking Camille, "Did your husband know Mallory?"

"Do you think I would allow my husband to be seen so publicly with another woman hanging off his arm?"

"Camille," I interjected, "does your husband drink alcohol?"

Camille looked to the wet bar and gave a chuckle. "Those bottles aren't just for me."

"Has Mr. Foster ever cheated on you, Mrs. Foster?" Erin's question got Camille to snap her head back to the center of the room. The questions were being slung like arrows and everyone was on the defensive.

"My husband is flawed, Ms. Tate, but," Camille pushed the gold bangles down on her wrists, "he's a good man."

"Would you say your husband has a type?" I asked.

"I hope Eric's type is me." She smiled.

Erin shared a knowing glance with me. I felt the blood leave my cheeks. I couldn't tell her that all of the victims *did* look like her.

"How did you and Eric meet?" I asked.

"Eric," she laughed as if the distant memory lightened the load, "was a man all the women wanted. Tall. Athletic. He had a knack for winning and he rarely lost." She dropped her gaze to her ring finger and paused. Then she swept her gaze up and grinned. "His friends called him The Lady Killer."

I swallowed down the stone lodged in my throat. Erin was equally tongue tied.

"Ironic, isn't it? To have a nickname like that. And now you're here, inside our house, with the gall to ask me if he has it in him to kill another human being."

"Does he?" Erin didn't miss a beat.

I held my breath, feeling my muscles quiver across my bones. We waited for an answer as time seemed to come to a halt.

"Do *you* think my husband is a murderer?"

Camille answered our question with a question. I wanted to shake my head and roll my eyes. Instead, I took my next breath and turned my thoughts to each one of the victims.

"We just want to know what he was doing with Mallory

and if you know anything that could move our investigation forward."

"I'm expecting Eric home soon. You can wait, or just leave your card for him to call you." Camille stood and threaded her fingers in front of her fashionable belt buckle. "But you should know, my husband is already cooperating with the police."

I fished out a business card and handed it to Camille.

"Before we go," Erin's posture straightened, "do you know who your husband left with last night after the gala?"

Camille's mouth pursed. "I'm guessing it was Bruce."

I took a step forward. "I'm sorry, Bruce?"

Camille tilted her head to the side. "Bruce Richards. The man who greeted you upon your arrival. He drives when Eric elects not to."

I pulled my phone from my pocket and turned it to face Camille, the picture from Susan on the screen. "Is this Bruce?"

Camille flicked her gaze to each of us before answering. "Honey, if that's Bruce, you and I have not been looking at the same man." The entire room froze. "I crossed paths with the man in your photo for the first time last night. He was friendly, so I greeted him. I was funding the event, after all."

CHAPTER FIFTY-ONE

THREE PADLOCKS LAY SIDE BY SIDE ON ALEX KING'S DESK. His eyes were red and gritty from his inability to stop staring. Since picking them up at the local hardware store, he had still learned nothing about this key.

His chair squeaked when he leaned back. Rubbing his face inside the palms of his hands, he sighed.

It seemed as if every new piece of information only complicated the case. One step forward was two steps back. He had the key but it didn't answer the important question: What lock did this key open up?

King flung forward, bringing the key Samantha had given him to the top of his desk. He brushed his thumb over the inscription, #67, knowing if he could answer where this key was meant to go, he could likely string together more of their leads.

Turning his head to the side, King wasn't certain this key even belonged to the case of these murdered women. To him, it didn't make sense going to someone like Samantha Bell instead of the cops if it was so important. But it was the message to Samantha's friend that King couldn't get past. It was the piece that linked the key to the murders.

Samantha Bell will solve this case.

It was a strange message to receive, and King doubted its authenticity. With no other details, he remained suspicious of its true intention. He'd dealt with cases where false leads were given to throw the police off. A calculated misdirection, and King thought maybe that was what this was.

He lifted his arm and plucked the photo of Eric Foster at the bar with Mallory Madison off his corkboard. His eyes darted back and forth between the key and Eric. When he closed his eyes, he could see the glimmer of belief shining in Samantha's eyes. Belief that she was on to something, but also fear that she could be in danger. He knew she believed there was a connection to these murders, and her instinct was something he could believe in, too.

Detective Alvarez snuck up behind King. "Where did you get that?"

King held the photo over his shoulder. Alvarez pinched it between his fingers. "I'd tell you, but I'd rather keep my source private."

Alvarez shifted his gaze off the image and arched a brow.

"It matches the surveillance video, but look how close they're getting," King pointed to Eric Foster's image. "You can almost see the glint in his eyes. He knows he has her wrapped around his finger and she is completely clueless to what is coming her way."

"What are you getting at, King?" Alvarez's eyes hooded while handing back the photo.

"When we interviewed Eric Foster, we never asked him about his shoes."

"We're going to need a better reason than shoes to bring someone like Eric Foster down to the station for a second interview." Alvarez rocked on his heels. "You heard what

Captain said after the last time we dragged Foster down here."

"Maybe you're right." King stared ahead.

"The easier plan would be to show Kristin Newsome this photo and see what she says."

King nodded but didn't bother looking up at his partner. He knew Eric Foster had been seen with each victim. Unfortunately for King, that was where their trail of evidence linking Eric to the murders stopped. They had nothing on hotel surveillance and no positive ID. According to what they'd uncovered, Eric was guilty of only flirtation.

"How is it that Camille Foster doesn't know about her husband chasing skirt?" King asked to no one in particular.

"She probably does," Alvarez answered. "But who says she doesn't have her own private affair going on, too?"

King's mind churned. He knew what they needed to do. If Eric Foster owned a pair of Neiman Marcus dress shoes, and if Kristin Newsome could positively ID Eric as being the man she ran from, then that might be enough to charge him with the murders.

King picked up a padlock and opened and closed it. "What do you use padlocks for?"

Alvarez raised his brows in thought. "Lockers. Storage sheds. Gun safes. Hell, lots of things. What's this about?"

King reached for the infamous key. "Somehow, this key is connected to these crimes."

"But you don't know what it goes to?"

King shook his head and shared a little bit about the backstory of how he'd acquired the key. "It's possible this mystery man either knows the killer—"

"—or is the killer."

The two men shared a knowing glance.

"Alvarez. King," Lieutenant Baker called from across the room. King stood. "A call just came in from a hotel manager on the east side. One of the employees discovered something in a room."

King tugged his sport coat off the back of his chair and felt his stomach drop. *Not another one,* he thought as he dropped Samantha's key into his pocket, promising himself to drop it at forensics on his way out the door.

Lieutenant's brow creased. "It appears that our killer isn't finished yet."

CHAPTER FIFTY-TWO

KING AND ALVAREZ ARRIVED AT THE HOTEL AS QUICKLY AS possible.

A handful of uniformed officers were already on the scene. They entered the building with the combined confidence of two of Denver's best homicide detectives. Though King's heart was heavy with the thought of another woman dying before they made an arrest, he refused to let his emotions dictate his better judgement.

The sounds of a man's feet clacking across the marble floor grew louder as he approached the detectives. King slowed his pace and watched as the man waved his hand through the air.

"Are you the manager who called?" King asked.

"Yes. Thank you for coming."

He was wearing a suit and red tie and had a nametag pinned to his left breast. His eyes were alert, his body pumping with adrenaline. King pulled his sport coat to the side and flashed his badge. "I'm Detective Alex King and this is my partner, Detective John Alvarez. Can you tell us what happened?"

The hotel manager nodded. "As soon as I was made aware of what our employee discovered, I called the police." He rambled, speaking a hundred miles per hour. "There were all these things, and it's not like any of us are oblivious to what's been going on in the news. We talk about it nonstop and have been fearing that we might be next." He turned his head away, his brow twisting with revelation. "Maybe that is why it happened?" His eyes swept back to King's. "My thoughts manifested until it became truth?"

"Wait, slow down," King said. "You mean to tell us that there isn't a body?"

"No." The man stretched his neck. "Just tools and... I don't know, toys."

Alvarez and King shared a glance. King's gaze skimmed around the front lobby, studying his surroundings, barely different from the last one. Another hotel chain with guests coming and going.

"Can we speak with the employee who found it?" Alvarez asked.

The hotel manager nodded. "She's there." He pointed across the room. "She's the maid who made the discovery."

On a stool behind the front desk sat a short woman with jet-black hair. Her eyes were cast to the floor when King asked the manager, "Anyone else been in the room since?"

"Just the officers who are up there now."

"Thank you." King stepped away. Alvarez followed. Dropping his voice to a whisper, he turned to his partner and said, "You speak with the maid and I'll head upstairs to see what we're working with."

Alvarez stared at the small woman and nodded.

"If you can, try to find out what name the room was registered to."

Alvarez looked King in the eye. "I'll dig for the surveillance video as well."

King headed up to the fifth floor. Upon stepping out of the elevator, he was quickly met by a uniformed officer. He flashed his badge and asked, "What do we have?"

"A room full of potential evidence." The officer wagged his head. "Follow me. I'll show you."

It was a strange feeling for King to be stepping into a room that didn't house a body. Police tape was up, sectioning off the room, but no crime had actually been committed. Relief relaxed King's shoulders.

"The maid was completing her rounds when she found it."

"Did she see anybody here?" King asked as he moved through the small room.

"Said she passed a tall man wearing a suit. They smiled at each other but didn't say anything."

"Any idea where that man is now?"

The officer shook his head. "Can't even be sure what room he was registered to or if he was a guest here."

King sighed. He bent over the bed and took a closer look inside the small roller suitcase. King noticed the same items used on the previous victims. Wrist and ankle binds, mouth gags, ropes, and blindfolds along with several other items.

"He already drilled into the bedframe," the officer said.

King dropped to a knee and plugged the drilled hole in one corner of the bed with his finger. The perp was set up, ready to go.

King stood and moved to the closet. Inside, an Armani tie draped off a hanger. He knew that this room was meant for Kristin Newsome and he was thankful she'd gotten away. But he wasn't satisfied. King needed more. Then, suddenly, his eyes landed on a dark object below.

Pulling out a pair of silicone gloves from his back pocket, he was drawn closer to the pair of shoes he couldn't take his eyes off of. "Just like she said," he muttered to himself. "Let's clear the room." King clapped his hands. "No one touches anything else until CSI gets here."

The room cleared and King hoped to find a fingerprint, hair strand, anything to make a positive ID on who left this behind.

Alvarez met him in the hallway. "John Doe," he said. "Can you fucking believe it? That was the name registered to the room." He shook his head. "I swear, this hotel has nothing but morons working here."

"Let me guess, paid with cash?

Alvarez nodded. "Security doesn't have anything either."

"No video?"

"They have video but nothing clear. Our suspect was dressed just like in all the other videos. Brimmed hat, heavy overcoat, and glasses. I searched everything hoping for a clear shot but got nothing." He frowned. "Besides knowing the man is white, we got shit." Alvarez rolled his eyes to King. "I hope you got more than I did?"

King grinned. "It's our guy, all right. Inside the closet was a new pair of Neiman Marcus shoes. Can you guess what edition?"

"Tom Ford?"

King gave a curt nod.

"That's it. I'm getting Eric Foster on the phone." Alvarez dove his hand inside his pocket and fished out his cellphone. "I don't give a shit what Captain says."

CHAPTER FIFTY-THREE

The Lady Killer woke from a groggy sleep.

It was what he needed. A deep rest to regain his footing. He had no idea what time it was but the apartment was dark, yet light peeked from behind his curtains. *Could he have slept through the night?*

Rubbing his eyes, he swung his arm off his bare chest and reached for his watch.

Slapping the palm of his hand around on the wooden coffee table, he finally found what he was looking for. His gummy eyelids were glued together. His vision one step behind his still-waking mind. Opening his eyes wide, The Lady Killer squinted at his timepiece, surprised to see it was still afternoon.

After a quick stretch, he swung his legs off the couch and planted his feet into the floor. Leaning over his knees, he scrubbed his face inside his hands and yawned. It didn't take long to remember the one he let get away.

His muscles flexed.

His breath escaped his chest as quickly as getting the air knocked out of him.

He watched the veins in his arms open and pulse with feelings of fear. Feelings of paralysis left him wondering what he should do next. A minute later, he stood and let the dizziness in his head disappear before moving to the window.

Peeking outside, the day seemed to drag on forever. Sleep was his only escape. A temporary relief to the immense anxiety sending waves of guilt up his chest. He knew he couldn't hide forever. People would begin asking questions, wonder where he was, and that was the last thing he needed to happen.

Act natural, he told himself as the muffled ringing of his cellphone broke the apartment's silence.

Turning his head, he followed the sound, trying to locate it. Not remembering where he'd put it last, he followed the sound to the kitchen table. Lifting the brimmed hat off the surface, his phone wasn't there. He finally found it in the pocket of his overcoat slung over the back of a kitchen chair.

Feeling the device vibrate in the palm of his hand, he stared at the name and number, knowing he couldn't speak to this person now.

The Lady Killer turned it to silent, set the phone on top of the table, and moved to the kitchen sink where he filled a glass of water. He chugged it down, then another.

Gasping for air, he gripped the edge of the sink and hung his head.

He needed a plan, and fast.

Except he didn't have one he was convinced would work.

Stuck between a rock and a hard place, he would never forgive himself for being so careless. That was what scared him most. He was a planner. Calculated his moves accordingly.

A knock on the front door.

Everything stopped.

He whipped his head around like an owl and stared.

His heart raced. It was the same knock as before—the knock he refused to answer. He had forgotten about it until now, having drifted off to sleep as he hoped whoever it was would leave. Now they were back and he found himself having to deal with the exact same problem as before.

This time the knock was heavier.

The door rattled on the hinges. He wished he had his bag of tools. He was the fool who didn't have the courage to retrieve them from the hotel room.

Biting his knuckles, his skin wouldn't break. He cursed the woman who refused to go inside the hotel with him. This was her fault. He wouldn't forget that. If only he had his equipment, then maybe he would have something he could defend himself with now.

The knocking softened and a familiar voice muffled its way through the heavy door. "Please. It's me."

His head perked up, his chest loosening with sudden compassion.

"Open up. I know you're in there."

The Lady Killer released a gasp of breath into the air and hurried to the door. Without looking through the peephole, he unlatched the door guard, twisted the deadbolt, and inched the door open.

A heavy foot kicked the door hard. Swinging open, it nailed The Lady Killer directly between his eyes. Feeling the warm blood run from his nose, he stumbled backward. He startled when the door slammed shut behind the intruder, who quickly came after him.

His eyes whitened as he ducked at the first onslaught of lashes. They kept coming. Striking with more intensity. He tumbled backward, dodging and blocking each blow coming straight for his head.

"Stop. I can explain." He unloaded his apologies as quick as an assault rifle.

Each strike delivered a sharper, more penetrating, sting than the last.

Then he tripped and fell.

He lost count of how many times he had been hit. It didn't matter. He deserved this.

Rolling on the floor, he soon found comfort by curling into the fetal position. Beginning to cry, his body ached and he moaned in agony.

"You have made a grave mistake."

"I'm sorry." He quickly submitted, knowing now who he was talking to.

A quick series of lashes hit him when his guard was down. The sharp cuts burned his skin and suddenly stopped when the cattail whip was tossed on the floor next to him.

He glanced between the person he called his and the whip.

A hand was lowered to his skull and pulled back his sweaty hair to palm his face. "Now, get on your knees."

The Lady Killer lifted his head and watched his person rise high above them. Lowering his gaze, he wrapped his hands around soft ankles, kissed the feet beneath, and said, "I deserve to be punished."

"I don't like it when you disobey a direct order."

"Understood, Master." He choked back the threat of more tears.

A hand hooked his chin and tipped his skull back. "Don't cry. I need you to be strong."

He nodded and blinked away the pools that had gathered in the corners of his eyes.

"There is more work that needs to be done."

CHAPTER FIFTY-FOUR

ERIN CLOSED HER CAR DOOR AND IMMEDIATELY TURNED TO me. "Why didn't you ask Camille if her husband owned a pair of Neiman Marcus shoes?"

I started the car. "I'll let King worry about those details." I flicked my eyes over to Erin. "Did you happen to notice what shoes the butler was wearing?"

Erin's head tipped back. "No."

"Me neither."

"Shit." Erin pushed her fingers through her blonde hair. "Should we go back in there?"

I put the car in reverse and said, "No. Camille thinks Bruce picked up Eric after Price's gala, but I believed her story about Mystery Man. Just because they were talking doesn't mean she knows him. She was right, she had to be friendly to everyone at the event whether she wanted to or not. Her reputation was at stake."

The vehicle's wheels rolled slowly through the upper-class neighborhood as we snaked our way to the exit. This time I kept my eyes forward, refusing the temptation of staring at the large houses.

"Both Mystery Man and the driver were wearing similar hats," I said, thinking out loud. "It could be the same person or someone who wants us to believe they are the same person. Or pure coincidence."

"Bruce would have inside knowledge of what their relationship is really like," Erin gripped her knees, "as well as what really goes on behind the scenes inside the Fosters' home."

I turned to look at Erin. "What are you saying? Bruce is our Mystery Man and Camille lied about meeting the man in the photo for the first time last night?"

Erin paused as I watched her expression pinch. "Maybe Eric crossed Bruce? Made him mad and this is his way of retaliation. Sending us the needed clues to catch Eric for murdering these girls."

"Without proof, anything is possible." I nodded to the man behind the security gate window as we passed. Then I pulled onto the main drag and turned the wheels toward downtown.

"But if Bruce knows Eric is behind these murders, he needs to be clearer with his message before another victim is targeted."

My brows pinched. Either theory was possible; Bruce could be sending us after Eric and was both Mystery Man and Eric's driver last night, or Bruce was only the driver and Mystery Man was meant to look like Bruce to appear innocent. Wondering how we could get Bruce alone to talk, I remembered Susan mentioning how she saw Eric and Camille arguing just before he left Price's party. What were they fighting about, and was it enough probable cause to have King bring them in for questioning?

When I mentioned it to Erin, she said, "So it's possible Camille didn't know who Eric left with last night."

"It's a pretty big assumption, considering she knows her

husband is a suspect in a murder investigation. Don't you think?" Erin nodded and I continued, "And then wouldn't she just say she didn't know? Wouldn't that be what most wives would do? Protect their husbands?"

Erin's nose wrinkled. "Do you think she's covering for him?"

"I wish I did." We shared a quick glance. "It certainly would be easier to explain than the alternative—she is on his hit list."

When we hit traffic, we both drifted off into our own thoughts. Mrs. Foster hadn't missed a beat. She'd come out swinging with a completely different tone today than last night. And when asked if she recognized Mystery Man, her explanation was reasonable. It certainly lined up with Susan's story from the surveillance video—a quick chat before the event.

"I need to talk with my editor," I said, turning to Erin. "How about you come with me to the newsroom and then we can get you back to your place so you can finish setting up your podcast?"

Erin checked the time on her wrist and agreed. "He's going to want a story from you."

"I know." I turned the wheel and let up off the brake. "Lucky for him, I think I might have something he'll like."

Erin angled her body toward me. "If I was your editor, I would request you write a story about how Eric Foster was connected to all three victims."

I smirked, continually amazed by how it seemed Erin could read my mind. "And not to forget, I also must mention how the police seem to be narrowing down their list of suspects and it appears Eric Foster is at the top of the list."

"And, if I were you," Erin's eyes sparkled, "I would also mention how the killer likes to drink Tom Collins and wear fancy shoes."

"But why stop there when we could also share how the killer likes to get off through fetish hotel romance." Erin arched a brow. "I mean, the story's purpose is to not only inform the public but also to instill fear."

"Fear sells papers."

We both busted up laughing and I wondered if Erin ever missed having to sell her ideas to an editor. I assumed she didn't. Her only concern was maintaining the reputation she had built for herself. It was all business and the more I looked at her future like that, the more attractive that independent lifestyle became.

I parked my car in the garage and together we walked up the concrete steps and pushed through the building's front entrance. Key-carding our way upstairs, Erin was one step behind by the time we finally arrived to the newsroom floor.

Immediately, I began searching for Dawson. Even on a Sunday afternoon, the newspaper never slept. When I couldn't spot him anywhere, I interrupted Trisha and asked, "Have you seen Dawson?"

She took her hands off her keyboard and looked at me. "In a meeting."

"Thanks," I said, staring at the closed-door conference room housing Dawson.

"Hey, Sam." Trisha spun her chair around and faced me. "Any closer to finding The Lady Killer?"

My heart stopped. Did I hear her right? "What did you say?"

"That's what we're calling him." Trisha blinked, dumbfounded. "You know, because he's killing women. I think it was first used by a TV anchor from Channel 4."

Now I was convinced Eric Foster was our guy. "I'm following some new developments."

"Should I worry?" Trisha's face drooped.

"No."

"Are you certain?"

"Yes."

"How can you be so sure?"

"Because your hair isn't blonde enough," I said, stepping away from Trisha's silly questions. I didn't like having to wait for Dawson, but we didn't have another choice. This was urgent. I had to know how Channel 4 got the idea to call this serial killer The Lady Killer.

"Did you hear that?" I asked Erin.

Erin nodded, her face pale. "Could Camille have mentioned Eric's nickname to anybody else?"

My shoulder shrugged. "Anyone who knew him back then would have known it."

"But to have the killer we're chasing be referred to by the same nickname as our prime suspect?" Erin followed me to my desk. "I don't know. Seems suspicious."

"Unless it's Camille's indirect way of asking for help? We can't be the only ones who've noticed all the victims look like her." I glanced back to the conference room. The door was still closed. Impatience was wearing on me when I turned to Erin. "Maybe you should just take my car and head home?"

"I'll give it a few minutes."

Erin lowered her tailbone to the edge of my desk. Picking up a pen, she said, "You know, I thought maybe I would miss the newsroom." She flicked her eyes down to me. "But I don't."

I hadn't had time to think about a life after this story. I just wanted to catch whoever was terrorizing Denver and make sure I was doing my due diligence in getting the facts straight. When I saw Dawson step out, I stood and we immediately locked eyes.

The buzzing between my ears went quiet. But the look he was giving me wasn't one that inspired confidence. He must have seen the urgency on my face because he came to me.

Erin's eyebrows were raised when she jumped off my desk. She'd seen the same thing and also knew it wasn't good. "I think you're right. Maybe I will leave."

I handed her my keys.

"You keep them." She refused to take them. "I'll catch a lift. You hang on to those in case you need them."

Erin rushed off to put the finishing touches on her podcast, passing Dawson along the way.

I stood and waited for Dawson with my hands buried deep inside my pants pockets.

"Sam, I've got bad news." His voice was so quiet I strained my ears just to hear him.

"I want a severance package guaranteed if you're going to fire me," I teased.

Dawson didn't react. "It's official. The *Times* will be sold and more of the city's best journalists will have to be let go." Dawson frowned and glanced around the newsroom as if reminiscing about better times.

"Am I one of them?"

He turned and faced me. "I don't know." His eyes fell. "But whoever does make the cut will be forced to move to our new office."

"What? They're closing down the newsroom?"

"The entire place. Too expensive to stay here."

Over his shoulder was the Capital, its gold dome shining like a beacon in the night. I felt my hand clench into a fist. This felt personal. They were destroying our careers but, beyond that, they were trying to rid the city of its checks and balances that were essential to our society. I couldn't help but feel offended—like they were doing this on purpose.

"I have an idea for a story I'd like to run by you," I said.

"There is nothing more we can do," Dawson muttered before looking me in the eye. "I'm sorry, what?"

"Hear me out," I said, rushing my words through in an

attempt to explain how I needed to present to the public what I knew about the murders. It was everything Erin and I discussed on our car ride here. We needed to do it. And the paper was a sure shot at getting the immediate local publicity I needed. "So, can I write it?"

Dawson angled his gaze down as he scratched his chin, mulling it over.

Then the doors burst open and a sudden commotion erupted on the other side of the room. I sprang to my feet and couldn't believe my eyes at what had burst into the building.

He was here looking for me.

I ducked my head. My heart raced. Then I flipped my head back to him and held my breath.

He was livid.

"Holy shit," I gasped.

Dawson's pupils dilated when he snapped his head to me. "Do you know about this?"

I watched Eric Foster stop a colleague to ask a question. My breathing became heavy as I watched their faces both turn in my direction.

Dawson's brows slanted.

"I swear. I don't know anything about this." How did he get in here?

A second later, the tsunami crashed into my cubicle. Eric's nostrils flared as he stared me down. "First Philip Price, now me?" he spat.

Feeling my body shrivel up and shrink against my desk, I gripped its edge tight to keep from falling. Mr. Foster was a large, intimidating man when he wasn't angry. I was afraid I might have poked the dragon. I hadn't seen this side of him and it was frightening.

"You're toxic," Eric growled, pointing his finger at me.

Rolling my shoulders back, I stood my ground but inside I

was quaking with fear. Everyone stopped what they were doing and had their eyes glued to the show unfolding at my desk.

I wondered why security hadn't arrived. *Where were they?* How the heck did Eric get past them?

Dawson stepped between us, using his body as a shield. "Mr. Foster, maybe we could discuss this in the privacy of my office."

Eric pushed Dawson to the side and kept his lion eyes on me. "Every single one of you is fucking unbelievable. Just because you work for a paper doesn't give you the right to publish whatever story you like."

I glanced to his shoes. They were dark and shiny but, honestly, I couldn't tell what brand he had on. "We're just trying to get to the truth," I said.

"I'll sue you for slander and put this paper six feet into the ground." He jabbed his finger to the floor like a pick axe repeatedly striking earth.

Not taking his threat lightly, I stepped forward, intentionally staying behind Dawson. "What were you doing with Mallory Madison the night she was murdered?"

Eric's eyes thundered. Dawson folded his arms over his chest, clearly wanting Mr. Foster to answer the question as well. Except he didn't respond.

"Don't want to answer?" My blood ran hot. "Then maybe you can explain the relationship you have to each of our victims?"

"What did my wife tell you?" He gritted his teeth.

"Were you having an affair with them? And, what, did they not like how you wanted to spice up their night? Is that why you killed them? Or did they threaten to tell your wife that you were busy banging them instead of her?"

"Watch yourself." He pointed his sword-like finger at me. "I know about you, Samantha Bell. What you do, where you live, and the pathetic little life you lead. You want to dig into my life, maybe it's time I push myself into yours."

Dawson threw his hands up as my thoughts immediately went to Mason.

"This conversation is over," Dawson said. "I'm going to have to ask you to leave."

Eric kept his eyes locked on me for a long suspenseful pause before turning away as quickly as he'd come. The hair lifted on the back of my neck as Dawson stared at me, not knowing what to say. As embarrassing as this was, I couldn't help but consider it a victory. Eric didn't like me poking around and that had me convinced I was close to discovering something he didn't want me to know about.

"Dawson, I'm sorry. I don't know what that was about." The way he was looking at me, I knew he was considering whether I was an asset or a liability.

But then Dawson surprised me by saying, "Write your damn story."

CHAPTER FIFTY-FIVE

An hour later I stood over Dawson with my finished story in hand. The only thing that had slowed me down was my call to Mason to make sure he was safe.

Dawson took his time finishing whatever thought he was working through before shifting his eyes off his computer screen and up to me.

"Here it is," I said, handing over my story.

Dawson pulled his glasses down on the bridge of his nose and read through my copy. When he was finished, he leaned back in his chair and said, "I can't promise you anything."

"I know."

"But, just to be clear," his eyes peered above the rim of his glasses, "I'm at the end of my rope, too."

I held his eyes with mine and I saw something that I hadn't seen before. There was more fear and uncertainty swirling inside of his irises than I had ever thought possible. Dawson was our fearless leader who wasn't afraid of taking on the largest issues that yielded the biggest consequences, good and bad. But now that all our careers seemed to be on the line, we could either play it safe or continue to push the boundaries until we were asked to leave. I was happy to know Dawson had my back and wasn't ready to dial our work down.

"Now what?" he asked.

"I'm going home to be with my son."

He nodded. "Would you like me to walk you to your car?"

I could feel my muscles still shaking from Eric Foster's surprise attack. "I'll be all right."

Dawson smiled and nodded. "Don't stop what you're doing. It's clear you're onto something."

"Thank you." I turned to leave his office but, before I left entirely, he had one more thing he needed to say.

"And, Sam, if this doesn't make the cut," he glanced to my story, "put it up on your website."

We shared a knowing look before I finally headed out.

I gathered my things and left the building with a desire to push all the dangers to the side and direct my energy toward being with Mason. I needed a break. And not just because of what Eric Foster threatened to do. But because if I allowed Mason to go any further without opening up about Gavin, I knew I would one day regret it.

Not even to my car, I received a call from a distressed Camille Foster.

"Slow down," I said. "Tell me what happened." I plugged my opposite ear with my finger in hopes of making it easier to understand what she was saying.

A blubbering voice drowning in emotion came spilling into my ear. I imagined Camille wiping her cheeks by the sounds I heard rustling through the phone line. "He lost it. I need to get out of here. You're the only one who knows what he's capable of," she cried.

Frozen, my knees locked as I glanced around the half-empty parking garage looking for my way out. Had she just confessed to her husband's guilt? I was afraid to say anything, terrified that I might have been the reason behind Mrs. Foster's anguish. "Camille, did Eric do something to you?"

A pause left my nerves jumping.

My mind played tricks on me and I assumed the worst. I questioned where Eric had gone after detonating his frustration on me, and I feared he'd taken that same anger back to his house and exploded on an innocent Camille.

"What did you say to him?" Camille asked.

"I didn't say anything to him."

She muttered a few choice words. "Oh, my God. I don't know who I married."

"What happened?" An intense swallow from Camille's side filtered through my ear piece.

"Can you help me?" she asked.

I blinked and looked for help, not knowing what to do. "I'm not sure I'm the person best qualified for this situation."

"You know I can't go to the cops." Her voice cracked. "That's what he would expect me to do. And our friends, well, he'd find me there."

An awkward pause left me spinning in circles.

"Samantha, there is something I should have told you earlier."

I dropped my head and pushed my finger deeper into my ear. "What is it, Camille?"

"Something big that might help with the case you're investigating."

"Tell me, Camille."

Silence.

I held my breath, anxiously awaiting her words.

"It's about my husband."

"You have my attention."

"You were right about him knowing the women who were murdered. But there is something that only I know. Something that you would understand."

"Camille, is he there with you now?"

She dropped her voice to a whisper. "I don't know where he went."

I lifted my gaze and felt my heart race.

"Recently, my husband's desires changed." A quick pause. "When we were intimate, he wanted our sex to be rougher. More experimental. He would bind me to the bed and blindfold me. I went along with it because he made it fun. But he took it too far."

"What do you mean?"

"What began as a game grew into something far darker than I ever could have imagined."

When I closed my eyes, I saw flashes of each of the victims' faces scroll behind my lids.

"Are you still listening, Samantha?"

"Yes. I'm still listening." I glanced to my car.

"He choked me as I sought orgasm."

"You need to get yourself away from him," I barked loud into my phone. "Do you have someplace you can go?"

Camille sniffled.

"Camille? Do you—"

"Yes. I have someplace I can go."

"Good. Leave now. Tell nobody. And when you get there, call the police. They can keep you safe."

"I can't."

"Camille, you don't have a choice."

"Exactly. It's not my decision. He has connections inside the department and if he finds out I'm telling anybody what I just told you," she sucked back a deep breath, "he'll kill me."

CHAPTER FIFTY-SIX

I DROPPED BEHIND THE STEERING WHEEL OF MY CAR LIKE A dead weight.

What began as a quake deep inside my core soon spread to each of my limbs. I lifted my hand and watched my fingers tremble. My lungs breathed short, hungry rasps until black splotches blinked in front of my eyes. I felt trapped, like I was losing control of something I should have had a tight grasp on.

I was terrified for Camille.

Afraid that Eric had finally snapped.

His secrets had caught up with him and now his inner lion was loose.

When I closed my eyes, I could still hear the fear sneaking its way into Camille's voice. I jumped when I thought about the way Eric charged across the newsroom floor in his attempt to intimidate me into backing down.

The first of my tears squeezed out.

Then the floodgates opened and I couldn't stop the river that flowed down my cheeks.

I wept for the victims, cried because I was exhausted.

But, mostly, I was just scared. I hated feeling helpless, like I might have been the cause of someone else's distress. It was a heavy burden to carry and the weight of it had finally caught up with me.

After a few minutes, I wiped my cheeks dry with the back of my hand.

Darting my gaze around the parking garage, I needed to clear my spinning head. But, more importantly, listening to Camille's call for help had me thinking about my own family's shortcomings.

I picked up my phone and called King.

"They're calling our suspect The Lady Killer," I said the moment he picked up.

"I heard." King's voice sounded equally as exhausted as my own.

"You know whose nickname that was during college?" I didn't allow time for a response. "Eric Foster."

"Who told you that?" King's voice perked up.

"His wife," I said. "Camille must have also been the one to tell Channel 4."

Another tremor rocked my body. There was no doubt Camille was scared for her life. Even before our conversation just minutes ago, Camille was searching for anyone to listen to her cry for help without making it super-obvious. But few —if any—of us were listening.

I pulled at my collar and sucked back a painful breath. "This is all my fault."

"You're speculating, Sam."

My head jerked up with a sudden revelation. "That's it."

"What's it?"

"That must be why Eric was so livid—the leaking of the nickname," I murmured.

"Sam, are you with Eric now?" King asked.

"He was just here an hour ago. You should have seen him,

Alex. He was inside the newsroom and I thought he was actually going to hurt me."

I heard King cover his phone's microphone with his hand and relay what I'd just told him to someone else. A man's voice in the background said, "That's why we can't track him down."

"Sam, where are you now?" King asked.

"He's a loose cannon," I barked. "Alex, Camille needs your help." I told King about my latest conversation with Camille. The distress I'd heard coming through the line, the fear I had that Eric might do something to her next, her fear of the same.

"Don't worry, Sam. I'll check it out. You stay safe."

My heart skipped a beat. "You, too."

"And, Sam, watch your back. You're an asset I can't afford to lose."

CHAPTER FIFTY-SEVEN

As soon as I ended my call with King, I called Mason.

My stomach muscles were still flexing with uncertainty as I listened to the line ring. Quietly, I said a quick prayer for Camille. I hoped King could get to her before a mistake was made. It was a race against the clock and I knew we didn't have much time.

My toes tapped anxiously, wondering why Mason hadn't picked up by now. His voicemail never clicked over and the thought of Eric's threat dropped my stomach to the floor.

Knowing it was worthless to sit here, I had to take action. Turning the key, I cranked the engine over and pointed the car home.

I pressed my foot heavily on the accelerator, battling traffic along the way.

My vision tunneled and I was still stuck inside my own head as I drove with aggressive precision.

I didn't like not having Mason answer the phone. If it hadn't been for me speaking to him right after Eric Foster left the newsroom, I would have already called the police.

Mason is home. He's in the shower, I reasoned. *Everything is fine. There is nothing to worry about,* I told myself.

It felt like I hit every red light on my attempt to rush home but, in the end, I made it in the time expected. The front porch light was on and a quick sigh of relief kept my hopes alive.

I grabbed my handbag and cellphone and hurried inside.

"Mason, are you home?" I said, closing the front door behind me.

Cooper jumped off the couch and wagged his tail as he bounded over to me. Pushing him down, there was no sign of my son.

I moved to the kitchen, setting my things down on the table, seeing Cooper had been fed. He stretched and groaned, demanding more petting. That was a good sign, an indication that made me believe Mason wasn't far.

Moving on tender feet to the back of the house, Mason's bedroom door hinges squeaked when I pushed it open. His room was dark and empty. The house was cold.

I spun on a heel and turned back to the kitchen with a pinched brow. *Where was this boy?*

Just as panic and frustration filled my chest, I flipped on an overhead light noticing a school paper on the counter.

The title caught my attention and drew me closer.

The Son of Sam by Mason Bell.

My breath hitched as I picked it up. The tips of my fingers went cold, wondering if Mason purposely left this out for me to find. I was scared to read it—fearful of gaining a glimpse of what was going on inside my son's head.

I backpedaled to the kitchen table and dropped my gaze to the text of what Mason had written.

It didn't take long for my eyes to water. It was the best poem I had read in a long time. Despite the immense pride blooming across my chest, it was impossible to not feel the sharp jab of guilt knowing I was at least part of the cause to my son's confusion and pain so eloquently expressed in his poem.

Damn it, Samantha, I cursed, setting his writing down on the table and grabbing my car keys.

Something told me I knew where Mason was—where he had been disappearing to—and his reason for keeping it a secret.

On my way out the door, I patted Cooper on the head and said, "Don't worry boy. I think I know where he is."

CHAPTER FIFTY-EIGHT

ALEX KING GOT OFF THE PHONE WITH SAMANTHA BELL and turned to his partner, Detective Alvarez.

Alvarez was still on the phone with Kristin Newsome but King knew this couldn't wait.

King reached toward the phone and hit the speaker button so he could be part of the conversation. "Ms. Newsome," King introduced himself, "if you don't help us catch this killer, who will?"

"I'm sorry, Detective King. I have a career to focus on." King shared a look with Alvarez and clenched his jaw. "Friends, family, and colleagues who would never look at me the same if they knew what happened. I just want to move on."

"And another woman could die because of that selfish desire," Alvarez said into the speaker box.

King knew Kristin had her mind set. He leaned across the table and said, "If you change your mind, please call us first."

Kristin promised she would and they ended the call with Alvarez directing his frustration at King. "What the fuck was that about?"

"She's not interested in helping. And who can blame her? She'll have a target on her back, whatever decision she makes." Alvarez lowered his brow and shook his head with disbelief. "Besides, while you were on the phone with her, I received a report of domestic violence."

"Isn't my concern." Alvarez pushed away from the desk, walked to the other side of the office, and began shuffling papers. "Send it to patrol."

King followed his partner, hovering over his right shoulder. "No, we'll take this one ourselves."

Alvarez rolled his head to King and arched a single eyebrow. "And why would we do that?"

"Because," King smiled, "it was about Camille Foster."

Alvarez dropped what he was doing and sprang into action. "That's why Eric didn't answer his phone."

"Could be." They grabbed their coats and hurried down the corridor. "Do you know what Eric Foster's nickname was in college?" King asked.

Alvarez shook his head.

"The Lady Killer."

Both men hit the brakes. "Isn't that what that anchor on Channel 4 has been calling our killer?"

King nodded. "Someone really wants this jackass to go down."

Alvarez planted his hands on his hips, his brow furrowed in thought.

"Could have been her?" King said.

Alvarez flicked his gaze back to his partner. "What? The wife?"

King nodded just as they heard their names being called by their captain.

"Get your asses down here." He waited for the two men to get closer before screaming, "You knew not to call Mr. Foster. You disobeyed a direct order." Captain fumed.

"Captain, he never picked up," King said.

"His lawyer just called. You know what he said?" The lines on Captain's face deepened. "That he should sue the department for harassment."

"Captain, listen." King's neck stretched. "We just received word that his wife might be in danger. We think Eric Foster might be behind it."

Captain snapped his head to King. "You better not be making this shit up." Captain's eyes jumped up and down both men's faces. "I can't afford to have the mayor breathing down my neck any more than he already is."

"It came from a reliable source," King insisted.

Captain breathed heavily before saying, "Then what are you waiting for? Get the hell out of here."

Alvarez and King hurried to King's car with hearts racing. Jumping behind the wheel, King sped out of the department parking lot, listening to his tires squeal. "This might be just what we needed to drag Eric down to the station," he said.

"He was never going to discuss his shoes, but now we have a reason," Alvarez agreed.

Upon their arrival to Cherry Hills, they were stopped by the gate attendant. "I'm sorry, Detectives. This is the first I'm hearing of this. Nothing came through my line."

"This isn't a game." King's tone hardened.

"I would have been the first to hear about a domestic dispute," the attendant said.

"We don't have time to argue." King banged his steering wheel with his hand. "If something did happen and you refused to let us through, who do you think they will blame?"

"It certainly wouldn't be us," Alvarez said.

The gate opened with the attendant only answering by a single look.

Alex King sped toward the Fosters' house. Slamming on the brakes in their driveway, both men flung their doors open and leaped to the front door with their hands firmly placed on their department-issued pistols.

King glanced to Alvarez. Alvarez nodded and King sucked back one final breath before pounding his fist on the door.

CHAPTER FIFTY-NINE

TEN MINUTES LATER, I PULLED UP TO THE CURB AND SAW my son sitting on the bench.

My lips tugged at the corners before curling upward.

I didn't react, didn't rush. Mason had come here for a reason and I wanted to give him all the time he needed before I interrupted his visit.

The sky was darkening and the clouds turned a brilliant orangey red as the sun set behind the Rockies. A dusting of snow whitened their peaks and I was reminded of the surrounding beauty that was so easily taken for granted.

I left my car and approached Mason, feeling my own heart shatter. It had been too long since I had been here myself. Part of me felt guilty for not asking Mason if maybe he wanted to visit together.

I walked up on him without making a scene, skirted around the bench, sat, and put my arm around him.

His head hit my shoulder like stone sinking to the bottom of a lake. My son was only two years away from legally being a man, but he held on to me like a boy still needing his mother.

I welcomed his embrace. Together we sat in silence, letting our actions speak for us.

I stared at the gravestone of my late husband, feeling the grief swell my eyes. And as the trees rustled around us, the emotions of the present collided with those of my past, and suddenly I doubted my ability to remain strong in the face of adversity.

"How did you know where to find me?" Mason asked.

My gaze drifted across the cemetery as I thought about each of the victims lost. "I found your poem."

Mason lifted his head and gave me a questioning look.

I held his curious eyes inside of my own. "I saw the photo you had out of you and Dad."

Mason frowned and dropped his head back down to my shoulder. "I can't sneak anything by you, can I?"

"You don't have to," I said. Our eyes were glued to Gavin's headstone as if willing him to come back to life and be with us now. "I brought something with me."

Mason sat upright and watched as I pulled old letters Gavin had written while away on deployment.

"Can I read them to you?" I asked.

Mason nodded.

Over the next half-hour, I read Mason the letters from Gavin. They brought back wonderful memories. We laughed and cried and I couldn't deny the chance to tell more stories of when Mason was little.

"He would really do that?" Mason asked.

"Your father could move Heaven and Earth." I smiled, reminding Mason what a loving husband and father Gavin was. "The world lost a good man and we should never forget that. But we shouldn't let what is missing from our lives define who we are today, either."

A sad look fell over Mason's face. Mason was quiet for a moment. His spine dipped and I knew he was taking it all in as best a teenager could. Then he asked, "Why is Dad buried here? I thought soldiers were buried in Arlington."

My arm was still around his shoulders. I squeezed his arm and said, "I wanted him close to home."

"Mom, have you forgotten that it's Dad's birthday tomorrow?"

I felt my throat close. Staring into his eyes, I shook my head. "I haven't forgotten, honey."

"Then why haven't you said anything?"

My gaze swept off the grass and I exhaled a soft sigh. "I've been busy, I'll admit that. But I didn't forget."

A text came through on my phone. Checking the display screen, I quickly read what it said. It was from Erin. *Podcast just went live. Cross your fingers our Mystery Man is listening. Keep your phone close. Not sure who he'll reach out to first.*

"We should do something for him, don't you think?" Mason didn't even think twice about me staring at my cellphone.

"That would be great," I said.

"Nolan is a good friend, Mom."

My brows pinched. "I know, sweetie." I put my phone back in my pocket and turned my attention to my son.

"And we weren't drinking." He raised his brows as if to highlight his serious expression. "We just wanted to hear the band playing inside. That's all. I swear."

"I get it. Good music is hard to resist." My smile hit my eyes.

"So you're not mad?"

I shook my head, still smiling. "I worry about you, that's all."

"Don't, Mom."

"I can't help it. And when I find you hanging around a crime scene—"

"That was coincidence," Mason interrupted. "We've already been over this."

"I know, but there was another crime unfolding last night, and today I learned it was linked back to where you and Nolan just happened to be hanging out."

Mason's shoulders slumped as he turned his head back to the tombstone.

"Hey," I heard my voice chirp up, "what do you say we go home and cook Dad's favorite meal?"

Mason turned to me and smiled. "I'd like that."

Together, we stood and walked to the car with a promise to finally have a meal we could both be happy with.

CHAPTER SIXTY

SUSAN YOUNG CHECKED HER SMARTPHONE FOR WHAT FELT like the hundredth time.

Nerves kept her jittery.

She paced her office back and forth, anxiously awaiting the arrival of Christy Jones.

Susan had requested the meeting with the hopes of having her identify Mystery Man. Since speaking with her friend, she had thought plenty about her call with Sam after viewing the surveillance from Price's gala.

Eric Foster seemed like the logical suspect. He could certainly be the one behind these murders and, if that was true, Susan wanted him caught as much as anybody.

She stopped, paused, and touched her forehead.

Her pulse throbbed loud and fast in her eardrums as she thought back to what she'd seen in the surveillance video. She had to approach this carefully. She certainly didn't want Christy to get the wrong impression. It was a fine line between politics and accusation but a risk she was willing to take.

Susan had a plan.

She would keep her conversation and questions simple by only asking if Christy could identify the person she couldn't herself. Then, she could relay what Christy had said to Sam, and have Sam take her investigation further.

The clock on the wall was a constant reminder of the minutes that passed. The ticking grew louder each second Christy Jones didn't show. Susan began to question if she had been stood up.

Falling into her desk chair, Susan stared at her computer screen. The video was paused and she swore she must have watched it a hundred times, trying to read lips.

Each review only took her further away from discovering anything new—the truth becoming blurrier. But she swore Camille Foster knew who Mystery Man was by the surprised expression at seeing him there at the same gala she and her husband had paid to host.

A subtle knock on the door.

Susan spun around in her chair and hurried to answer it with a warmth radiating through her body. "Christy, thank you for coming." She answered the door.

Christy smiled. "Not a problem."

"Would you like some tea or water?"

"No, I really can't stay long." Christy clutched her purse inside both her hands and let her gaze take in Susan's office. "Nice place."

"Thank you." Susan directed Christy to an empty chair at her desk. "Then I won't waste any more of your time. The reason I asked you to come tonight is because you have been inside the Fosters' inner circle."

Christy glanced to the exit.

Susan chuckled. "Don't worry, I'm not looking for dirt on them. Quite the contrary. Rather, I'm hoping you can help me identify a man at Price's gala."

"Okay." Christy pursed her lips in thought.

"The strangest thing happened to me just before the gala started." Susan folded her hands on her thigh, keeping Christy's eyes locked with her own. "A man approached me with an envelope addressed to Samantha Bell. You know my friend Samantha, right?"

Christy nodded.

"This man said that Samantha would be the one to solve the case of these murdered women. I'm sure you've been following the news."

Christy's cheeks paled as blood left her face. "I'm devastated by the news. Never in my wildest imagination would I have thought something like this could happen in a city like Denver." Christy played with the jewelry on her wrist. "And you, what, want me to try and identify this man who approached you?"

"Yes."

Christy turned her head and took a moment to think it over. "I have to be honest, Samantha Bell's column hasn't particularly been friendly to Price's campaign."

"I can't speak for Sam, but I can assure you she is only trying to find the truth."

"They made an agreement and, from the way I heard it, Samantha didn't keep her word."

Susan looked Christy directly in the eye and said, "I don't know the details behind the agreement to which you're referring. And, frankly, I don't want to make this into something it's not. Sam was wrong in thinking Price was behind these crimes, I'll give you that. This isn't about politics, Christy. All I'm asking of you is to help me figure out who this man is."

Christy sighed.

"Please, can you just have one look?"

Christy was reluctant but agreed.

"There are two clips I'd like to show you." Susan hit the play button on the first.

The first clip was of Eric Foster leaving the gala. She paused on the man driving the limo.

Susan glanced to Christy. Christy shook her head. Susan wasn't surprised; the image wasn't clear.

Then Susan showed her the second clip from before the gala where it looked like Camille was talking to Mystery Man. "Do you recognize him?"

Christy squinted her eyes and said, "Play it again."

Susan rewound the video and hit play.

Christy tipped forward in her chair and stared with recognition flashing in her eyes.

"Who is he?"

The room fell silent. Christy continued to stare at the bright screen.

"I can see you recognize the man," Susan said. "Have you met him before?"

"I've never seen him with Eric," Christy said without taking her eyes off the computer screen.

"But you have seen him?" Susan's heart raced with a sudden surge of adrenaline.

Christy's blood left her face as she nodded. "Only once." She flicked her wet eyes to Susan. "He was with Camille one afternoon Price and I stopped by their house."

Susan's spine straightened. "Do you know his name?"

Christy moistened her lips with her tongue, dropped her voice down to a whisper, and said, "I believe Camille said his name was John Standard."

CHAPTER SIXTY-ONE

ALLISON DOYLE STAYED IN HER OFFICE, AFRAID THAT IF SHE left she'd miss the Facebook account coming back online. It was something she couldn't risk. She wanted to help her friends any way she could. This was the least she could do, considering the high stakes.

They were onto something big, she could feel it in her bones. Tossing a tennis ball between her hands, Allison's stomach grumbled with hunger. She didn't want to leave, debated ordering in, but instead pushed her hunger out of her mind by weighing her stomach down with a glass of cold water.

Erin's voice came through Allison's computer speakers, and Allison paced the room while she listened to her new friend's podcast. It had just gone live and she was one of the first to hear it. Erin broke down the case, explained the facts, and presented her listeners with the evidence.

Allison's cellphone chirped with a new message.

Stealing her attention, she spun on a heel. Her hair flinging over the backs of her shoulders, she picked up her phone. It was Erin.

Anything? Erin asked in a text message.

Setting her tennis ball on top of her desk, Allison leaned over her keyboard, curled her fingers, and tapped at the keys. There was no sign of movement on the inactive account.

Nothing yet, Allison messaged back.

She caught her own reflection in the dark window glass when she turned back around.

If Mystery Man was watching Erin and Sam as closely as they all suspected, Allison knew he should be listening to Erin's episode now. Allison crossed her fingers and began pacing back and forth across her floor again. She couldn't sit still. Her blood shook with adrenaline and nerves, the same feeling she got when she drank too much coffee.

Suddenly, Allison stopped.

Her heart raced.

Standing in her office facing the front door, she held her breath.

There was movement at the entrance.

Jabbing her finger on the space bar, Allison muted her computer speakers and focused her attention to the sounds coming from the front.

The front door shut and the white in Allison's eyes went electric.

"Hello?" she called out.

Nothing.

Allison clenched her jaw and wiped her clammy hands on her thighs.

A noise from the kitchen made Allison tense with fear. Gripping her cellphone tight, she was ready to call the cops if something were to happen—if this was a break in, or something worse.

Removing her pumps, Allison tiptoed through the office as quietly as she could. She pressed her back up against the walls and held her breath. A shadow danced across the floor.

Allison watched wide-eyed for a second before gathering the courage to peek her head around the corner ever so slowly.

Inside was a figure.

Allison's hand flew over her racing heart as the gasped. "Patty, oh my god."

Patty O'Neil let out a shriek. "Allison, I didn't realize you were here."

"Surprise." Allison turned her palms to the ceiling as she giggled uncomfortably. "I didn't expect to see you here this late."

Patty finished making her tea. Dipping her tea bag in and out of her steaming hot water, she said, "I wanted to catch up on some work before Monday."

Allison leaned a shoulder into the doorframe and folded her arms over her chest. She appreciated Patty's dedication to the job. "Yeah, me too."

"Now, if only I can dial in a couple of our clients' ads, maybe I'll be able to rest easier." She laughed.

"Hey, can I ask you something?" Allison asked.

"Sure." Patty curled her lips around the rim of her mug, sucking back her first sip of tea.

"What was it like working with Eric Foster?"

"Fine." Patty's brow knitted. "Why?"

"Did he ever make you feel uncomfortable?"

Patty's expression pinched as she thought it over. "No. Why? Something going on? I can check the ads he has us running for Price, but they were receiving a great return last I looked."

Allison felt her arms tense as she wet her lips. "Have you been following the news about those women being killed?"

Patty stared. Her eyes flared with connection. "O.M.G." She touched her heart. "Has me afraid to walk to my car." Patty did a double take at Allison. "Wait. Are you suggesting..." her nose scrunched. "Is he the one who is killing these women?"

A beeping rang loud from Allison's desk.

Allison pushed off the door and rushed into her office. Patty followed, asking what the alarm was set for.

Allison stared at her computer, her fingers tapping fiercely over her keyboard. "The account has been reactivated," she muttered.

Patty's gaze darted between the computer and printer, connecting the dots to what Allison was doing.

Allison's system swept the account's backend, and soon began spitting out its report from the printer. She peeled the first sheet off and immediately dove into the report. Her eyes scanned, looking for a name. She combed through the account's connections before looking up to Patty and saying, "It's a fake."

"Allison, what is going on?" Patty's eyes were wide. She was no longer holding her tea. She stood with legs wide, as if ready to spring to the exit at a moment's notice.

Allison stared into Patty's eyes, deciding how best to explain Mystery Man to her colleague without scaring her into silence. Then, the fake account sent a message to Erin. Allison flipped her head back to her computer screen and read what it said.

You called? I'm here.

Patty's hands began to shake as if knowing something bad was about to happen. They both leaned close the monitor. Allison's heart stopped as a second message came through the account and she realized what she was looking at. A photo of Erin and her dazzling blonde hair lay perfectly framed in the center of her screen. Erin was at home, alone, the image taken only seconds ago through her front window.

"Shit. It's a trap!" Allison jumped to her feet, reaching for her phone.

"What is going on, Allison?" Patty asked, hugging herself tight.

Allison frozen when her eyes met with Patty's. "He's going to kill her next," she whispered.

Patty started hyperventilating as Allison explained the message, Mystery Man, and the key that probably went nowhere.

"And now Erin and Sam fell right into his hands," Allison rambled, "asking him to come to them."

"You need to do something," Patty blubbered.

Dialing Erin, Allison knew her friend was in danger and that she was being stalked by what could be the killer.

The line rang and rang but Erin never answered.

CHAPTER SIXTY-TWO

Mason was still laughing beneath his Colorado Rockies baseball hat. My cheeks hurt from smiling so hard and I was having a wonderful time with my son. Over our beef taco dinner, I shared many more stories about Gavin that Mason had never heard. It felt great reliving the happiest time of my life—brought back memories I had stored away long ago but would never forget.

With our stomachs full, Mason cast his gaze to the table.

I watched his smile flip upside down and I knew something was wrong.

"Mom," he glanced up at me from under a heavy brow, "do you miss Dad?"

"Every day," I said, feeling my eyes swell with renewed sadness.

Mason lifted his eyes further and stared into mine for a moment before asking, "Did Dad not want you to marry again?"

I cast my gaze to his Tom Petty and the Heartbreakers t-shirt. "Why would you say that, sweetie?"

"It's just... since... I figured..."

I reached my hand out and touched Mason on the shoulder. "There isn't a day that goes by that I don't think about your father."

"Do you not want to marry again?"

"What is this about?"

Mason shifted uncomfortably in his seat. "You spend all your time working. It's like you're running away from something. I mean, are you even happy?"

I felt my throat close up as I stared into my son's eyes. His dark hair spilled out of his hat and, in that moment, he looked like his father. Even his attitude was a direct reflection of Gavin. Strong willed, curious, and straight.

My lips curled upward and I felt the twinkle return to my eye.

As long as I had Mason, I would always have a piece of Gavin. But Mason was right. Something inside of me was missing—had been absent from my life for a long time. I'd lost my rock. Life got away from me after Gavin died and it hadn't slowed down. I did my best to hide my feelings of depression and sadness. Some days were better than others but, apparently, I didn't do a great job at disguising the pain I stubbornly refused to let go of.

"I still have you, and that's all that matters," I said.

"What about when I'm gone?"

My brows slanted and my chin quivered. "You mean when you move out?"

Mason sat on his hands and nodded. "Will you date again?"

There was a stone in my stomach. "I don't know," I whispered.

Mason shifted his eyes to his empty plate. "I don't think Dad would be angry if you did."

A weak smile twitched at the corners of my lips. "No, I don't think so either," I murmured just as my cellphone rang.

Mason lifted his head, his face falling with the assumption that our night was over. I had the same feeling. I didn't want to let him down but I had to answer it.

Stepping over Cooper, he followed me across the floor with his tail wagging. I swiped my cell off the counter and headed into the living room with my heart leaping into my throat.

"Allison, was the account reactivated?" I asked.

"Erin," Allison fired off. "She doesn't know what's coming for her."

My head whipped around to the kitchen. Mason was still at the table, lost in thought. "Slow down," I said. "What do you mean?"

"Mystery Man. The message came through. He's there, Sam. Outside Erin's house. He's watching Erin!"

I paused, quickly planning for obstacles and ways to overcome them. "Does Erin know this?"

"She's not picking up. Oh my god, Sam. What if something happened?"

"Relax. Erin wanted this. She's prepared," I lied.

"You need to get over there."

Mason picked up his head and stared. "I'm on it."

"Stay vigilante, Sam. We don't know what this guy is capable of doing."

I ended my call by telling Allison to stay put and keep her phone close. I wasn't sure what I was going to find at Erin's or what I was walking into. Erin's house wasn't far from my own and I knew that if I left now, I could get there within ten minutes. But ten minutes was an eternity when danger lurked.

Rushing into the kitchen, Mason was placing his plate in the dishwasher. "Something has come up," I said.

Mason nodded without looking. He knew. Was listening in on my conversation and could hear it in my voice.

My heart squeezed the last bit of life out when I heard

myself saying, "My friend, Erin, needs my help. I shouldn't be long."

I didn't want to leave him, but Erin was in danger.

I kissed Mason goodbye, told him to lock the door behind me, grabbed my car keys, and raced to Erin's. Ten minutes later I arrived to mostly empty streets. No one was around. It was eerily silent as I ran up to her door, knocking like I was the police.

Erin answered with a smile. "Hey, Sam."

She was alive. And apparently had no idea that she was even being watched.

I swung my head back to the street, hoping to see something different. There, across the street, a dry patch of pavement revealed itself from Erin's porch. The car was gone, along with Mystery Man and whatever else this person seemed to know.

I dropped my head into my hand, feeling the pressure build.

"Everything all right?" Erin asked.

Why did he leave? And what was his reason for giving me the key?

We were spinning in circles. It felt like I was chasing a ghost.

My eyes closed when I shook my head. "No. I'm not okay." I picked my head up and looked Erin in the eye. "And neither are you."

CHAPTER SIXTY-THREE

AFTER THE INITIAL SHOCK WORE OFF, I SAW NOTHING BUT strength inside of Erin's eyes.

She wasn't afraid. Instead, she was ready to tackle the issue head-on. Maybe even more so than I was. But one thing remained true, there was no way I could leave her alone until we knew who had taken that photo of her inside her own house.

With goosebumps still standing tall on both of my arms, together we jogged up and down the block, covering both sides of the street looking for any signs of Erin's stalker. Besides the dry patch of pavement, we found nothing.

"Let me see it again," Erin said the minute we were back inside.

I pulled up the enhanced picture Allison had created and handed Erin my phone.

The quality was better than what Erin received inside her own Facebook account and was no doubt taken shortly before I'd arrived.

"I can't believe I missed it." Erin sighed. "I was even waiting to be contacted."

"It's not your fault. Besides, Allison had your back."

Erin was still staring into the palm of her hand. "That dry patch of pavement is at the right angle. There's no doubt about that."

My gaze drifted over Erin. She was still wearing the same clothes—a fleece zip-up and blue jeans—and drinking from the same cup of tea.

"Send it to me." Erin met my stare. "I want a copy of it for my own records."

I took the phone back as chills crept up my spine and made me shudder. Just the thought of someone watching without her knowing had me creeped out. "There," I said. "Sent."

"Sam, our plan worked." Erin grinned.

"Except he left." My eyes felt heavy with grief. "Why?"

Erin's mouth pinched.

I rolled my head to the window. The drapes were drawn and we were tucked inside her warm house with a false sense of security. "He was spooked, that's why."

Erin folded her arms across her chest and said, "Maybe he wanted to establish his dominance?" She flicked her gaze to me and arched a brow. "Just like the killer is with his victims."

My eyebrows slanted. "You mean he wants us to know he knows where you live and can watch you without you ever knowing it?"

"Exactly." Erin's neck muscles tensed.

My thoughts wove back and forth, connecting, trying to see it from Mystery Man's point of view. "That's why he gave me the key at Price's gala," I said quietly. "He wanted to show us that he could get inside an event like that, be seen, and not have anyone know who he was."

Erin was light on her feet as she moved to the window. Cupping the side of her eye with one hand, she peeled back the drape and peered into the dark abyss outside. "How can we be sure he's not still here, watching?"

A zap of electricity hummed in the air between us. The hairs on my neck prickled when I responded, "That's what I'm afraid of. I'm not certain he's gone."

"But what is he waiting for then?" Erin dropped the drape and came back to the couch. "He gave us no other clue to go along with the key. That's all he's given us so far."

"And the Facebook account Allison said was a fake."

"And that."

I sat on the couch, resting my sharp elbows on the points of my knees. Staring at the floor, I needed to get inside this person's mind. "Why say I'm going to solve this case if he's not willing to give us anything else to work with?"

"What did you do with the key?" Erin asked.

I glanced at Erin from behind a dark curtain of lashes. "I gave it to Detective King."

"And?"

"Nothing yet." Erin seemed frustrated with King's ability to control the speed of our own investigation and, truthfully, I was, too. But I trusted King and expected to be hearing back from him soon. There were no other obvious connections pointing to any of our other leads. This was so bizarre. "Maybe he wants us to chase him?"

"And what? Follow him to where? The killer?"

"If he isn't the killer himself." I shrugged and glanced to my watch. It was after 7PM. Time was passing with no clear action to take next. It left me feeling unsettled, inadequate. I needed to do something before I went insane. But maybe that was Mystery Man's intention. "Something happened after you left the newsroom."

Erin stopped pacing, glanced over her shoulder, and met my gaze.

"Eric Foster found his way to my desk."

Erin angled the rest of her body toward me. "What did he say?"

My eyes glossed over as I remembered the terror I felt smashing inside of me. "Threatened to come after me if I didn't back off the investigation."

"Christ, Samantha." Erin dropped her arms to her sides and took two steps forward. "Now that is the kind of stuff that scares me. What if it was him outside my window?" She pointed her index finger to the front of the house. "Allison swore this was a trap to lure us into danger, and now I'm starting to wonder if maybe she was right."

I was still staring at the floor when I began shaking my head. "Eric didn't bring me the key. He's not Mystery Man. He would have shown his face tonight." I swept my gaze up off the floor and looked into Erin's dark eyes. "He's not afraid of confrontation. This has to be somebody else."

"How can you be so sure?"

I was slow to respond. "I can't," I murmured as my thoughts drifted to Camille.

I was still waiting to hear back from King and I wasn't going to cross any assumptions off my list until evidence suggested otherwise. If Eric was behind these murders, and what Camille said was true, Eric was focused on keeping his wife silent which didn't allow for time to be stalking Erin. It couldn't have been him tonight.

Our heads snapped to the front of the house when we heard the sounds of tires squealing across the pavement outside. We jumped to our feet and rushed to see what the commotion was.

My heart thrashed loud in my ears.

Erin's eyes were wide as she pulled the drapes fully open across the window.

We ducked in the spotlight we found ourselves suddenly inside. A sedan's headlights shined directly into the house and

I feared our cover had been exposed. Thinking we were targets in the line of fire, I shouted, "Get to the side."

We both dove for cover behind the wall, assuming our positions in opposite corners, continuing to keep our eyes on the dark sedan. The headlights dimmed and suddenly the driver door swung open.

I blinked, cursing my eyes for not adjusting to the change in light quick enough.

Squinting, I followed the dark shadow as it got closer to the house. "It's Susan," I exhaled, watching her leap to the front door.

Erin lunged across the floor and ushered Susan inside. "Thank God it's you."

"Allison said I would find you here." Susan smiled and reached for both our hands. "She told me everything. I'm glad you're both safe." Susan squeezed our hands.

"What are you doing here?" I asked.

"I was just with Christy Jones." Susan dropped Erin's hand and turned to face me. "Sam, she identified Mystery Man."

I shared a knowing glance with Erin over Susan's left shoulder. "Who is he?"

"If her memory is correct, she said his name is John Standard and is the owner of Thornton Storage Units."

"The key!" Erin moved to her opened laptop on the kitchen table.

"Storage unit #67." I flipped around and gathered my things.

Erin followed my shadow, quickly shouting off the address in Thornton. "Sam, it still could be a trap," she warned.

"We have to try," I said. "Something is there this man wants us to know about. Something he insists will get me—get us—to solve this case."

Susan stepped forward. "Erin is right, Sam. This doesn't feel right."

The ringtone from my cellphone sliced through the tense air. Reaching for it in my coat pocket, I glanced to the screen and said, "It's Detective King."

"Tell him, Sam," Erin insisted. "Tell him everything."

I answered his call and held my phone to my ear. "Alex, please tell me you have good news."

"No one is at the Fosters' house, Sam."

"Shit."

Susan's eyes danced across my face.

"I also spoke with the gate attendant and he hadn't received notice of any domestic violence. You haven't heard from Camille again, have you?"

"No," I said, hearing my voice crack. I then caught King up on learning the name of Mystery Man. "According to Philip Price's campaign manager, Christy Jones, his name is John Standard. Owns Thornton Storage Unit. That's where the key goes, Alex." I flicked my eyes to Erin. "We need that key. I'm sending Erin to get it now."

The phone line crackled.

"Did you hear what I said?" I wondered if I had lost him. "Erin is coming to get the key." I could still hear him breathing but something had distracted him. "Alex, did you hear me?"

"Hang on," King said.

"I don't have time for this." I clenched my jaw. "John Standard might have just been here."

"I'm going to have to call you back."

"What?" I barked.

"Sam, Eric Foster just pulled into the driveway."

My heart stopped. "Is Camille with him?"

King's pause was long enough to tell me she wasn't. But then he confirmed what I already suspected. "No. There is no sign of Camille. Eric Foster is alone."

CHAPTER SIXTY-FOUR

ALEX KING FISTED HIS SMARTPHONE INSIDE HIS HAND and watched as Eric Foster stepped out of his car, stumbling.

Alvarez held up his hand and shook his head. They would wait for Eric to come to them. The approach was slow and it gave King time to assess his suspect.

Eric's hair was disheveled and a cocky grin split his face in two. His collar was open, his shirt untucked. *Where did Eric just come from and was he the person stalking Erin Tate?* King's gaze fell to the suspect's feet.

Eric stepped into the light.

King couldn't identify the make of his shoes. He allowed his gaze to float back up to Eric's face but stopped short when he noticed blood on his collar.

"What happened?" King pointed to Eric's neck.

"It's been a doozy of a day," Eric slurred.

King felt his brows pull together. "Are you drunk?"

Eric's head floated back and forth on his shoulders as he chuckled.

King shared a look with Alvarez. They both took a step

closer, carefully approaching the suspect in case he decided to try to flee the scene.

"Why don't we talk inside?" King offered.

Eric's eyes couldn't look at him straight. King noticed his body tipping forward and, before Eric could fall, King caught him by the arm and told him to take a seat on the front steps leading up to his million-dollar home.

Alvarez moved to Eric's car and peeked his head inside the opened door. Sniffing around, Alvarez looked up at the house and nodded at his partner. He could smell the scent of booze, and Mr. Foster had been drinking and driving.

"It will come off," King said, staring at Eric wiping the scuff mark from his right shoe. "Those look nice. What are they, Neiman Marcus?"

Eric laughed. "My wife loves these shoes." His glossed eyes lifted to King's. "Don't tell her, but I think it's stupid to spend so much on a pair of shoes."

Alvarez joined them at the steps with his hands buried in his pockets. "Tom Ford edition?"

"That's right." Eric stared at Alvarez, looking genuinely impressed.

King flinched when a whiff of Eric's flammable breath hit him in the face. The dude was toasted. "Where is your wife, Mr. Foster?"

Eric continued shining his shoes. "Not here."

"Did you take her somewhere?"

Eric's chin hit his chest and King watched his head bob like a buoy in the ocean.

"Mr. Foster, how many drinks have you had tonight?" Alvarez asked.

Eric's eyes hid behind hooded lids when he looked up. "Not enough."

"What is it a man like you drinks, anyway?" Alvarez scratched his chin.

"If I had his kind of money," King smiled with delight, "I would drink nothing but rare imports."

"No, I would keep it real. Coors Light would be my drink of choice." Alvarez flicked his gaze to Eric. "So, what is it, Mr. Foster? Foreign imports or Coors Light?"

Eric perched his elbows on his knees and said, "You're both wrong. Me, I like Tom Collins."

"Huh. That's interesting," Alvarez said. "Now that you say it, you look like a Tom Collins kind of guy."

"We would really like to talk with your wife," King said.

"So would I." Eric's spine rounded as he inhaled a deep pained breath. Then he closed his eyes and murmured, "But I don't think she'll be talking to anybody anytime soon."

King and Alvarez shared a knowing look. Alvarez nodded to King. Afraid their assumption about Eric was right, they could only assume Camille might now be dead.

"How did you get that blood on your shirt?" Alvarez asked.

Eric tucked his chin into his chest and struggled to see what both detectives saw. "That's not blood. Must have been from lunch."

Unwilling to believe Eric's story, King asked, "Did you do something to your wife, Mr. Foster?"

Eric rolled his neck and glanced at King. "Is that what this is about? Did she call you? Is that why you're here?" He shook his head and started laughing. "Mother fucker. That bitch just couldn't keep her mouth shut."

"How about you come down to the station with us and answer a couple of questions." Alvarez's tone had changed. He took a step forward and hovered over Eric Foster.

"Over my dead body." Eric stood and stared. "I'm calling my lawyer."

"Fine. But you'll have to do it at the station. After you've been booked for drunk driving."

King tossed on the cuffs and escorted Eric Foster into the back of their cruiser without much resistance. When the door was shut, he turned to his partner.

"What are we going to tell Captain?" Alvarez's head tipped back on his broad shoulders.

"The truth."

Alvarez answered with a look.

"Captain will understand." King lowered his voice, staring through the glass at a drunk Mr. Foster. He had his eyes closed, slumped in his seat with a look of defeat on his face. "Besides, you heard what he said his preferred drink is."

"And the shoes." Alvarez nodded.

"That's no coincidence. This bastard killed those women and he probably killed his wife, too. If that isn't reason enough for the judge to sign off on a warrant to search this place, we've got bigger problems on our hands."

Alvarez nodded. "You thinking what I'm thinking?"

"I wish I wasn't, but until we see what's inside that house, finding Camille Foster remains our highest priority."

"If she isn't dead already."

CHAPTER SIXTY-FIVE

"No, I just won't let you do it." Susan blinked rapidly.

Erin shifted her weight and couldn't stop staring. Her round eyes followed me wherever I moved. The way she was looking at me was something new. I had never seen it before. Not on her. Erin cared and was worried that I might be making a mistake.

"This isn't your decision to make," I said to both of them.

Erin folded her arms tightly across her chest and cocked out a hip. "I'm with Susan. I don't like this idea."

Tying my hair up into a messy knot on top of my head, I said, "There are only three of us." My eyes shifted between them. "We have to split up."

"No, Samantha." Susan shook her head adamantly. "You can't go chasing someone you know nothing about."

My toes curled into the soles of my shoe. "Who do we think is killing these women?"

"Eric Foster," Erin said.

I raised my eyebrows. "And King said that Eric Foster just

showed up to his own house. We know where the danger is and the police have him contained."

"Maybe you're right," Susan's jaw loosened, "but we still know nothing about this John Standard guy."

"If John Standard is Mystery Man, he's been our invisible friend throughout all of this. There is nothing to worry about." My stomach clenched, hoping what I said was true.

Erin shared a look with Susan. Then Erin rolled her eyes back to me. "You have a point."

"Thank you." I sighed and pulled my car keys out of my pocket. "I'll have my cellphone with me at all times and if something doesn't feel right, I'll get out of there."

I stared into Erin's eyes, taking in the beautiful golden hair cascading down the front of her shoulders. If there was anybody's safety to worry about, it was hers. She had already been stalked tonight but, on top of that, she also shared enough of the qualities that seemed to be getting our victims killed. As far as I was concerned, if anybody was in danger it was Erin. She would go to the station to get the key. King would make sure she was safe. And Susan would go to my house to make sure Mason didn't become a target.

"The storage unit probably won't even be open," I said, reaching for the door handle.

"We'll call you as soon as we have the key." Erin blew out a heavy sigh.

"Looking forward to it." I smiled, shared one last look with each of my friends, and stepped outside into the dark cold night, determined to finally face Mystery Man once and for all.

I blasted the heat on my short drive north, despite my hot blood pumping and keeping my core warm. The dropping temperature outside was the least of my concerns. I drove without being overly aggressive. My mind jumped between scattered thoughts that led me nowhere good.

I thought about where our investigation had begun and what information led me to chasing after a name I had never heard of until tonight. Christy Jones identified Mystery Man and connected him to Camille Foster. She was someone I could trust, even if we weren't the best of friends. But Susan saw Camille act surprised by Mystery Man showing up to Philip Price's gala and that was something I believed in 110%. Then there was the call from Camille, and me seeing Eric's rage first-hand. I wasn't making any of this up. It was as real as the night.

I'd solve this case.

That's what Mystery Man had prophesied. It could only mean one thing. That he knew the Fosters intimately and had dirt on them that no one else knew. And, for whatever reason, wanted me to know about it, too.

I crossed the line into Thornton and pulled into the poorly lit storage unit. My nerves kept my face tight and I was surprised it was still open. Parking my car in front of the office, I pulled my keys from the ignition, preparing myself for the worst.

The breeze caught a loose strand of hair when I stepped out. Zipping up my coat, I was completely alone. Not even another car was here, but the lights were on inside and I headed to the front door.

I pulled open the glass door only to find the office completely empty.

Nobody was around but it had the feeling of someone not too far away. Slowly, I moved to the desk, perking my ears at the slightest of sounds, beginning my search.

"Hello," I announced my arrival.

My head swiveled around on my shoulders.

Again, no response.

I felt my heartrate tick up a notch higher with each minute that passed.

Pushing my way through the back-office door, again the overhead light was on but nobody was around. I searched on top of the desk, looking for clues. There were no photos I could turn to, only Denver Bronco memorabilia. It gave me nothing.

Then I hit the brakes and stopped breathing.

There, on the coatrack behind the door, hung a brimmed hat and matching overcoat. It was the same as the one Mystery Man wore in the video surveillance.

"Christy was right," I whispered to myself.

Mystery Man *was* John Standard.

But where was he, and why wasn't his car outside? And why did he leave Erin's if he truly did want to help us solve this case?

I turned slowly to the front of the building with the strange sense of being watched. Holding my breath, I listened closely for sounds while my mind raced.

Feeling my muscles shudder, I didn't have a good feeling about this. But I couldn't place what or where that feeling was coming from other than the man I'd come to speak with was nowhere to be found.

I pulled my cellphone from my pocket and snapped a quick photo of the brimmed hat and overcoat. Then I sent it to Erin with the message, *It's him. John Standard is Mystery Man. Except he's not here. I'm heading to the storage unit now.*

CHAPTER SIXTY-SIX

ALEX KING STARED FROM ACROSS THE ROOM AT ERIC Foster, a scowl permanently stamped on his face. "Why isn't he in the interrogation room for questioning?"

Alvarez shrugged. "Procedure."

King shook his head. "We need to get him talking while he's still drunk."

"Go ahead. Disobey another direct order. Me, I'm going to wait."

Lieutenant Baker walked up on them. "Read your initial report. Good work, men."

"He has blood on his collar, Lieu." King flipped his palms to the ceiling, anxious to keep working. "We're wasting time."

"You heard him. He requested his lawyer and that's it." Lieutenant's look hardened. "This isn't new, King."

"Did you see what shoes he's wearing? I did. The same shoes our witness, Kristin Newsome, said he was wearing the night she escaped. What more do we need?"

"He admitted to drinking Tom Collins tonight, too," Alvarez added.

"I'm not going to argue." Lieutenant stuffed his hands inside his suit pants pockets. "His lawyer refused to answer any questions until he reviewed the evidence presented by the DA's office." He cocked a brow and rolled his eyes to King. "Any word on the whereabouts of Camille Foster?"

Alvarez furrowed his brow. "Still no sign of Camille Foster. No one has heard or seen her since early this afternoon."

"Her cell is off," King added. "We have a patrol car parked outside their house giving us updates."

"And?"

"The house is still quiet. No has been in or out since we left."

"The bastard probably offed his wife and dumped her body before we found him," Alvarez grumbled. When no one responded, he lifted his head and said, "Why else would he have blood on his collar?"

Lieutenant's gaze never left Eric Foster. "Mr. Foster maintains his innocence and says he has been set up but can't say by whom."

"He wants to talk," King said.

"But not without his lawyer."

"We need to get a confession." King's phone buzzed. It was a text message from Erin Tate. He glanced to his partner. "I gotta go retrieve this key."

Alvarez folded his arms and puffed out his chest. "I'll call if there is any movement."

"Don't let that asshole out of your sight," King said, pointing his finger at Eric.

Pushing his thick fingers through his hair, King took the stairs down to forensics. He was sure they had caught their killer. Eric Foster acted guilty. But what really kept King itching was the fact that he had to wait while knowing Camille Foster was still missing.

He hoped Camille was alive, but where would she be? It wasn't like someone of her status to completely go off the grid without someone knowing something. They had to keep talking, keep looking.

King stiff-armed his way into forensics. The doors shut behind him. He greeted the officer working the desk. "You have the key I asked you to check out?"

"Got it right here." He produced a key inside a plastic bag and handed it over to King.

King stuffed it inside his breast pocket. "Anything?"

"Mark, in the back, knew what it was and where it went the moment he saw it." The officer nodded. "Goes to a lock issued by Thornton Storage Unit."

"And Mark knew all this how?" King suddenly remembered Sam and not following up with her after Eric Foster arrived at his home. She'd said something about the same storage unit, and now he wanted to know what.

"Said he has a unit there himself." The officer locked eyes with King. "Recognized the engraving immediately. He has the same key, just a different number."

"Thanks," King said.

His heart raced. He started back upstairs, putting a call in to Sam. The line clicked over to voicemail. He cursed and then left a message. "Sam, I have the key. You were right. It goes to Thornton Storage Unit. Call me back. We need to go there together. Pronto."

As soon as he hung up, he pushed his worry for Sam to the side and messaged Erin.

Got the key. Where are you?

Once back on his floor, King approached his partner and said, "Key goes to Thornton Storage Unit."

Alvarez gave King an arched look. "Who's the unit rented out to?"

King shrugged. "I'm going to check it out."

"What? Now?"

King's phone buzzed with a text from Erin.

Outside the station. Coming up now.

King nodded and moved his eyes to Eric Foster. He lowered his jaw and said, "Something tells me that whatever is there might help lock him away for good."

CHAPTER SIXTY-SEVEN

I EDGED THE BUILDING WITH MY BACK PRESSED UP AGAINST the wall. My nerves jumped and I fumbled when pulling up the flashlight app on my cellphone. But, before flicking it on, I took a moment to catch my breath.

The hum of traffic filled the air.

John Standard was here. I could feel it.

My pulse throbbed in my neck and it was all I could hear in my ears. The office lights shone to my left but, to my right it was pitch black. I stared into that dark abyss, knowing it was the direction I needed to head. Something told me John was already waiting. He was there, inside unit #67 as if knowing I would come for him tonight.

Beneath my coat, I was sweating despite the plummeting temperatures. Each breath I exhaled reminded me of the season. Winter was coming and I shivered, but not because I was cold. When my thoughts returned to Susan and Erin making the case for me to not go this alone, I now understood their concern. But it was too late. I was here and determined to finally speak with John, the Mystery Man who seemed to have all the answers.

There is nothing to be afraid of, I tried to convince myself. But it was useless.

Even I couldn't fool myself into believing that I wasn't walking straight into a trap. I was so close I couldn't back out now even though I'd promised I would. Being only feet away from discovering what waited for me, I couldn't resist the temptation it presented.

Samantha Bell will solve this case.

I kept hearing the statement play on repeat inside my head. I wanted it to be true.

This case was mine.

Since Mallory, I had never wanted to write the end of the story as badly as I did this one. It kept me from quitting. Picked me up when I lost steam. This was more than solving a case. It was giving each of the victims the tribute they deserved.

I picked up my feet and began to move.

My pupils were fully open as I swept my eyes across the dark horizon in front of me. I was light of my feet, moving stealthily in the cover of darkness. The stars were twinkling bright on this moonless night and I was thankful for what little street light made its way into these dark corners I traveled.

Rounding the building, I tripped over a stray cat. It screeched and darted into the shadows as I fell heavily into the cold metal siding. My heart was still lodged in my throat and I felt it beat wild against my trachea for a minute before finally catching my breath.

Somewhere in the distance, sirens wailed.

I flipped on my flashlight. The sword of light shone bright and I turned to see what unit I was leaning against.

Fifty-five.

Time to move.

Crouching low, I counted the numbers up until I found myself slowing one unit before 67.

Inhaling a deep, frozen breath, I inched closer. Shining the light on the lock, my eyes widened as I gasped. "Holy shit, I was right." The padlock dangled open but the door was latched close.

My heart knocked loud and fast against my chest.

I looked behind me before sliding the padlock free. Bending at the knees, I slid open the door—it rattled loud— and I shined my light inside.

I stared with bulging eyes, feeling my jaw come unhinged.

A large, attractive man sat in the back corner, staring bright-eyed directly at me, wearing only his underwear. It was easy to imagine his charm, the way he would turn heads when wearing a nice suit. He had that look about him, even as he shivered in the cold and tried to speak past the ball gag strapped to his head.

I approached slowly, wrestling with my own thoughts to turn back and call King.

Blood dribbled from the bridge of his nose. His eyes were bloodshot red and full of terror. He didn't move—couldn't because of the restraints.

On a foldout table lay boxes of equipment. I shined the light inside each, quick to recognize the items. They matched the evidence collected inside each hotel room the victims had been killed in. Next to them, pictures of Eric Foster with Mallory, Darcy, and Jaime. *Where was Kristin? Why wasn't she here?*

Turning my head slowly, I looked to the man. "Are you John Standard?"

He nodded his head enthusiastically, his words muffled and incoherent.

"Is this what you wanted me to know about?" I asked, pointing to the boxes and pictures.

John nodded his head again. His breathing was loud as he worked deep, wheezy breaths through his broken nose.

Keeping the light on John, I assessed the way he was masterfully bound. My scalp prickled with fear but I knew I needed to help him. Kneeling in front of John, I perched my cellphone on the table behind me and worked to unclasp the mouth gag from behind his head. His shoulders were covered with swollen lash marks. Small cuts across his back had bloodied and dried. He had been beaten, but by whom?

John didn't resist.

His body continued to shake against the cold and I knew he was close to hypothermia.

"We need to get you out of here," I said, peeling the gag away from his head and hearing the sound of suction pop as it was freed from his mouth.

John coughed and gagged. "It's too late," he said. "I thought I could help but I can't."

"It's not too late," I tried to reason.

The big man started to cry. "I should have been clearer in my message. I waited too long."

With one hand on his bare shoulder, I asked, "Who did this to you?"

He lifted his head and I watched his eyes land on the person behind me. His gaze was full of love and regret that didn't match the next words he uttered. "She did."

A loud pop blasted in my left ear.

An explosion of red detonated from John's shoulder.

John's hot blood splattered on my face as I gasped.

I whipped around without time to duck. Time slowed to a crawl as I watched the blunt edge of a hard object connect to the side of my skull. The intense stinging of pain was all I registered before I realized what had happened. Everything came to a screeching halt.

Losing my balance, I fell onto my back. The back of my

skull cracked on the concrete floor—my head ringing loud in my ears—and then my lights went out.

CHAPTER SIXTY-EIGHT

ALEX KING MET ERIN TATE AT THE ENTRANCE OF THE Denver Police Station.

He pinched the storage unit key between his fingers and dangled it in the air between them. "It's a storage unit in Thornton."

Erin's lips parted. "Shit," she breathed.

King's brows slanted and watched Erin turn sideways and thread her fingers through her hair.

She twisted back to face Alex. "Sam is there now."

"You let her go alone?" King's pulse quickened.

Erin tossed her hands down to her sides in frustration. She craned her neck and said, "She tried to tell you."

King stared, realizing the severity of his mistake. Knowing they didn't have time to debate who was in the wrong, King said, "We'll take my car. Let's go."

Erin kept pace with King as they weaved their way through the rows of parked cars. King lifted his key fob and pointed it toward his sedan. The lights flicked as it beeped unlocked. Jumping inside, King was quick to start the car and race to the exit, telling Erin, "Hold on."

Erin gave her seatbelt a couple hard tugs, testing its integrity. She nodded, deciding she was safe.

Pointing the vehicle's nose into traffic, King flipped on his emergency lights and raced north.

"How did you two figure it out?" King asked, keeping one hand on the wheel and an eye on the road.

Erin kept her eyes forward, wanting to give King an extra pair of eyes when blowing past the posted speed limit. "It started with a Facebook message," Erin began. "Then Sam's friend, Susan Young, connected Camille Foster to Mystery Man," she turned to look at King, "the same man who gave Sam that key."

"But how did you connect that key to Thornton Storage Unit?"

"Susan asked Christy Jones if she could identify the man who'd given her the key."

King flicked his eyes to Erin. "Christy Jones, from Philip Price's campaign?"

Erin nodded. "Christy had met him. Was introduced to him by Camille Foster. His name is John Standard, owner of Thornton Storage Unit."

"Jesus." King's muscles flexed.

"Alex," Erin sat up in her seat, "John is the one who said Sam would solve this case."

King swerved around traffic, his brow deepening with worry the more Erin explained the sudden connection to both the storage unit key and Camille Foster.

"Whatever is inside that storage unit..." Erin's voice faded.

"Will implicate Eric Foster."

Erin nodded. "John Standard knows something and wants Samantha to share it with the world. And whatever it is will tell us who has been killing these women."

King scrubbed a hand over his face and rolled a heavy gaze to Erin. "We can't find Camille."

Erin gripped the grab handle above her head, squeezing the crease between her eyebrows tighter. "Alex, where is Eric Foster?"

"Eric is in custody." He pressed his foot down on the accelerator and increased his speed exponentially. "He's lawyered up. Isn't saying shit." King weaved through traffic with a steady hand.

"But he killed those women, right?"

King lowered his brow and didn't answer.

"You don't know or can't to say? This is all off record," she reminded him.

King flicked his gaze to Erin and held her stare for a second.

"Alex, do you think he's the one behind these killings or not?"

"Let's hope he is." King paused. "Because, if he's not, then the killer is still out there hunting his next victim."

Erin's eyes rounded into large discs as she turned her focus forward. A stone lodged in her throat, which Erin struggled to swallow down.

They were both afraid to admit what King knew they were both now thinking. His knuckles went white on the wheel with anger. He wanted to lecture Sam on the dangers of going to the storage unit in the dark of night alone. He promised he would when he found her.

His stomach flopped.

Though he didn't want to admit it, the thought had crossed his mind, and he began imagining a world without Samantha Bell.

King glanced in Erin's direction. Though she didn't turn to look, he knew she was also thinking the same dreadful thought.

"I need you to be on top of your game," he murmured.

Without looking, Erin nodded.

But what King couldn't say was how he not only needed Erin's mind to be sharp, he needed her to stay strong, remain confident, and not fall to the temptation of being timid. There was too much at stake and he couldn't be sure what they were going to find once they arrived.

Spinning the steering wheel, King applied pressure to the brakes and slowed the car when passing through the storage unit's entrance gate. His heart knocked against his ribs, the sound of his blood thrashing inside his ears. Keeping his clammy hands on the wheel, he crept closer to the office.

"The office lights are on." Erin released her grip above and began looking around. "It's still open."

As difficult as it was, King remained optimistic. "And there is Sam's car." He pointed.

Erin's knee bounced and she was already out of her seat-belt by the time King parked next to Sam's car. King kicked his door open and they stepped out, looking around for any sign of life.

"It's too quiet," Erin whispered against the breeze.

The cold air caught beneath King's collar as he headed inside. "They're not here," he said, finding the office completely empty. He turned and glanced to Erin

"They must be at the bin."

"C'mon, let's go," King skirted around Erin, pushing his way through the glass door.

Erin followed.

"Stay behind me." King put his hand on his gun, safely tucked away in the holster attached to his hip. "I don't know what we're walking into, but something tells me it's not good."

CHAPTER SIXTY-NINE

THE PRESSURE IN MY HEAD WAS UNBEARABLE.

The vice squeezed, then released, and did it all over again.

I blinked, as if waking from a dream. My eyes were glued shut by my gummy lids. It felt like I had been drugged, my mind not quite fully awake. Certainly not present to the reality of the situation I was in. And when I went to move my arm, I couldn't.

My arms and legs felt paralyzed—heavy and stiff.

I lifted my head, pushing through the intense agony of pain, and glanced down the length of my body.

Again, I tried to move but couldn't. I squinted but couldn't see my feet. They were there because I knew I was wiggling my toes. "I'm not dead," I said when I released my neck muscles and allowed my head to sink into the soft mattress where I lay.

After a couple excruciating breaths, I rolled my head to the side and peered at the restraints binding my wrists to the bedframe. "No," I cried. *What did I do?*

The strength of my eyes was back but did me little good. I couldn't see where I was, couldn't gauge my surroundings. It was just me, tied to this bed, struggling to remember how I'd gotten here in the first place.

A bright light shined directly down upon me, making it impossible see past the barrier of light. It was a curtain of blinding white and was certainly done on purpose.

Movement perked my ears.

I felt my pulse quicken as I watched a shadowy silhouette drift behind the curtain like a shadow caught in the wind.

The smell of booze had me even more confused. My skin felt drowned in it but I knew I hadn't been drinking. "Where am I?"

"A place they won't find you," a familiar voice said.

I focused on my breathing. *Was I at a hotel or motel?* "You're making a mistake."

"I'll be the judge of that."

I snapped my elbow, cracking the restraints tight. *Snap!* There was little give and the more I thrashed in an effort to set myself free, the tighter it seemed to get.

A small cackle filled the air.

I felt the mattress dip beneath her weight. Camille's eyes raked the length of my exposed body, trailing her sharp nails up my bare leg before landing her reptilian eyes directly on mine. The memory of John Standard getting shot sent tremors of fear throughout my body.

"How did you get me here?" I asked.

Camille swung her right leg over her left knee and folded her hands on top of her thigh. She stared and smirked like she was genius at being able to figure out the logistics of kidnapping me without raising suspicion.

I hated how amazingly put together she looked. Her evenly pressed dress and flawless hair. I despised everything about her. Camille's makeup was as perfect as her diamond earrings catching the light, sprinkling the glittering rays of light to the far corners of the motel room.

"Incredible what people believe when the story is spun right." She grinned.

I coughed. The scratchy itch in the back of my throat was relentless. Each cough sent another throb of pain through my skull, reminding me of the taste of blood that left me suddenly counting each of my wounds. Squeezing my eyes shut, I inhaled a deep breath, finally getting myself to stop coughing.

"Do you recognize this room?" Camille asked.

Opening my eyes once again, Camille angled the light to the wall, allowing me to finally take in the room in its entirety. My gaze traveled the nondescript walls all the way to the toilet. Yellow stains spread like liquid tattoos on the ceiling and there was a musty smell filling the air in the room which was in serious need of a good clean.

"Her name was Mallory Madison and she was the first woman to find herself in a similar room," Camille said as she made her way to the small round table near the cushioned armchair.

"You won't get away with this," I said through clenched teeth.

Camille didn't bother looking up. She opened the bottle of gin, squeezed a couple squirts of lemon juice into her tumbler, mixed in a splash of seltzer water, and finished it off with a sprinkle of sugar.

"Tom Collins," I whispered, kicking myself inside for never suspecting Camille simply because she was a woman. King had profiled the murderer as a man.

Camille wiggled her eyebrows, curled her lips over the rim of her glass, and swallowed down her first sip. "My husband's favorite."

"It's no longer a theory, Camille." Hot air breathed through my nose. "The evidence points to you. We know you

killed Mallory, Darcy, and Jaime." We didn't. We thought it
was Eric.

Camille pulled another sip from her glass, this one bigger
than the last. "Oh, yes. Back to your original question." She
held her glass in front of her as she paced at the foot of the
bed. "How did I get you inside this room, past so many eyes
when you were unconscious?" She stopped, turned to me, and
stared. "You're smart. How would you do it if you were me?"

I felt my heartbeat tick up another notch. "I'd use what
resources I had."

Her lips curled at the corners. "Money does make things
easier. If anyone says it doesn't, it's because they don't have
much." She laughed and took another sip. "Yes, I did use
money, but not much. And that wasn't the genius behind
getting you here without strangers asking too many
questions."

"You didn't drug me—"

"Didn't have to." She floated back to the round table,
picked up the bottle of gin, and flung her hair over her shoulders when she turned to face me.

"So, how did you do it?"

Lowering her brow, her evil grin spread just before she
came to me. I watched her push the flair of her hips wide
with each step she took on her way to me and, when her
thighs came into contact with the edge of the mattress, she
lifted the opened bottle of gin and turned it bottoms-up.

The clear liquid gurgled out of the bottle and spilled
across my chest.

I turned my head away and scrunched my face.

The liquid splattered off my sternum and onto the bed.
The scent of it burned my nostrils raw. I was drenched—
drowning in Camille's gin bath.

Suddenly, it stopped.

"Look at me," Camille demanded.

Slowly, I turned my head and met her gaze. The same smell that I'd woken with was back, ten-fold.

"I said you were drunk and that I needed help carrying you inside." Her eyes flickered like candlelight. "Genius, right?"

My jaw clenched in anger and I flinched with pain shooting down my spine. The swelling on my face felt like a balloon about to pop and I couldn't be sure if my jaw was broken or if my skull had been cracked.

"Really," Camille tilted her head to the side, "men become pathetic little puppy dogs desperate for attention when in the presence of beauty."

At Price's gala she'd made me believe it was her husband who was the narcissist. But it was her. She was the person controlling the room. Like puppets on a string, how many people did she manipulate with her lies? Just me, or were there more?

I stared into Camille's beady eyes, seething with anger, as if finally seeing her for the very first time. She wasn't crying for help. She was the dark, manipulative, controlling figure I had labeled her husband as. Camille was a woman bent on seeking revenge and pursuing it without remorse. She represented everything I despised—everything I wanted to expose. "And that is how you got John to work for you?"

"John was the same as all of them." She giggled and began pacing. Back and forth, back and forth her heels clacked. "From the moment we first met, I knew that I could control him." Camille stopped, hovered over my head, and gripped the restraint on my wrist, testing its strength. "It was his job to lure the women in and get them in a position where I could finish them off. All the while making Eric look guilty. You have to admit, the shoes and drink were genius."

"You sicken me." My breath quickened along with my pulse. "Your husband—"

"Is a fool," she snapped.

Silence filled the room as I stared into her wild eyes.

Then she tossed back her head and released a fitful cackle that electrified the air.

"Did he help you kill these women?" I gripped my restraints and lifted my head off the bed. "And you shot John!" My veins opened up, I was so mad.

"No." Her voice lowered when she pointed her finger at me. "I killed three women. Not Eric. Not John. Only me. I did it myself."

"I don't believe you."

"Eric was the reason I had to kill them." She sucked her cheeks in.

Suddenly, it all made sense. Eric's affairs, the photos of him being seen with each of the victims. It was how Camille knew about them, how she knew where to find them and lure them in. "The humiliation you must have felt," I said.

Camille turned her back and stared at the drawn drapes. She said nothing for a long pause and then turned her head toward me and whispered, "Eric should have never been so open with his affairs."

"Why kill the women?" I asked. "Why not kill him instead?"

Camille cast her gaze to the floor and lightly chuckled. "You must admit, The Lady Killer was a nice touch, don't you think?" Camille faced me head-on. "And the connection to Price?" She arched a brow. "It was so much fun watching you and the police chase your tail in circles."

"Then why shoot John tonight?"

"Because he ruined what was the perfect plan." Camille set her empty glass down on the table. "It was perfect. I had it all laid out. Eric would be accused of the murders and, just when the police were closing in on him, I would disappear and make it look like he killed me, too."

The distress call, I remembered. She'd played me when she'd called, all worried that Eric would kill her next. I wondered if King had found a way inside the Foster house and what was waiting for him inside when he did.

"What you don't understand about my husband," Camille folded her fingers in front of her, "besides that he is a cheating bastard, is that he doesn't understand consequences. For a man who believed he could get away with anything and not have to face the penalties of his actions, I wanted him to know what it felt like to have the entire world turn on him."

"What happened to you?"

"John had a change of heart. And when I discovered what John was trying to do with you—" she dropped her head into her hand, pinched the bridge of her nose, and shook her head. "John wasn't the man I thought he was."

"He did the right thing when giving me the key."

"It was an idiotic thing to do," Camille snapped. "You were looking at everyone but me. Your silly theories only strengthened my own. Even the ones yet to be told."

"You killed him!" I spat.

"He killed himself the moment he stopped following orders," Camille screamed.

Her chest rose and fell as she stared. I watched her eyelids hood and I knew she was no longer present. Stuck somewhere deep inside her twisted head. I glanced to the exit with an intense desire to flee.

The room darkened.

My pulse ticked hard and fast when Camille dove her hand inside a black duffel bag on the floor. When she came up, I yelled, "Help me!"

Her hand flung over my mouth.

Jumping on the bed, Camille straddled my waist and pushed a pillow over my face. Picking my head up, I fought back as best I could but it was useless. I couldn't move— couldn't fight back.

Camille pressed the pillow harder into my mouth.

I gagged and coughed, struggling to breathe.

When the pillow came off my face, I gasped once and filled my lungs before I felt the rope Camille worked around my neck during the struggle, tighten and squeeze.

My eyes bulged and now I was certain I would die.

Baring her teeth in front of my eyes, she said, "Shame that I have to kill you, too. You had so much promise." She twisted the stick tied to the rope tighter around my arteries. "Then again, so did the others."

CHAPTER SEVENTY

"THIS WAY." ALEX KING'S HANDS WERE SWEATY AS HE counted off the numbered bins.

Forties, fifties, sixties.

Erin was one step behind, her hand lightly touching King's shoulder for guidance while running in the dark. When King slowed, she hit the brakes and they both dug in their heels when King stopped and shined the light on bin #67.

He turned and glanced over his shoulder, sharing a knowing look with Erin.

They breathed hard, their lungs desperate for air, each breath crystalizing against the cold temperature. Time slowed and sounds ceased to exist when King lowered the beam of light to the lock.

A padlock dangled on the door.

Erin lunged forward, impatience getting the best of her. She pulled on the padlock as hard as she could. It rattled but refused to open. She jerked and tried again, this time putting more muscle and weight into her tug. Still, nothing happened.

King grabbed her arm. "It's locked."

"This doesn't make sense," she said, taking a step back. "Sam should be here."

King fished out the key from inside his jacket pocket. Inhaling a deep breath of air, he lined the key up with the keyhole but the key refused to fit. "Shit."

"It doesn't work?" Panic rose in Erin's voice.

King shook his head, bending closer to the padlock. "It's the wrong key."

"It has to fit." Erin held her stomach with both hands.

A grumbling sound rustled from inside the bin.

They both held their breath and angled their ears closer to the door.

Another grumble.

"Someone's inside." Erin pounded the flat of her hand on the door. She feared it might be Sam. Adrenaline pumped fast through her veins. "Sam, is that you?"

"Help me," a weak voice said against chattering teeth.

"Did you hear that?" Erin turned to King. King nodded. "What do we do?"

King glanced to his palm. His mind scrambled as he searched for a plan. The key matched the bin number but why not the padlock? It must have been changed. With a racing heart and the persistent fear that something had happened to Sam, he said, "Stay here."

"Where are you going?"

"If anyone comes, hide." King took off, running.

Erin tossed her hands up and cursed.

King's strides lengthened as he darted straight for the trunk of his car. He popped the latch with his key fob and dug his heels into the pavement, skidding to a stop at his car. Diving his hands inside the trunk, he searched.

King had a shotgun, extra ammunition, a first aid kit, and bolt cutters. He grabbed the bolt cutters and first aid kit, slammed the trunk shut, and took off running back to Erin.

When Erin was sure that the figure sprinting toward her was Detective King, she hurried to him, reaching for the first aid kit. King fought with the cutters, growling through gritted teeth and straining muscle until the lock finally snapped.

Bending one knee, he swung the bin door open and Erin shined the light inside.

A nearly naked man lay in his own blood on the cold concrete floor, struggling to breathe.

They both stared speechless for a moment that suspended time. Ignoring the items on the table, King raced toward the wounded man and skidded on one knee, beginning to apply pressure to the stranger's injury.

"It's a gunshot wound," he said to Erin. "Call for help."

Erin pulled out her phone and dialed 9-1-1.

"What's your name?" King worked his arms free, took his coat off, and wrapped it around the man, hoping to keep him warm long enough to survive.

"John." His teeth clacked. "John Standard."

"John, you're going to be all right."

"I'm going to die."

"No, you're not." King pushed into his wound harder. The pulse of blood grew weaker by the second. "Help is on the way."

John closed his eyes and sighed.

"John, I need you to look at me." John's eyes formed tiny slits when he opened them. They lacked life, like water freezing. "Who shot you?"

"Camille Foster." He struggled to swallow. "She kidnapped a woman—"

"Samantha Bell."

John's eyes closed as he gave a small nod.

Erin stepped back inside the small rectangular box. "An ambulance is on its way."

King twisted around and flicked his eyes on Erin. "Camille has Sam."

Erin's brow wrinkled. "Where are they?"

John's eyes were closed again, his breathing fading in and out.

"John, stay with us. You can do it. It won't be long." King tipped John's face up. John opened his eyes and stared through a dull gaze. "Do you know where she took Samantha Bell?"

John parted his dry, cracked lips. He tried to speak but nothing came out.

King lowered his head and put his ear next to John's mouth. "Can you say that again?"

John whispered the location in King's ear. King whipped his head around to Erin. "She's at a motel in Northglenn. I-25 and 104th. Not too far from here."

"Go." Erin sprang forward and pressed the palm of her hand over King's. "I'll stay with him."

King pulled his hands free and sprinted to his car, determined to save Sam before he lost her for good.

CHAPTER SEVENTY-ONE

I FLEXED MY THIGH MUSCLES IN AN ATTEMPT TO KICK MY feet. Each second without a fresh breath of air was a second closer to death. But I could hardly feel the pain in my lungs, only feeling the pain in my heart at what would happen to Mason.

I needed to fight back. Camille was more determined than ever to see her plan through. I'd gotten in her way. Given her a hurdle to jump over, and now I wondered if I hadn't made a grave mistake in doing so.

Camille's facial muscles strained as she twisted the rope around my neck tighter.

I bucked my hips but Camille absorbed each thrash—each bump—with her thick thighs.

"When they find you dead, everyone will think it was Eric, too."

The rope fibers cut into my neck. The restraints dug deeper into my ankles and wrists. I felt my life being taken away with each new twist. With watering eyes, my vision blurred.

I don't fit the profile, I wanted to respond.

"Too bad you aren't his type," Camille said, as if reading my mind. "I suppose if your friend, Erin, would have taken your place, it would have been more fitting. What is it with blonds anyway?" Her eyes narrowed. "Doesn't matter. The evidence left behind here will be too overwhelming to not make the connection. Tom Collins, check. Tom Ford shoes, check."

I held her eyes inside of mine, not wanting to concede to the reality of her already having won the fight. My heart still beat, my mind still scrambled to find a way out.

Saying a quick prayer, I had to keep the faith.

I was afraid I only had minutes to live. This wasn't how I'd seen my life ending.

Camille squeezed and my fight dimmed.

I thought about Mason and him visiting both his parents' gravestones. Tears fell from my eyes. I blankly stared at the ceiling with an aching heart. I wanted to say goodbye to my girlfriends, thank them for being the support system I needed in my life. For all the laughs and cries we'd shared, and the future ones I would miss. They had always been there for me, and I hoped they knew I would always be there for them as well.

"You're almost there," Camille breathed.

My tongue swelled. My body jerked as the cells in my body begged for oxygen.

When my vision tunneled into a dark abyss, I saw Alex and felt the pang of regret twist my side. Suddenly, I wished I had acted on the feelings I had for him.

"There you go, baby." Camille stroked my cold cheek with her free hand. "I can see it in your eyes, Sam." She tapped my cheekbone. "Look at me."

I refused, enjoying my thoughts drifting someplace else.

Camille pinched my cheeks and jerked my head, forcing

our eyes to meet. "I want my face to be the last impression you see before you depart this earth forever."

My limbs went limp. The blood slowed and I felt a strange sense of contentment fall over me. Camille proved too strong. There was nothing I could do to stop her from killing me.

I was just like the victims. Where they were lured in with the promise of sex, we were both surprised by the betrayal. Even the strongest among them didn't have a chance. We all would go into the next life remembering the person who'd put us in the ground.

A splintering sound exploded from behind Camille.

The door flung open with a bang.

Camille tightened her grip, even as she turned her head to look behind her.

Suddenly, a large body flew through the air, tackling Camille to the ground.

The first full breath of air stung like hell, but I kept gulping down the oxygen my body craved. Slowly, my vision came back, the strength in my limbs along with it. There wasn't an ounce of me that didn't hurt but I kept sucking back more air.

King's head popped up over the side of the bed and I wanted to laugh. Instead, I cried. Tears streamed down my cheeks. He'd saved me, but it felt like divine intervention.

"Are you okay?" he asked.

I nodded. "I'll live."

Camille struggled and cried out as King pinned her to the floor with his knee. He slapped a pair of cuffs around her wrists and read her her rights. She responded with threats King chose to ignore. Standing, King yanked Camille off the floor and moved her to the opposite side of the room. Sitting her down against the wall, King turned to me.

My stomach fluttered at the sight.

I smirked, so happy to see him.

He peeled the sheets back and respectfully covered me up —always the gentleman—before moving to unclasp my limbs from their restraints.

"Alex," I watched him work, "Camille shot the owner of Thornton Storage Unit."

King was gentle and quiet as he worked. "We found John. Erin is with him now."

"Is he going to be all right?"

King shared a small glance. "I don't know. He was in pretty bad shape when we got to him."

He helped me sit up when I was free. I stared at Camille and rubbed life back into my raw wrists. "She confessed. Told me everything about how she murdered the women and why." Camille scowled. I turned my head to King. "She wanted it to look like it was her husband."

Alex gave me a knowing smile. "Relax, Samantha. It's finally over."

King might have been right but I didn't know how I could relax. I needed a cool down from the race we'd just run. Needed a shower to clean off the scum left over from Camille breathing down my neck. Wanted to hug Mason and see my friends. There was so much I wanted to do, including getting this story right.

King gathered my clothes up off the floor and turned his back as I slipped my body into them. When I stood, King turned to me and lifted his hand to my face.

My heart beat wild inside of my chest as I stared into his blue eyes.

His rough palm gripped my soft cheek as he tilted my head to the side, wanting to inspect my wounds. "We need to get you to the hospital."

My eyes swayed with his. "I'm all right."

He lowered his brow. "Are you going to fight me on this?"

"I'm not sure I have any fight left."

We both smiled.

A flood of sirens wailed outside the motel. Backup had arrived.

"How did you find me?" I asked.

King pulled his hand away from my face but I wanted to tell him to put it back. I liked having it there. The heat, the security, the deep sense of trust that came with it.

"John knew where Camille would take you."

I cast my gaze to the floor. "He was her accomplice but had a moment of regret when he gave me that key. Maybe he has a conscience after all."

"That won't save him from what's coming his way." King flicked his gaze over my shoulder and glanced to Camille. "Apparently, he helped set up the room so that it would stay out of her name."

Feeling slightly dizzy, I needed to sit.

King stepped into the hallway, ready to direct incoming traffic.

I still didn't understand why Camille would risk everything she had—the life, prestige, and power—only to throw it all away over her husband's infidelity. She had options—so many alternatives that could have brought insurmountable shame to him. Instead, she let revenge control her actions and chose to kill innocent people rather than be humiliated by divorce. It was something I probably never would understand, why people did the things they did.

When Detective Alvarez arrived at the door, I stood up.

He stared into my eyes without saying a word.

A second later, Erin popped her head into the room. She paused when she met my gaze and, when I smiled, she leaped over Camille, ran across the room, and flung her arms around my neck. "Don't you do that to me again."

I tensed in her embrace, her squeeze inflaming my injuries once more. "I can't promise you that."

Erin pulled her head back and gave me a sideways glance. "Fine. Then, next time, you're letting me come with you."

"Deal," I said, falling into her open arms as we shared a laugh.

CHAPTER SEVENTY-TWO

I FLINCHED AGAIN. THE ANTISEPTIC USED TO CLEAN MY wounds stung but paled in comparison to what I'd experienced tonight. Besides, my mind was someplace else.

I stared at Alex, unable to take my eyes off of him. He commanded the situation with the confidence I'd come to expect of him. But, tonight, I saw a new side of him that I hadn't seen before. Humility. And as he was showered with the new status of being called a hero, he deflected the podium, deciding to share it with all who were involved.

The corners of my lips curled upward, a sense of pride blooming in my chest with renewed warmth. "Am I fine to go home?"

The paramedic tilted her head and paused. "You have a concussion, Mrs. Bell."

"But no broken bones." My eyes met with hers. "You said it yourself. My wounds are mostly superficial."

She pursed her lips and looked down. "No broken bones."

I nodded. "Then I'm not going to the hospital."

Her eyes flicked up. The emergency lights still flashed on the various vehicles parked outside the motel and caught in her pupils, causing her eyes to sparkle. "I suggest you take it easy for the next week or so."

I smiled. "Thank you."

She nodded and stepped to the side. The moment I stood, I caught Alex staring.

My breath hitched and I froze, locked in his intense gaze.

With his hands inside his pockets, he strode to me with an even gait. Gripping my elbows tight, I hugged myself warm. Alex closed the gap between us and tucked his chin into his chest. I raked my gaze over his strong jawline before drifting my eyes up to his.

"I owe you one," I said.

Alex stroked his chin and chuckled. "The paramedics let you go?"

"I'm fine."

He showed me his palms and leaned back like an intense wind was threatening to blow him backward. "Then let me take you home."

I smiled. "I'd like that."

Our ride started out quiet. My mind was stuck on Mason and needing to make sure that he was safe. I thought about how nice it was of Erin to offer to retrieve my car from Thornton Storage Unit and drive it home. I shared small glances with Alex, not sure I had the words to express my appreciation for what he'd done to save my life.

"What is going to happen to Eric Foster?" I asked.

"He's already on his way home." King rolled his gaze over to me. "And you were right, their home was destroyed, made to look like a fight broke out."

"Camille's work?"

"Seems like a safe assumption." He focused on the road.

"I can testify," I said, fiddling with my fingers in my lap.

"You'll probably have to."

"What about John? Will anything happen to him?"

"He'll get treated and then processed into the system. Hopefully Kristin Newsome will agree to identify him as the man she escaped from, and then we'll officially charge him with kidnapping and accessory to murder."

"It's a shame," I muttered. "I bet he wishes he died."

King flicked his brows. "I wouldn't be surprised if he makes a plea deal with the DA in exchange for testimony against Camille. We wouldn't have caught her without that key."

I nodded. If it hadn't been for him arriving at Price's gala, we'd still be chasing after Eric.

King rolled his head to me. "We couldn't match John or Camille to the crimes because neither of them had a criminal history."

"She's smart." My head shook. "Maybe too smart for her own good."

King smiled but I could feel that something was on his mind.

"What is it, Alex? I can see you have something you want to say to me."

King sighed. "Sam, you did great, but you really should have let the police—or even me—check these things out before running into the fire."

"Alex," I said softly, "I didn't know what I was walking into tonight."

He frowned. "It's just that..."

I reached over and draped my hand over his. His skin was warm, his hand strong. "When I thought tonight was my last," I stared into his eyes, "I thought about how I wished I could have said goodbye to you."

King pulled to the curb in front of my house and parked. He turned off the engine and stared at the steering wheel for a moment before finally turning his eyes to me. "I wouldn't have let it happen."

"It almost did."

Alex squeezed my hand. I stared at how my hand looked inside of his. I liked the way it fit—how it felt like it was meant to be. Even if it reminded me of Gavin, I welcomed it fully.

King's eyes drifted over my shoulder and I turned to see my front door wide open. Cooper came running with his tail wagging, Mason hurtling after him.

"Mom," Mason said, flinging my door open, "oh my god." He hugged me. When he pulled back, he paused at the sight of my fresh wounds.

"I'm okay," I smiled. And I was.

"Susan and Allison are inside," he said. "They told me everything."

I stepped out of the car and hugged Mason.

"Mom, you look like you got in a fight."

"I'm hurt but I'll heal," I said, hanging on to him. I couldn't forget the fear of what his future would have been if Alex hadn't saved me.

Headlights lit up the sidewalk and a car pulled in behind King. I recognized my car immediately and, when Erin stepped out and walked up to us, I said, "Thank you."

"Figured you might need it." She shrugged.

With my arm hooked around my son's waist, we stepped inside to a commotion of cheers and hugs. Allison and Susan swarmed me with their unconditional love.

"You're tougher than you look." Allison hugged me again.

In that moment, I looked around the small living room and felt more loved than I had in a very long time. All my friends, all the people I cared about, were there, smiling, waiting their turn to tell me how stupid I was for doing something that almost got me killed. And I loved them all for it.

When the front door opened, I wondered who else could possibly be coming.

Ryan Dawson showed his face and immediately made his way to me.

"And who told you that I almost died?" I asked him.

"The police scanner." He winked. "I knew you were involved the moment I heard it."

"I couldn't resist the makings of a good story."

"You never could." Dawson hugged me. "I'm glad to see you're all right."

When he pulled away, I watched King interact with Mason. Mason responded to him well—always had. Watching them laugh confirmed that King was someone I couldn't let go of—someone we could both use in our lives.

"I guess I'll be the first to tell you to take the next week off." Dawson lowered his gaze, hiding his hands inside his pockets.

"You know I can't do that."

Dawson answered me with a look from under his brow.

"Not with us moving offices."

"Maybe you're right." He arched an eyebrow. "I'll leave the decision up to you."

Before Dawson could get away, I caught him by the arm and lowered my voice. "You can't run the story I wrote."

"No, I can't. I guess you won't be taking that week off after all."

"Hey, I haven't made my decision yet."

"No, but I can see it in your eyes."

"Sometimes I think you know me better than I know myself."

"I'll need a new story, and I think you might have one you're itching to write."

"Thanks, Dawson." My ear pressed against his heart as I hugged him.

Soon, my house cleared and Mason disappeared to his room with Cooper. The house was quiet and it was just Alex and me, sharing awkward glances as we shuffled our feet over the old house's floors.

"Now what?" I asked.

He stepped closer. Then I closed the gap that remained.

Tipping my head back, my eyes hooded with feelings of seduction taking over. It was an intense feeling—a lively emotion that brightened up the dark room. Sliding my hands up his muscular chest, I hooked my hands around his neck and pulled his mouth over mine.

The fireworks exploded. I kissed Alex until my lips went numb. And when I finally dropped my heels back to the floor, Alex asked, "So, does that mean we're dating?"

"If you want to call me your girlfriend," I bit the edge of my lip, "you'll have to ask me out on a date first."

King blushed and laughed. "Have dinner with me."

"Are you asking me or telling me?"

His smile hit his eyes. "Asking."

"Then I would love to."

I pressed my lips against his once more and melted into his big arms, knowing that everything could only get better from here.

CHAPTER SEVENTY-THREE

I SLEPT LIKE A LOG AND DIDN'T WAKE UNTIL MID-MORNING the next day.

I was too exhausted to be tormented by the terror of yesterday. My heart too filled with joy and excitement for my future with Alex to let someone like Camille drag me down. But when I woke, there was one last thing I needed to do before finding absolute peace with this story.

I tucked my hair behind my ear as I walked up to the mansion's entrance. After ringing the doorbell to announce my arrival, I turned and let my gaze drift over the incredible view.

It was a bluebird day and not a cloud was in the sky. Though I heard snow was on the way, I was going to soak up today's sun and remind myself of all I was grateful for.

When the front door opened, I turned with a smile on my face.

"My god, Samantha." Christy Jones swept me up in her arms. "I heard what happened. How awful. I'm so sorry."

"Water under the bridge."

Christy pulled back but still clung to my shoulders. Her

brows furrowed as she gave me a look. "If I would have known..."

"Thanks for agreeing to see me on such short notice."

"Yes. Of course." She released my shoulders and turned on a heel. "Please, come inside."

When I entered the home of Philip Price, I was immediately reminded of the early stages of my investigation. Now, knowing the outcome and who was involved, I felt mildly embarrassed for wrongly accusing the man who wanted to be Colorado's next governor.

I floated one step behind Christy, feeling unusually relaxed. I promised to keep an open mind and was more willing to see Price in the same light I knew Susan saw him standing in.

When we turned into the living room, Price was already waiting. He turned away from the window and met my warm gaze. He was slow to approach, but eventually he did. Keeping his hands tucked deep inside his pants pockets, he stopped a short breath away from me.

"I wanted to apologize," I said.

"You were right."

I cast my gaze to the floor, shaking my head.

"You were only doing your job. If only there were more reporters as bold as you, then maybe we'd all clean up our acts." Price laughed.

"Samantha, it's as much your fault as our own." Christy stepped forward with bright eyes. "We should have done better research on where our money was coming from and who was sponsoring events."

"Eric's only crime was having multiple affairs outside his marriage," I said, surprising myself that I felt the need to defend him.

I didn't know why I did. It wasn't like I felt that what he'd done was okay, but maybe it was the guilt I felt for accusing him of murder when he had nothing to do with it.

"I want to make it up to you." I lifted my eyes to Price's. "I gave you my word. I want to stick to our agreement. No spin. No shooting from the hip. Just straight talk."

Price turned to Christy. "We have an idea of our own," Christy said.

I arched a brow. "Okay."

"We're going to highlight good journalism," Price said, "and make you the face of my new agenda."

"I'm not sure—"

"You're a hero, Sam."

"There are many heroes in this story. Only one true villain. If it weren't for Christy identifying John Standard, the police would have never been able to arrest Camille, and maybe even arrested the wrong man."

"It's already done." Price's tone was matter-of-fact. "If it weren't for your persistence, Camille might have actually gotten away with the crimes she committed." Price paused. "Sam, you want to make it up to me?"

"I do."

"Then just say yes."

My fingers throbbed as my pulse quickened. There wasn't much to debate. With the current status of *The Colorado Times,* the opportunity sounded fantastic. Even if it was only soundbite material or a brief answer during a political debate, my colleagues and I needed anything we could get to highlight the importance of a free and open news media.

"So, what do you say?"

"Sam, say yes," Christy chimed in.

My smile spread to my ears as I began to nod. "Okay, I'll do it."

CHAPTER SEVENTY-FOUR

ONE WEEK LATER.

I stood behind the couch, intently watching Philip Price speaking on television. My hair was still damp from my morning shower. King, who had arrived to the house early, was sitting on the couch, Mason next to him. He tipped his head back and angled his face to share a small smile with me before turning his attention back to the television screen.

Philip Price couldn't stop highlighting the brave work of journalists throughout the state, always quick to drop my name in nearly every interview since the last time we'd spoken.

It was strange to be suddenly thrust into the spotlight and labeled a hero. I was taking it in stride as best I could. But that still didn't stop this day from coming.

My wounds were healing nicely and I had written the story Dawson requested. It was therapy in and of itself, reliving the investigation from the beginning. It allowed new perspective to what I'd accomplished, with plenty of time to reflect on the areas I could have improved.

There were so many things I would have done differently if given a second chance. I made many poor decisions I wished I hadn't but, even now, one week later, I was accepting each decision and treating it as a necessary stepping stone which eventually led us to catching Camille Foster.

We caught the killer.

Made Denver a safer city to live in.

And even with the high-powered lawyers someone like her could afford, the judge had denied her bail and granted us our second win of the week.

Camille Foster was looking at a life sentence. I felt good about that. As for John's future, it was still uncertain. Kristin Newsome positively identified him as being the man she denied. It helped our case but, in the process, we also learned that Kristin wasn't a target of Camille's. She was purely John's mistake and probably what got him and Camille caught.

Though Eric Foster had nothing to do with the murders, he wouldn't escape without receiving a few bruises of his own. Thanks to his wife, his reputation was now being questioned. What kind of man was he? Was his money in politics worth the baggage he brought to the table? All sorts of questions were being asked about him, and not just because of what his wife had done. There was infidelity but, beyond that, Eric's sex life with the women he dated was anything but conventional. Camille knew it, too, which was the reason she had made the victims look like they had died during sex.

Price turned and looked into the camera. "If only we could all be as brave and have the integrity of Samantha Bell, then the world in which we live would be a better place for all."

"Mom," Mason twisted around and looked at me, "he's talking about you again. Did you hear that?"

I grinned. "I did."

Mason's face beamed with pride.

Pointing the remote at the TV, I clicked it off. The screen went black. "You two better get going; you don't want to be late."

Mason jumped off the couch and stuffed his school bag full of books. King edged the couch and approached me. His eyes sparkled as he smirked.

Placing my fingers on both sides of his tight stomach, I tipped my head back, looked into his eyes, and said, "Thank you for doing this."

"It'll be fun."

"Mason is beyond excited to bring you." I clasped my hands behind the small of his back. "Have you ever been interviewed by a school paper before?"

King's eyebrows pulled together. He tilted his head to the side and said, "No. I don't think so."

"Don't let them know your lack of experience, Detective. If you think I'm tough, wait until you see what high schoolers bring." My eyes glowed. "Teenagers will surprise you and are relentless when going after what they want."

"Thanks for the warning," King said, just as Mason ran back into the living room and came to a full stop when catching us holding each other in our arms. His face was deadpan.

Both King and I laughed. He released me but not before I stole one last kiss from him.

"C'mon, Alex," Mason said. "I don't want to be tardy."

I hooked Mason's elbow and spun him around before he could leave. "Give your Mom a kiss." My lips pressed in the center of his forehead before I whispered into his ear, "Keep an eye on him, will you?" Mason nodded. "It's been a while since he's set foot in a high school and I don't want him to get lost."

Mason squeezed his arms around me and pushed off, sprinting to the door.

"I'll call you after work." King's lips brushed my cheek.

With Cooper leaning against my leg, I watched my boys tuck themselves inside King's dark sedan from the front window. A smile was permanently stamped on my face and had been for the last week. I was happy, content. Everything coming together again.

Alex had taken me out on our first date two nights after I said yes to his invitation. It went extremely well, as I knew it would. We joked about it being long overdue but he understood my hesitation, knowing I only wanted what was best for Mason. Then he asked me out on a second date before our first was even finished, and of course I said yes. But this time he had a stipulation. We had to bring Mason along with us.

Mason had loved it and the three of us had a blast. We'd been seeing each other every day and sleeping in our own beds. I wasn't sure where we were going from here, but I wasn't in a rush. And neither was Alex. He was a friend, the best of male friends, and the perfect role model for my son. He was a dream in every way imaginable, and that was what mattered most.

I finished getting ready and soon was driving across town, heading into the office. The snow was flying but the roads were clear. Winter was maybe my favorite season of all. It was quiet, forced the world to slow down and rest. I looked forward to warm cups of tea, curled up with a book on the couch, deciding what story I would write next.

When I parked in the parking garage—the same garage I'd started my career in—I felt my throat close up. It was bittersweet. Sad to think that we were on our way out.

It wasn't how I imagined it ending. Not like this.

By the time I stepped onto the newsroom floor, I headed

straight for my desk. The air was still, quiet murmurs breaking out every few minutes, but mostly just sounds of people packing up their desks.

I lowered myself into my chair and stared at my blank computer screen. It was my first time back at my desk since the night I almost died. In the end, I'd followed Dawson's advice. A week at home wasn't so bad after all but that hadn't stopped me from working. I'd written from home, inside busy coffee shops with Erin, and couldn't stop myself from looking for my next story.

My cellphone vibrated with a new email.

It was another message from a new fan.

Mrs. Bell, I love your website and the stories you write. Don't ever stop writing! Your newest and biggest fan, Martha.

I read it and smiled, still in disbelief how my *Real Crime News* blog's readership had suddenly exploded overnight. Thanks to piggybacking off of Erin's successful podcast as well as my name being mentioned repeatedly in the media, we were well on our way to reaching new heights.

My thoughts drifted to Erin and I put a call in to her.

"I just stole another one of your subscribers," I said when she answered.

"You're welcome. This publicity you brought both of us has been incredible." Erin spoke rapid fire. "I've been receiving messages from people across the state wanting me to investigate potential crimes."

"Anything worth pursuing?"

"I have a pile of potential cases we should research. You name it, I have it. Missing persons, child sex trafficking, business corruptions, even cold cases that have been sitting dormant for years."

Leaning back, I knew we needed content, and I could sense Erin's restlessness to making a decision soon. Erin and I had finally rebranded ourselves to act as one and, over the past week, my webmaster worked tirelessly to merge Erin's podcast onto our new website. But I still had a job with the paper—even if Erin wished that I didn't.

I heard somebody sneak up behind me and, when I turned, Dawson smiled.

"I'll call you back," I said.

"Wait," Erin protested, "just give me an idea of what you're interested in most."

"I'll think about it." I ended my call, turning to greet my incredible editor.

"Welcome back," he said.

"Thank you."

"Though I can't help but wonder why you even bothered."

His comment struck me like a punch to the gut. I didn't see it coming and had no choice but to responded with a smile. "Because you need me."

Dawson stepped into my cubicle and rested his backside against the edge of my desk. His eyes moved casually around my mess before he said, "Except you don't need us."

"What are you saying? You know that's not true. Much of my success is because of you, Dawson."

He flashed a thin-lipped smile. "Run with it, Samantha."

My breathing grew shallow.

"The future isn't here," he said, looking around. "Not anymore. I know you see it. Look around yourself."

I lifted my gaze to the lights above.

"The enthusiasm has dried up. We're drowning in our own tears."

"I'd miss it too much," my voice cracked, suddenly choking up. The thought of losing something I loved was breaking me down. My knees were weak and my eyes swollen with the threat of tears.

"Our days are limited, Samantha." Dawson grinned. "But I don't have tell you that." He stood and shoved his hands inside his pants pockets. "Soon, everything we write will be censored by those who control us." A nostalgic look fell over Dawson's face. "We'll work for their agenda and not the public." He turned to look at me. "Listen to me. I'm washed up and rambling about something I know nothing about."

I reached for his hand. "That's not true."

"I guess I'm just an old school journalist caught up in the tsunami of technology."

"You may be right about that, but I can't leave. Not yet. I still have Mason to think about."

Dawson smiled. "I'll keep you for as long as you'll have me."

"Thanks, Dawson."

Trisha ran over. The look on her face had me standing. "Sam, did you hear?"

My brows knitted as I felt my heart race. "Hear what?"

Panic filled Trisha's eyes as she said, "There's been a shooting. North High School."

Mason's school.

I didn't wait for her to finish. I sprinted across the floor and dove into Dawson's office, flicking on his television. "Oh no," I gasped as I stared at the breaking news hitting the television stations. "No. No. No."

I covered my mouth and listened.

Breaking News. North High School is currently on lockdown as an active shooter is on scene. One student has already been confirmed dead but authorities and emergency services are expecting the number to rise.

"Sam, is Mason there now?"

I didn't know who asked. All I could think about was how Mason looked so happy when he left this morning. I prayed that King was by his side and was keeping my son safe—that Alex was carrying his handgun today. But I couldn't be sure of anything.

"I've gotta go," I said, exiting the building and sprinting to my car. With one hand on the wheel and an eye on the road, I dialed Mason's cell, reliving the terror all over again.

Continue the series by reading Bell Hath No Fury. Click here and start reading today!

AUTHOR NOTE:

Thank you for reading Dead and Gone to Bell. If you enjoyed the book and would like to see more Samantha Bell crime thrillers, please consider leaving a review on Amazon. Even a few words would be appreciated and will help persuade what book I will write for you next.

ABOUT THE AUTHOR

Waldron lives in Vermont with his wife and two children.

Receive updates, exclusive content, and new book release announcements by signing up to his newsletter at: www.JeremyWaldron.com

Follow him @jeremywaldronauthor

facebook.com/jeremywaldronauthor

instagram.com/jeremywaldronauthor

bookbub.com/profile/83284054